Hanging out to dry . . .

Jack DuBois's eyes snapped open and he blinked through the fog in his head, remembering. He had been the last man to jump out of the plane, and the wind had gusted him past the LZ. He must have slammed into some rocks or a cliff.

He had no idea how long he had been unconscious, but he knew the rest of the team would be gearing up and moving out. With the storm raging, they wouldn't go far, anyway. DuBois looked around, trying to get his bearings. He looked up, and the rain blinded him. Then he looked down. All he saw was the rain falling into blackness.

He thought, *Uh-oh.*

His chute must have snagged a ledge or an outcropping of rock, and now he was suspended in midair as he literally twisted in the wind.

"Anybody out there?" he whispered into his comlink. He wasn't sure why he was whispering, but maybe it was because any sound, any disturbance, might undo his chute's tenuous hold on the cliff and send him falling like a stone.

"This is DuBois calling," he said, "and I definitely have a problem here . . ."

Also in the TALON Force Series

TALON FORCE

SECRET
WEAPON

Cliff Garnett

A SIGNET BOOK

SIGNET
Published by New American Library, a division of
Penguin Putnam Inc., 375 Hudson Street,
New York, New York 10014, U.S.A.
Penguin Books Ltd, 27 Wrights Lane,
London W8 5TZ, England
Penguin Books Australia Ltd, Ringwood,
Victoria, Australia
Penguin Books Canada Ltd, 10 Alcorn Avenue,
Toronto, Ontario, Canada M4V 3B2
Penguin Books (N.Z.) Ltd, 182–190 Wairau Road,
Auckland 10, New Zealand

Penguin Books Ltd, Registered Offices:
Harmondsworth, Middlesex, England

First published by Signet, an imprint of New American Library,
a division of Penguin Putnam Inc.

First Printing, June 2000
10   9   8   7   6   5   4   3   2   1

PUBLISHER'S NOTE
This is a work of fiction. Names, characters, places, and incidents either
are the product of the author's imagination or are used fictitiously,
and any resemblance to actual persons, living or dead, business
establishments, events, or locales is entirely coincidental.

People sleep peacefully in their beds at night only because rough men stand ready to do violence on their behalf.

—George Orwell

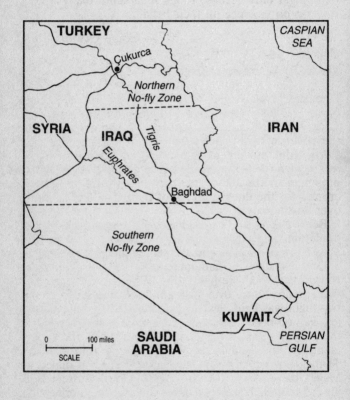

Prologue

Underneath his oxygen mask, U.S. Air Force Captain Mike Daniels was smiling in spite of everything. The night was dark and foul, with spider lightning signaling the advance of thunderheads on the leading edge of a storm front moving in from the west. Daniels's F-16C was bucking a heavy headwind as he and his wingman prepared for the 180-degree turn that would bring them around for the downwind leg of their oval flight pattern over northern Iraq.

Below them a low cloud cover obscured the rugged mountain range that was a no-man's-land between Saddam Hussein's forces and the Kurds of northern Iraq.

Daniels knew he had more than the weather to be concerned about. He had put in his share of "vul time," vulnerability time, over Saddam's turf and he knew his two-flight was being watched by Iraqi air defense batteries. His on-board threat warning system had alerted to their radar signals twice already. Both times, the system identified the signals as broad-beamed transmissions. That meant search radar, no big deal. He had dialed up Magic, the Airborne Warning and Control System Boeing E-3 orbiting high above them, and asked for verification. Magic confirmed both impulses were nonthreatening.

If the Iraqis spiked him or his wingman, that *would* be a big deal. A spike meant target acquisition radar. Which would mean Saddam's SAM jockeys weren't just watching, they were about to launch on his ass. It happened often enough to keep the American pilots on their toes, but so far nobody had been hit. Rules of engagement said if they spiked you, retaliation was authorized in self-defense. That meant locking on the radar sites and feeding them a dose of HARM air-to-ground missiles. Even Saddam's diehards had to get tired of playing that game after a while.

Some of them were crafty, though. They used truck-towed launchers like the SA-6s that could fire three missiles at a time. Intel said it was an SA-6 that knocked down an Air Force F-16 in Bosnia in '95. They could latch onto you, get their three surface-to-air missiles off, and hightail it before you got a fix on them. Hell of way to lose a $20 million airplane.

So it wasn't like Mike Daniels had no worries as he banked left into the gentle 180-degree turn that would bring him and his wingman around into the sixty-mile downwind leg of the oval. That was the mission profile—around and around the oval at 15,000 feet. At 400 miles an hour, the F-16s made a lap around the oval about every twenty-five minutes. It was a "Deny Flight" mission, making sure none of Saddam's pilots violated the northern No-fly Zone.

They were nearing the halfway point of their mission. After two more laps, they would divert to rendezvous with a KC-135 tanker for a dip—a midair refueling. Though always dangerous, it was a pretty routine exercise, except on a moonless night in high winds with bad weather moving in.

But Daniels couldn't help smiling. He was due a week's leave in three days—R&R in Italy. And Stephanie was going to meet him there. Thinking about Stephanie and sunny Italy with no Iraqis to worry about, he couldn't keep the smile off his face.

As they leveled out, Daniels checked his wingman. Visibility wasn't the best, but the F-16's unique one-piece bubble canopy let him scan a full 360 degrees. Lieutenant Freeman was right where he was supposed to be, in tactical line abreast, a mile away and a thousand feet above Daniels. In a two-flight, the wingman is the lookout. His job is to maintain formation and keep a sharp eye out—

visual and instruments, especially radar. Daniels was the flight leader. He called the shots.

It had begun with a standard pre-mission briefing. Deny Flights are never routine and nothing is taken for granted. He had run it all down from the top, starting with the mission objectives. It was to be a four-hour mission, including roundtrip transit time and at least one refueling dip. He ran through what pilots called the motherhood—the basic principles. That included the rules of engagement, the two pilots' "contracts" as flight leader and wingman, radio procedures and contingency plans, the weapons systems their F-16s would be configured with, and a review of their squadron's SAR—Search and Rescue—procedures for a downed pilot. And they had reviewed the video and audio-tapes from the on-board recorders on their last mission.

That was followed by a weather report and intel brief. Then they sanitized their flying suits by peeling off the Velcro wing and squadron patches and drew their personal equipment—G-suit, parachute harness, survival kit, and sidearm—and hopped a ride to the flight line.

Daniels knew every mission began long before takeoff. He and Freeman had put in an intense two hours before they even climbed into their aircraft. It was deadly serious business, and Daniels prided himself on being good at it.

But the smile kept creeping back every time Stephanie popped into his mind. She was a tall blonde, a southern belle from a blueblood Virginia family. He was a Michigan autoworker's son, a wiry little bantamweight with a crooked nose from his Golden Gloves days. If it hadn't been for the air force, he would never have even crossed paths with a girl like Stephanie. Now she was going to be all his for a week in Italy. And he was trying to come up with a classy way to ask her to marry him.

He stole a second to look down at her photograph taped to the pad strapped on his right thigh. Even in the eerie light of the illuminated dials of the control panel, he could make out her perfect smile, her eyes. He couldn't see the blue sky or puffy white clouds in the photo, but he knew they were there. He'd taken the picture at her daddy's farm. She had tried not to laugh at his awkward attempts at horseback riding with the little English saddles they used in Virginia.

The alarm from his radar warning receiver sounded in Daniels's headset and his eyes darted from Stephanie's smile to his threat-warning screen. Confirmed—target acquisition radar. But there was something odd about it, a second impulse or echo. He had been spiked before, but this was different.

"Striker One, I have a contact," Daniels squawked on their tactical frequency to alert Freeman. He was surprised at how calm his voice sounded.

"Striker Two," Freeman answered. "I've got something, but—"

Two seconds after the spike alert, Daniels heard the programmed female voice over his headset, "Counter, counter."

He shifted his thumb to the countermeasures switch on his control stick to deploy his chaff flare system to blind the Iraqi radar, but even as he did he knew something was terribly wrong.

The recorded voice in his headset deteriorated in an instant from feminine to masculine to guttural and then growled to silence.

Daniels blinked in disbelief as his instruments scrambled, flickered through a cycle of false readings, and then flat-lined and went dark.

"What the hell—" he muttered.

The sudden silence that enveloped him registered an instant later. He heard the wind whistling by his canopy and that was all. No power—a flame-out. His engine was dead.

This can't be happening, he thought. He fought to trim the ship and keep her flying as his mind raced. At the same time he frantically scanned the sky beneath him, looking for the glowing trail of a missile. He saw nothing but that didn't mean it wasn't down there, climbing like a bat out of hell.

What are the odds, he found himself thinking as he

tried desperately to restart his crippled ship. What are the odds of a shutdown at a time like this?

Lieutenant Freeman, flying Daniels's number two, stared dumbstruck at the night sky ahead and below him. Striker One wasn't there any more. His flight leader had disappeared. One second he was there, the next he was gone. No fire, no explosion, no trace.

Freeman called Striker One and got no answer. He called him again. Then he dialed up Magic and asked for a fix on his flight leader.

"We've lost him," was the report. "He's just . . . gone."

"You've got to be kidding me," Freeman said, not realizing he was thinking out loud.

There was nothing below him but the roiling cloud cover and the mountains.

Off to the west he saw lightning and heard the thunder. The storm was rolling in.

Striker One was gone.

Chapter One

The SAR alert was out before Lieutenant Freeman had collected himself enough to dial up the command frequency and report Daniels missing to the squadron command center. Their radio traffic was being monitored aboard Magic. The AWACS plane circling high above had followed the whole flight on its radar screens. The Magic crewmen were the air traffic controllers who tracked everything that flew in the theater of operations, and they had passed the word to scramble SAR immediately. But Magic's commander aboard the command post in the sky had no more idea what had become of Mike Daniels and his F-16 than Lt. Freeman did.

"Striker Two, this is Magic."

The AWACS commander had opcon—operational control—until SAR assets arrived on scene, and he wanted Striker Two to snap out of it.

"Striker Two."

"I'll give you our last fix on Striker One. You get down on the deck and fly me a figure-eight until SAR converges on you. Advise if you can confirm impact."

"Roger that."

Freeman wasn't thinking about his fuel load yet, but he would be soon when the alarm bells went off. He and Daniels had been due for a dip after their next lap, and he was going to have to break off, maybe before SAR ships could get to him.

*　　*　　*

It all happened in milliseconds, but Mike Daniels saw it like a slow motion, out-of-body dream—the product of his mind's defense mechanism of denial. His airplane was falling out of the sky. It was as if the whole thing, the whole multimillion-dollar marvel of space-age technology had shorted out. He quit worrying about the Iraqi radar spike and missiles when he got no response from any of his control systems, main or backup.

The control panel sputtered back to life for a second but it was all screwed up, like R2-D2 after a kick in the head. Then all the instruments flat-lined again and went dark. That was it.

The F-16 was a computerized, fly-by-wire machine. There were no mechanical systems to operate any of the steering or flight surfaces. The only reason the pilot's control stick moved at all was to give him a sense of "feel." Everything was electronic, computer driven. And somehow the whole system was fried.

Daniels's mind was racing a million miles an hour, even as he watched his hands moving in nightmare slow motion. In his peripheral vision, he could see the choppy cloud cover that hid the jagged mountain peaks screaming up at him as the wind roared over the unresponsive wings of his ship. He knew he was running out of time as he groped between his legs for the ejection handle. The yellow handle with lettering that said PULL TO EJECT was right there, but it seemed to take forever to get a grip on it.

As he finally grasped the handle and pulled, Daniels was praying the ejection system wasn't fouled up, too.

"Please, Lord," he muttered. "I promise—"

He felt the inertia reel straps yank him snugly back against the seat. He had to be in the correct position or ejecting could be as lethal as a crash. It was dangerous enough when you had time to do it right. The canopy's jettison mechanism fired a fraction of a second before the rocket catapult beneath him blasted Daniels's seat up its guide rails and launched him into the night sky.

Daniels forced himself to open his eyes. He was falling face down, still in the seat. He knew the automatic ejection system was designed to deploy the parachute packed inside the headrest of his seat, but he also knew he was already dangerously low and there was no way of knowing what lay beneath the cloud cover that was racing up toward him. He grabbed the manual override chute handle on the right side of the seat and drew it back hard to fire the mortar cartridge that launched his parachute.

There was an immediate pop as the small drogue chute deployed, then he felt a jerk and took a deep breath as the main chute billowed above him and jerked him vertical. At least he wasn't falling like a rock anymore. Now all he had to do was get rid of the seat, fall through the cloud cover, and hope he got lucky and came down in a good place.

He thanked the Lord for getting him this far. He had never ejected from a jet before. It wasn't something you could practice.

1525 hours EDT
The Pentagon, Washington, D.C.

"What's up?" the gangly young man with the bifocals asked as he spied a familiar figure hustling down the corridor, going in the same direction. "All I got was a beeper code to report."

"Not here," the second man shot back. He was in his late fifties and bald, dressed in a rumpled suit without a tie, his shirt collar bulging open around his bullish neck.

Both men presented ID badges to the armed guards at the checkpoint set up where the subterranean corridor that led from the Pentagon elevator bank made a T intersection with a second corridor. There was nothing perfunctory about the way the guards eyeballed the men and their credentials before they waved them through.

"I'm just asking," the first man said when they were out of earshot of the guards. He was a civilian, a technology wizard with a DOD contract think tank. He wasn't sure all the hush-hush stuff was strictly necessary. "In general, you know."

"In general, shut the hell up," the second spat. His name was Mac and he was CIA. He thought wizards should be kept in cages and fed as often as they proved themselves useful.

Mac knew no more about the summons than the wizard did. He had not been given a sitrep—situation report—just a message to report immediately. But he had problems of his own. Mac and his colleagues had been working overtime out at Langley trying to get a fix on Osama bin Laden. The millionaire son of a Saudi prince and at the moment the world's most wanted terrorist mastermind, bin Laden had gone missing from his camps in Afghanistan. All the sigint and humint—signal and human intelligence—the CIA and NSA could get their hands on, which meant everything from encrypted satellite transmissions to cell phone traffic and cocktail party gossip in capitals around the world, had not yielded a clue to his whereabouts.

Mac had his fingers crossed that the subject of this Pentagon briefing was not another bombing with bin Laden's fingerprints on it. The Saudi fanatic was already linked with the two simultaneous American embassy bombings in Africa and was a suspect in the World Trade Center bombing in New York City.

As they made their way down the second corridor without any more conversation, the two men were joined by others, all hurrying to a secure room deep underneath the Pentagon.

After passing through another security checkpoint where their credentials were even more carefully scrutinized, the men collected in a SCIF—a Special Classified Intelligence Facility—to get the word.

The SCIF was basically a room within a room, a 15 by 30 foot chamber suspended inside a larger room, with floor, walls, and ceiling specially designed to defeat electronic eavesdropping. It was like a large-scale version of the cone of silence gizmos on TV and in the movies.

And they were Hollywood's takeoff on the real things in American embassies.

The CIA man had been through this drill more times than he liked to remember. He particularly didn't like remembering the long night he had spent in one of these rooms monitoring satellite feeds and radio traffic as the operation to rescue American hostages from the embassy in Tehran turned to shit in a fireball at Desert One. That was over twenty years ago, but it stuck with him.

This time the briefer was air force, a one-star general assigned to the Joint Chiefs of Staff. The crisis was in northern Iraq, the general said. The Air Force had lost an F-16. It was early Saturday afternoon in Washington, a couple of hours after midnight in Iraq. And the weather was so bad on-site that SAR operations had been suspended, the general said. Bad business risking SAR crews when there was so little chance the F-16 pilot had survived. His wingman had been unable to confirm ejection, or even a point of impact.

The man from the CIA was more curious than interested. Didn't the military have an off-the-shelf plan for situations like this? Why the top-security huddle?

The wizard looked bored until the air force general told the little group that data from the aircraft involved, the lost F-16, his wingman, and the AWACS, had been transmitted by satellite and downloaded for analysis, digital and analog. That interested him.

"Excuse me, sir."

The general acknowledged the man in the corner. It was clear by his squared-away haircut and lean, mean demeanor he was a military man, his knit shirt and jeans notwithstanding. It was the weekend and the summons had been come-as-you-are.

"You have a question?" the general asked.

"Commander Greeley, attached to the staff of the Chief of Naval Operations, sir."

"Recently attached, I believe," the general smiled.

"Yes, sir. My question is, if the ragheads shot down our airplane and we've got a pilot missing, why haven't we gone in and lit their ass up? Sir."

"You're the specwar rep on the admiral's staff, aren't you, Greeley?" the general asked.

"Yes, sir."

Special Warfare, in the navy, meant SEAL. Greeley was fresh from a SEAL team, probably just promoted, and newly assigned to a ticket-punching tour in a staff slot.

"It shows," the general said.

There was quiet buzz around the little room, the intelligence agency reps and military officers sharing knowing nods and eye rolls. The technical types were oblivious, already thinking about their analysis of the data from the aircraft.

"I appreciate your directness, Commander," the general went on. "And I'm sure you are aware we have contingency plans for just such an event. If you had been a little more patient, though, you would have heard me say that this appears to be an anomaly."

"I see," Commander Greeley said, standing at attention. "Thank you, sir."

Greeley took his seat. If he wasn't sure what the general meant about an anomaly, he sure as hell wasn't going to ask. He'd stepped on his dick once already, and that was plenty.

"Preliminary evaluation of the aircraft telemetry indicates it was not a SAM that took down the F-16. We don't know what the hell it was. That's the problem. Technical analysis shows none of the profile elements of a missile strike or even a launch. And the radar spike that preceded the event was irregular. You'll be able to see and hear that for yourself as the data is presented on the monitors behind me. We want your ideas on this. It's a puzzle, Commander Greeley, which is why we haven't initiated reprisals. We're not sure what happened out there and we don't want to act until we know. Does that answer your question?"

"Yes, sir," Greeley announced firmly from his corner seat.

"Good. Now, I'll leave you men to get to work. You

represent a cross section of the military, scientific, and intelligence communities. We're counting on you to put your heads together and give us an answer on this. We've also taken this show on the road, approached some specialists who may be able to shed some light on it. Time is of the essence, gentlemen."

Sunday, June 11, 0040 hours
The mountains of northern Iraq

Mike Daniels froze in his tracks and held his breath. He heard voices.

He had jettisoned his seat a few seconds after his parachute opened, just as the low cloud cover enveloped him. He had descended blindly, cursing the clouds and fog and waiting for impact.

Now he realized the soup had been a blessing in disguise. Somebody was out there, probably looking for him. And they weren't speaking English.

He had come down pretty cleanly, everything considered, with his survival kit strung on a twenty-foot cord beneath him. Try to relax, he had told himself. Don't stiffen up and break a leg when you hit.

As it happened, the impact was so sudden he didn't have time to tense up. Drifting downward through low clouds that turned into ground fog, he didn't even see what he hit. It must have been the side of a mountain, because he struck it at an angle and bounced. When he hit again, it was on steeply sloping ground that sent him rolling thirty meters downhill before he came to rest against a fallen tree, wrapped in the shrouds and canopy of his parachute.

It had taken him a couple of minutes to cut himself loose with his issue K-Bar knife. When he was free, he gathered the chute and scraped out a hollow under the dead tree with the knife to bury it. He also buried his G-suit, the elongated vest designed to control blood flow to keep a pilot from losing consciousness under the gravitational forces generated by a high-performance jet. He wouldn't have any use for it on the ground.

When he had finished the little burial detail, he took a quick inventory.

He was battered and bruised, but nothing seemed to be broken. His Global Positioning System receiver was still in the inner pocket of his survival vest. He had his handheld radio, his Baretta 9mm pistol, and the survival kit with food, a camouflage blanket, and some other goodies. Okay, he was alive and kicking. Now what?

The first thing is to figure out where I am, he thought. That meant finding a clear spot and trying to get a reading from a couple of satellites with his GPS receiver.

Wrong. He cursed himself.

Get your act together, Daniels, he thought. We briefed on this. First thing, get on the radio. Squawk on Guard to let 'em know you're alive. Then switch over to Bravo and try to raise the SAR ships.

Guard was the international distress channel. It was not secure, but it might be his best chance to be heard, and it was monitored by intel units at Wing. Bravo was one of the two secure SAR channels, the one designated for his mission.

The first order of business was to let his friends know he was alive. They'd be looking for him, and they were his only chance of getting out of this in one piece. Step two was escape and evasion—don't let the bad guys find you first. Then he could try to pinpoint his location.

In the air, the rule of thumb was aviate, navigate, and communicate, in that order. But he wasn't in the air anymore. This was a whole different ball game, and he knew he would have to play by SAR rules if he was going to live to tell about it.

He sat quietly and listened before he talked on the radio, but he couldn't hear voices any more. Sound carries at night, he told himself. They could be a mile away.

There was no response on Guard. As he switched to Bravo and began transmitting, two things happened at once. The heavy whup-whup of a helicopter sounded off to his left, which almost certainly meant SAR was on the scene. Iraqi choppers would not be up this far north.

Daniels had a rough idea where he was—southeast of the Iraqi town of Amadiya near the Turkish border, in the mountains east of the Tigris River. Erbil lay somewhere to the south and the 35th Parallel was a hell of a long way beyond that. He was in what the Kurds liked to call Kurdistan, a no-man's-land where rival bands of Kurds were in a perpetual state of war with the Iraqi army when they weren't fighting each other.

The SAR choppers had arrived on scene in record time, and he knew they must have been staged somewhere in southern Turkey or else they had already been airborne, orbiting on station somewhere for just such an occasion. There was no way they had come from anywhere near his own base at Adana.

At the same time he heard the helicopter, a flash of lightning splashed across the sky followed a moment later by a crack of thunder that shook the ground.

The lightning showed Daniels his situation like a camera flash. He was about halfway up a ridge above a deep valley that ran as far as he could see in either direction. The sound of the chopper died away, and he realized it had crossed over the valley he was in, some distance away. If they were flying down along the valley, he might have a chance of making radio contact. But as it was, there was no way they would hear him. His handheld radio transmitted line-of-sight, which meant he would have to work his way up to high ground where he could get out a clear signal. Even if he didn't raise anybody from there, he could switch the transmitter to beacon and hope somebody homed in on him.

What he hadn't seen in the momentary illumination of the lightning was the squad of men with AK-47 assault rifles who were working their way along the ridge toward him. It was their voices he had heard moments earlier, and now they were closing on him. They hadn't seen him yet, but it was only a matter of time.

Another lightning bolt flashed, followed by thunder that sounded like artillery. This time, Daniels looked the

other way, up the valley in the opposite direction from
the sound of the helicopter. And he saw the armed men
coming his way.

There wasn't time to run far. He turned and scrambled
twenty meters up the slope from the dead tree where he
had hastily buried his chute, trying not to leave too much
of a trail. He found the stump of a tree and dropped
behind it. In the darkness he couldn't tell if he had good
cover, and he was afraid more lightning would give him
away. But there was nothing else to do.

He eased the Baretta out of his shoulder holster and
gently tugged the slide to the rear, chambering a round
as quietly as he could manage. He would make a fight
of it if he had to. But if he had a choice, he would lie
low and let them pass.

"Lord," he whispered, "it's me again."

Chapter Two

The guy on the screen looked like a character out of a bad movie, a nutty professor type straight from central casting. His hair looked like he combed it with an egg-beater, and he couldn't keep his thick-framed glasses from sliding down to the tip of his nose.

He was a little guy, scrawny like he might forget to eat if somebody didn't bring him his meals. And his voice was the kind of high-pitched nasal whine that reminded Mac, the CIA man, of fingernails on a blackboard.

But what the nutty professor was saying was interesting in the extreme. Somebody at the Pentagon had piped the downloaded telemetry from Captain Daniels's F-16—everybody in the SCIF knew Daniels's name by now and everything else about him—to the nutty professor's lab. His lab was way the hell up in the New Hampshire woods where he worked in near isolation on projects for the government, according to the note Mac had been given.

Mac figured if the brass wanted this goofy little man to have a go at the telemetry, he must be sharper than he looked. He must be a wizard, like the gangly kid with the glasses who wanted to talk out in the hall.

By now, Mac knew the gangly kid's name was Bob something. The way things had worked out, Mac and Bob were buddied up, trying to figure out why the hell a perfectly good F-16 had fallen out of the Iraqi sky.

Bob had been poring over all the stuff downloaded from the aircraft involved in the incident, mumbling a lot of crap that didn't make any sense to Mac. But that

was all right with him. Mac knew he wasn't there to
decode the technobabble. He was there to put the pieces
together once the geeks had reached consensus.

"Damn," Bob muttered over Mac's shoulder as the
two of them looked up at the nutty professor on the
wall-mounted television monitor. "He could be onto
something."

"You think?" Mac asked, humoring the kid.

"Aren't you listening?"

"Intently. So what's he saying?"

"He could be onto something, I'm telling you."

"You said that already."

"We've got to get him in here."

"Excuse me, Colonel?" Mac motioned to the officer
who had been detailed to chaperon their little study
group. The man, a ramrod-straight air force type who
looked like a bird colonel even in his golf togs, came
over to them. "Bob here says the professor may have
something. Can we get him in here, you think?"

"Being taken care of as we speak," the bird colonel
assured him. "What you're watching was taped earlier
at his lab. We're flying him in, should be here within
the hour."

"I take it we're not the only crew working on this,"
Mac said. He had figured there were other teams seques-
tered in rooms just like this one.

"Let's just say Bob here isn't the only one who thinks
Dr. Fensterman may be onto something," the bird colonel said with a wink as he turned away.

Then Mac made Bob tell him what the hell this Dr.
Fensterman was talking about. It took a few minutes, but
finally Bob broke it down into simple enough language
for the CIA veteran to get the picture.

And once he got the picture, Mac knew what would
happen next. At last he knew part of it. He had seen
spooky *Mission Impossible* deals like this before. He
knew there would be a huddle and a high-priority pitch
to the Joint Chiefs. Once they gave their "hack" to the
preliminary-ops plan, it would go up Pennsylvania Ave-

nue to the White House and the National Security Council. The lights would be burning late up there, maybe all night. After that the details would get murky, but somewhere out there a collection of very serious operators would be getting some heavily coded instructions and then things would start happening. Mac had seen it before, and he had seen things done that nobody was supposed to be able to do. He didn't understand how it all worked exactly, and he didn't want to. But whoever it was out there who made those things happen, Mac had sat in a SCIF like this one more than once and watched the show unfold from thousands of miles away through satellite transmissions. And it had almost made up for Desert One. Because, whoever they were, those people out there were better than anything he had ever seen before.

Mac noticed Bob staring through his bifocals at him with an impatient look, and he realized he had been lost in thought for a moment.

"RF," Mac said, nodding at Bob to show he had been listening. "What'll they think of next?"

Sunday, June 11, 1100 hours
Adana, Turkey

Travis Barrett got his wakeup call as requested, the KC-135 crewman nudging him lightly with the toe of his boot to let Travis know they had set down in Adana. Welcome to Turkey.

"Thanks, partner," he drawled goodnaturedly at the crewman who had awakened him.

It was high noon or damned near it, Travis figured as he looked out the hatch of the big tanker at the hangars and buildings of the air force base. He zipped up his flight suit and squared the blue air force cap on his head as he followed the crew off the aircraft to the truck waiting to take them to the ops shack for debriefing. As far as anybody could tell, Travis was just another flyboy back

from a refueling flight over the Mediterranean somewhere.

He was traveling light. All his gear was back in
Aviano, Italy, where he had stopped over briefly after
hopping a ride on a Black Hawk helicopter out of the
Kosovo area of operations. At Aviano, he had checked
in with Sam Wong at the NSA via secure satcom to
find out why he had been summoned by coded pager, a
summons that meant turning over his command in the
field to his executive officer and leaving without explanation. Sam's info was skimpy, some kind of a CSAR—
combat search and rescue—op into northern Iraq. Sam
described the area and said they'd be looking for an F-
16 jockey lost on a Deny Flight out of Adana, Turkey.
But there was a wrinkle, something spooky about the
deal, details to follow. In the meantime, the rest of
TALON—Technologically Augmented, Low Observable,
Networked—Force was assembling.

Travis had left his camouflage fatigues and everything
that identified him as Major Travis Beauregard Barrett,
U.S. Army Special Forces, in Aviano and wrangled a
ride on the KC-135. Now he was a mystery man traveling
without written orders, just a code word that opened any
door, no questions asked.

If anybody along the way wondered who he was or
what he was up to, they knew better than to ask. That
went for generals right on down. Once they verified his
code word, all any of them wanted to do was get him
where he was going and then forget they had ever seen
him.

Travis left the crew of the tanker at the ops shack and
found his way to the base commander's office, where he
had no trouble getting in to see the head man.

The base commander found himself looking across his
desk at an impressive individual. Travis was clean-cut
and appeared to be in his late thirties, with eyes that
could be scary if they fixed on you a little too tight. He
was six foot two and built like the fitness fanatic he was.
A man who whips himself through 300 sit-ups and 300
pushups every day of his life for twenty years naturally

has a way about him. He was a Texan and fourth-generation army, the first West Pointer in his line. He knew what he was doing and it showed.

The base commander had never heard of TALON Force and Travis intended to keep it that way. He was there to advance-prep his team's mission, and for that he needed the commander's cooperation. All he owed the man in return was the code word.

Travis looked out the window at the base shimmering under the noon sun as the commander made his calls, rounding up the people who would do the briefings. He could see mountains in the distance and they put him in mind of Texas. He flashed for a moment on the Davis Mountains and the Big Bend country, driving up in there in his daddy's old truck and getting away from it all. Then he turned away from the window and brought his focus back to the job at hand. This trip into the mountains was not going to be any getaway.

In a couple of hours, Travis would know all there was to know about Captain Mike Daniels, his wingman, and the mission that had led to the loss of the F-16. He would know everything Adana knew about the terrain, the politics, and the military situation in the mountains between Amadiya on the north and Erbil on the south, the Tigris on the west and Iran on the east.

Then he would request another secure satcom link for an intel dump from Sam. By suppertime, he would have all the information he was ever going to get on his team's mission environment. He hoped that by then he would know what they were going to be up against—including that nasty wrinkle Sam had warned him about.

1100 hours
The mountains of northern Iraq

The Russian looked through the 4x PSO-1 scope of his SVD Dragunov sniper rifle and thought he saw something move on the hillside across the valley.

Mikhail was a hunter by instinct, *Spetsnatz* by training. His bad luck to come along just when everything went to hell in Mother Russia and now here he was out in these Muslim mountains soldiering for pay like a common mercenary. But he couldn't help that. A kill was a kill, and the main thing was to keep yourself sharp, to practice what you had learned.

He thought of his teacher. Nikolai Dobniak was a legend in the Soviet Union's special warfare family. The man had won Olympic medals with his rifle and he taught generations of men like Mikhail how to kill the enemy economically. A good hunter doesn't squander precious ammunition, Dobniak always said.

"You're a long way from KGB Group Alpha these days," Mikhail told himself silently, adding a heartfelt curse for the politicians who ruined everything that was worth living for in his homeland. He thought with disgust of the group he had hired out to for this operation. The boss was a Saudi madman with a cadre of fools looking for their chance to be martyrs and a pack of Iranians scared shitless of the Iraqi Republican Guards and the Kurds who claimed these worthless mountains for their homeland. A bunch of ragheads, like the *mujahideen* bastards he had fought in Afghanistan.

At least you're not a hired gun for the mafia pimps and drug dealers back in Moscow, he thought to himself.

Mikhail could do this, divorce a part of his mind and let it roam while his hands and his shooter's eye attended to the business at hand. It was a part of the discipline he had learned from the master. And the business at hand was the American pilot.

Pretsky the technician—he called himself a scientist, but Mikhail knew better—had given him the coordinates where he claimed to have intercepted the pilot's beacon signal. According to Pretsky and his equipment, the beacon had moved during the night, popping up briefly in one place and then another. Which meant, if Pretsky knew what he was talking about, that the American was alive and mobile. There weren't likely to be any beacon signals now, in daylight—not unless the American helicopters came again. More likely, he will lie low during the day, Mikhail thought.

But lying low isn't as easy as it sounds. Mikhail knew that better than most. Dobniak had drilled it into him—how to find a good hide and burrow into it, then remain perfectly still for hours at a time. After the shooting and the ability to memorize details with a glimpse, it was the third hardest thing a sniper had to learn to do. Mikhail had been lying in his position a hundred meters below the skyline of a ridge on the south side of the valley since first light, scanning the slope opposite him for any sign of the American. If Pretsky's coordinates were right, the last beacon signal had come from over there somewhere.

And the American was a jet pilot, not a sniper. Mikhail knew that most American pilots went through what they called E&E—escape and evasion training. But that was hardly the same. Such a man would not find it easy to lie utterly motionless while the sun traveled from horizon to horizon. Sooner or later, he would grow restless and give himself away, even if it was only to stretch a leg to fight off a cramp. If he was injured from the crash of his precious F-16, that was even better. After a night in the mountains, he would have fever from his wounds and he would sleep fitfully, if at all.

Mikhail knew he did not need a big mistake by the American pilot. The rocky slope peppered with stunted trees on the other side of the valley was just over 600 meters away—well within range. With its 7.62mm x 54 rimmed Soviet machine-gun cartridge, the Dragunov had an official range of 800 meters, and Mikhail had scored one-shot kills at even greater distances in Afghanistan. There's another stupid mess those drunks at the Kremlin got us into, he thought bitterly.

No, the American need not make a big mistake. Any movement at all would do.

Sunday, June 11, 0300 hours EDT
The Pentagon, Washington, D.C.

Inside the SCIF deep in the bowels of the Pentagon, Mac, the CIA man, had heard enough of the technobabble. He knew they were talking about some of the stuff the Russians were supposed to have been working on for years—directional radio-frequency, or RF, energy wave generators that theoretically could knock out cars, tanks, missile systems, anything with computers. The West was doing some work on it now, too, but by all accounts they were playing catch-up with the Russians.

Of course, if this Dr. Fensterman was right—if it was some kind of RF gizmo that brought down Captain Daniels's F-16—it didn't figure it was the Russians who were behind it. They were still palsy enough with Saddam and the Iraqis, but they weren't looking for that kind of trouble, not in that part of the world. They had their hands full running interference for the Serbs in the Balkans.

But Mac knew Russian technology and the men who made it run were for sale to the highest bidder since things went to shit over there. They had top-flight scientists getting paid with bread and sugar because there was no cash in the till. So he figured this was some kind of rogue operation. It could be Saddam. He had spent millions on Eastern European scientists and equipment to get his nuclear and chemical weapons programs up and running. But why would he risk a one-shot deal like this with a weapon system that is so high-tech, in a part of the world where he's sure to be fingered? This was not an attack, taking down one plane. It was some kind of a field test, somebody wanting to see if the gizmo actually worked.

The way Mac saw it, that made it unlikely Saddam was calling the shots. Why risk massive retaliation from the United States by testing your secret weapon on your main enemy? He's got plenty of his own planes, Mac was thinking, MiG-21s and Su-25s and some Mirage F-1s he could spare. If he wanted to test the thing, he would try it on one of his own. If Saddam had this gizmo, we'd never know it until he used it on a massive scale in an attack of some kind.

Which led him to think it was a rogue operation for sure. Somebody operating on their own, with the money to hire a Russian scientist and build a prototype and then test it in one of the hottest spots in the world. Mac had been in northern Iraq working with the Kurds before the Gulf War. He knew that part of the world was literally a powder keg just waiting for somebody to drop a match. Now somebody was in there playing with fire. Who could that be?

Mac had a pretty good idea. He knew the old saying that if your favorite tool is a hammer, every problem looks like a nail. But he didn't think he was working from an obsession on this. He had thought it over and the pieces fit.

He dialed up a secure line to Langley and got through to the task force he had left to answer the Pentagon summons hours before. He told them what he knew and what he was thinking, and argued for a priority request to the NSA to re-target some of their satellite and earth-bound interception assets to the Iraqi mountains in the north, east of the Tigris. Mac knew that if he was right the man behind all the trouble up there would not sit silent. He knew the man had to keep in touch with his associates around the world. And that meant satcom traffic of some kind at some point.

Mac made his case and he was persuasive, because he knew what he was talking about and because if he was right it was worth all the trouble and expense of redirecting intelligence-gathering satellites and even shifting their focus from other trouble spots around the world.

Because if he was right, the man behind the downing of Captain Daniels's F-16 was rich enough and crazy enough to use his new RF toy on anything from civilian airliners to Air Force One.

As Mac told his boss out at Langley, "If our boy has gotten his hands on RF technology capable of knocking an F-16 out of the sky, there's no telling what he's got in mind for his next trick."

Satisfied that he had convinced his boss and the satellites would be redirected, Mac leaned back in his chair in the SCIF and wished he could smoke. He needed a smoke, or a stiff drink. Anything to settle his nerves at the thought of Osama bin Laden hiding out in the Iraqi mountains with his finger on the button of a real-life death ray.

Chapter Three

As it happened, Travis Barrett did finish his briefings at the air base in Adana, Turkey before suppertime. But there was no time for chow. He hopped a flight out on a C-130 Hercules as soon as he wrapped up things in the Ops Center and waited until they were over the Mediterranean to tell the pilot to change course. There was the usual drill, the pilot taking umbrage at Travis's intrusion. But once he had checked in with the base by radio and been told that whatever Travis said was how it would be, Travis gave him his new course and they were on their way.

Travis settled in for a nap during the flight because there was nothing else to do and he knew he would need all the rest he could get. There would not be much time for sleeping in the days ahead.

"You know what you are, surfer dude? You're a bus driver. A freakin' glorified bus driver!"

"And I guess you're hot shit because you can drive a boat, Stan. Like a zillion drunks out on the lake every Sunday."

"Next time I get you on the water I'll show you driving a boat, pretty boy."

"Hey, you guys," the woman put in. "How about a little officer-and-gentleman decorum."

Captain Hunter Evans Blake III, United States Air Force, flashed her his Val Kilmer smile right out of the movie *Top Gun.* He and the woman were both in their late twenties, younger than the hairy barrel named Stan Powczuk. Hunter had grown up in California as much as anywhere else in his travels as an air force brat and he did have a surfer look about him. But he was an Air Force Academy grad and one of the best pilots around if he did say so himself. In what he called his "day job" with the SOA—Special Operations Aviation—detachment, he was known as the guy who could fly anything with wings or rotors.

"You'll have to excuse my friend Stan," he offered charmingly. "I'm afraid he's vertically challenged and it wears on him."

"What the hell you mean by that?" Stan growled. Though his records listed him at five-nine, he was closer to five-seven. So he was used to looking up at people, but that didn't mean he took shit from anybody. You don't get to be a lieutenant commander in Uncle Sam's navy and wear the SEAL Team 6 emblem by taking shit from people.

"I mean if you were tall enough to reach the pedals maybe you could learn to operate a real machine someday. That's all."

"It's clear to me your last ass-whipping has just about worn off, flyboy."

Sarah Greene saw Stan, a fireplug of a man, move menacingly toward Hunter, who turned to face him with his smile still in place.

"Gee," Sarah muttered, "wouldn't Mom and Dad be proud if they could see me now."

An army doctor with the rank of captain, Sarah Greene hardly looked like the type of person you would find in an army tent on a hilltop in the middle of a mountain range, not unless she was attending an alternative rock festival in support of Greenpeace.

A willowy five-four, she was in the habit of surprising

people with the kind of strength and athleticism that had gotten her through Airborne and Ranger qualification. She looked like she might enjoy hiking and snowboarding, which she did. But she did not look like a black belt martial artist, which she was. She often thought of her mom, a radical from the '60s, and her dad, a Vermont country vet, when she found herself in strange places with strange people.

This was a strange place and Hunter and Stan qualified as strange people, each in his own way. She had been through a lot with them and loved them both like brothers. But that didn't mean she felt like trying to break them up if they really went at each other, and this was no way to start a mission.

Sarah didn't like to admit it, but she missed the other female member of their little family, Jen Olsen. Lieutenant Jennifer Margaret Olsen, USN, was as different from Sarah Greene as you could imagine. There was show business in her background and she had the looks that went with it. Sarah had a kind of girl-next-door good looks; Jen was a blonde bombshell who could take the art of makeup well beyond glamour into the realm of outright disguise. Sarah had no way of knowing what role Jen would play in the mission at hand. It was not for Sarah to question. Like everything else about the team, information about assignments was doled out on a need-to-know basis.

The roar of rotors announcing an incoming helicopter ended the fight before it began. There had been no arrivals since Hunter came in around noon and they were expecting Travis with the skinny on their next mission.

As the three of them stepped outside the tent, the helicopter, a Sikorsky MH-60A special operations version of the Black Hawk, sat with its rotors still spooling down near the rim of the little plateau that overlooked a river valley. The river was a silvery stream far below, dividing the steep mountain slopes that surrounded them into a deep valley.

In the windstorm of backwash from the chopper, they

saw Travis shuffling their way. He was bare headed, wearing an air force flight suit.

"Trav, you look good in that," Hunter announced. "You finally transfer to a real outfit?"

"I'm in-cog-nito," Travis said dryly, drawing the word out with a Texas twang. "Don't want anybody to know I'm an operator."

"That's what I'm saying," Stan said with a throaty laugh. He made a circle with his figure to include everybody except Hunter. "We're operators, me and Travis and even Sarah there. You, you're just a bus driver."

"Stan—"

"Knock it off, you two," Travis said. "We've got work to do. Where's Jack?"

"Right here, sir."

Captain Jacques Henri DuBois, USMC, seemed to appear out of nowhere as he uncoiled from the knee-high grass beside the tent to his full six feet five inches. Like Travis, he was an impressive specimen, but on a larger scale. He assumed an easy slouch, his XM-29 rifle like a toy dwarfed in his catcher's mitt of a hand.

"Where have you been?" Hunter asked.

"Out here surveiling the perimeter," Jack said softly. "Keeping an eye on things."

"Nothing out here to keep an eye on," Hunter scoffed.

"Don't know about you," Jack said with a twinkle in his eye, "but I've sneaked up on a lot of men that thought that way."

"Man's an operator," Stan muttered.

"Like Geronimo said, 'There's old Apaches and foolish Apaches, but there ain't no foolish old Apaches,'" Jack said, laughing to himself.

Twenty minutes later, Travis had finished his private briefing of Hunter, who climbed aboard the Black Hawk and flew away down the mountain on the first leg of his part of the mission. Hunter didn't bother to say goodbye to the others and Travis didn't offer any explanation. That would come later, when he would tell them everything they needed to know.

0730 hours EDT
The Pentagon, Washington, D.C.

Things weren't going Mac's way back at the SCIF. He had pitched his theory to the others in his group, but the military types weren't buying it.

"Summing up," the bird colonel chaperoning the party said, "the majority view is that Saddam Hussein is our most likely suspect. It is in his backyard."

"Yeah, but—"

"You've made your case," the colonel said, cutting Mac off. "It's an interesting take on the situation, I grant you. But a little too cloak-and-dagger, it seems to me. I mean, you don't have any real evidence to support your theory."

"If it's our boy, he'll have to communicate with the rest of his network sooner or later," Mac said. "We know he has satcom capability, takes it with him everywhere. When he goes up, our satellites will intercept him. If they don't, the ground-based assets will. We've got that area covered now."

"We can't afford to wait," the colonel said. He checked his watch. "I'm due at the JCS in a few minutes and they expect a report they can act on. I believe we're all agreed on the technical side of things of what happened to the F-16."

There was a murmur of consent around the room.

Mac looked at Dr. Fensterman. Someone had put a doughnut and a cup of coffee in front of the little man and he was eating like he hadn't seen food in a week.

Yeah, Mac thought, we all agree Fensterman was right. There's an RF gizmo out there somewhere that could mean more trouble than we can imagine.

"But I still say it's Osama bin Laden," Mac said, thinking aloud.

"You've made yourself clear on that," the colonel said. "And I hope you don't mind my saying that you might be obsessed with the man. I know you people have been scrambling ever since he went missing out of Afghanistan, and it's understandable that you would see him everywhere."

"I know him," Mac said plaintively. "That's the thing."

"I'll do this," the colonel said with a tight smile. "I'll include your theory as a minority opinion. But the recommendation of this group will be based on the assumption that Saddam Hussein is the mischief maker here."

"And then what happens?" Mac asked.

"What do you mean?"

"After you present our report to the Joint Chiefs. We going to bomb Baghdad, or what?"

"You know better than to ask that."

"I'm just wondering. Because if I happen to be right about bin Laden—"

"Even if you are, that only means bin Laden is in cahoots with the Iraqis. Saddam is still behind this thing."

"Not necessarily. That's the thing about bin Laden. He's a tricky bastard."

"In any event, your bin Laden theory will be included."

"As the dissenting opinion, like with the Supreme Court."

"As the minority opinion. The JCS will make the call."

Meaning they'll kick it up to the NSC, Mac thought. This thing is playing out just like I thought it would. Except that he had a hunch the whole thing might be going off the track if they zeroed in on Saddam this time. Mac had no soft spot in his heart for Saddam Hussein, far from it. But you don't want to go bombing the wrong guy, even if he is a son of a bitch. There could be serious blow-back from that kind of a mistake with all our Arab friends—and enemies—in the region.

Worse than that, though, it would mean Osama bin Laden got away with it again. He would be free to duck out of there and nobody the wiser. But the really bad part was he would still have this gizmo and God only knew where he would turn up with it next time.

1600 hours
The mountains of northern Iraq

Captain Daniels opened his eyes under the cover of the survival blanket and hoped that it was night. But he knew better. He could see sunlight filtering in around the edges of the blanket. Which meant he was stuck in his hideout for at least a couple more hours.

He was lying in a shallow depression among some rocks, within a few feet of a stand of scrubby, twisted trees that might have been some kind of cedars. He had chosen the spot in the darkness early that morning, when he knew it was time to take cover and get some rest. No way he could afford to be stumbling around these mountains in the daylight.

With his right hand, he gently shaped the edge of the blanket in front of his face into a little tent so he could see out. His range of vision was limited to about 30 degrees directly to his front. When he had laid down here and covered himself with the blanket, he had positioned himself so he could see to the west. That was the direction the men had come from the night before, the armed men he had seen and heard making their way along the side of the mountain in the darkness.

He had taken cover behind a tree stump and waited with his pistol in his hand, but they had turned back before they reached the tree where he had buried his parachute. It stood to reason that if there was going to be any trouble it would come from that direction. But Daniels could see nothing through the opening in his blanket, looking out between two large stones—just the rocky slope running down to his left toward the valley floor.

The stones reflected bright sunlight, which told him two things. For one thing, there was a break in the weather, the storm front that had come in the night before just minutes after he bailed out of his crippled ship. For another, the stand of trees he had counted on for cover was smaller or farther away than it had seemed in the darkness, or else they would have made shade on the rocks. That meant there was no way he could move before nightfall. He would be exposed among the rocks as soon as he stood up.

And that was a problem, because his assessment of his physical condition moments after his parachute landing had been a bit optimistic, obviously clouded by the adrenaline rush of bailing out of his jet and falling through a blinding fog onto a mountain. Now that he had time to feel it, his body was racked with stiffness and pain. He still didn't think anything was broken, but he felt like he had fallen off a building. And his legs were starting to cramp up. If he could just stretch them a little—maybe, if he kept low among the rocks, he could even crawl out of his hole and find a place with better cover. Then he could check himself out more thoroughly.

He knew his only hope of getting out of this alive was to activate his beacon at night and try to get a radio message out. Somebody out there was looking for him and he had to let them know where he was. He had not heard or seen anything of SAR since the helicopter that flew across the valley not long after he landed. They don't know where I am, he thought.

If he did raise them by radio or they homed in on his beacon, they would come in hot and he would have to be ready to make a run for it. That was why he was thinking about taking a chance, a calculated risk. He was thinking about crawling out of his hole and finding a place with enough cover so he could stretch his legs and limber up.

Chapter Four

Travis's briefing was sobering to say the least, and after
he had finished, none of the team members argued about
running a little practical exercise in the surrounding
mountainsides. They all wanted to make sure everything
they had—including lungs, legs, and brains—was good
to go.

Some of the most interesting things Travis had learned
at the air base in Adana had come from a Turkish officer
assigned as the base commander's liaison. The rest had
come from Sam Wong—the payoff on his hint earlier
about a spooky angle, more to follow.

The Turk had shown Travis a map and pointed to a
large irregular oval drawn with a grease pencil. The oval
took in territory in northeastern Iraq east of the Tigris
and northwestern Iran along its borders with Iraq and
Turkey. It also included most of the panhandle of northeastern Syria. But the biggest part of it lay in southeastern Turkey, marking off an area roughly the size of Israel
and Jordan combined.

"Kurdistan," the Turk explained. "That's what the
Kurds call it. They claim it for their homeland."

Travis knew about the Kurds, as anyone did who had
spent any time in the region. There had been a CIA
operation before and after the Gulf War to help organize
Kurdish resistance to Saddam. The hope was that it
would play out like Afghanistan, but it had gotten all
screwed up. He knew that his area of operations on this

mission was in a rough patch of mountains in the heart
of the Iraqi Kurds' turf.

"I call it Indian Country," the Turk said with a smile.
It turned out he was a fan of American westerns. He
particularly liked the 1965 film *The Glory Guys* starring
Tom Tryon, which he thought was a particularly interesting portrayal of the Custer Massacre.

Travis knew something about Indian Country, the real
thing. He had grown up on land that used to be Coman-
che hunting grounds, and he knew what taking that land
had meant, on both sides of the fight.

The Turk went into more background than Travis
needed to hear on the history of Kurdish uprisings—he
called it terrorism—in southeast Turkey. Trouble had
been flaring up there from time to time since the fabled
Mustafa Kemal Ataturk, the father of modern Turkey,
had unified the nation following the defeat of the Otto-
man Empire in World War I. The original treaty in 1920
called for a Kurdish homeland, but much of the territory
was incorporated into Turkey instead. Their Kurds were
Turks now, he said, minorities like the Greeks and Ar-
menians. They are Sunni Muslims, most of them, and
cling to their own language, which is similar to the Farsi
of the Iranians.

In 1984, the Turkish officer explained, a man named
Abdullah Ocalan—his Kurdish followers call him "President Apo"—founded the Kurdish Workers Party, the
PKK, to launch a campaign of violence. In the fifteen
years since, over 30,000 people had been killed.

"Most of them were PKK guerillas," the Turk pointed
out.

And a hell of a lot of civilians, Travis thought.

"As I'm sure you know," the Turk went on, "Ocalan
was captured in Nairobi by our commandos and brought
back to Turkey to stand trial. He was found guilty of
treason and sentenced to hang. He is imprisoned on Imrali Island while his appeals run their course. The sentence must be approved by Parliament and President
Demirel as well."

Travis knew a little about the capture of Ocalan. The

word was that American intelligence assets had been used to locate him for the Turks. When word got out about that, it won America no friends among the Kurds, even those who didn't particularly support the PKK.

"Since the verdict, the PKK has been on the warpath," the Turk said. "All over the southeastern territories, even in Ankara. Their political front in Brussels has called on the Kurds to rise up. Maybe they hope to intimidate us into commuting Ocalan's sentence."

"Any intelligence on activity across the border?" Travis asked.

"The natives are restless," the Turk smirked. "Especially here."

He pointed to the map, his finger coming to rest in precisely the area where Captain Daniels's F-16 had gone down.

"The Kurds are not very sophisticated in their weaponry," the Turk went on. "We are thankful that your CIA did not see fit to equip them with Stinger missiles as they did the mujahideen in Afghanistan. But they can be fierce when they're stirred up the way they are now. And, if you don't mind my saying so, there are a hell of a lot of them."

"How many, exactly?" Travis asked.

"Twelve to fifteen million in Turkey, another ten million in Syria, Iraq, and Iran."

"I reckon that's a hell of a lot," Travis said.

In a satcom hookup with Sam later, Travis had learned about the stateside theory that an RF weapon had been used to down the F-16. Passing along the intel briefing from the NSC, Sam had told him that the most likely suspect was Saddam Hussein, possibly working through a third party. He said there was a minority opinion that the mastermind might be Osama bin Laden, acting on his own or with allies unknown.

Even over the satellite, Travis could tell something was wrong. He could hear it in Sam's voice. When he asked, the commo wizard was not bashful about explaining.

"I'm airborne, that's what's the matter! I'm in an airplane."

"What kind?"

"How should I know? A big one, eastbound over the ocean."

"Why?"

"Nobody would tell me, they just hustled me out to a base somewhere and here I am. You know I'm not crazy about flying, Travis."

"Don't worry about it," Travis joked. "It's all part of the master plan."

"That's what I'm afraid of."

Sam Wong was a cocky, skinny kid in his early twenties whose parents had left China for New York City shortly before he was born. He wore glasses and was not career military like the rest of them. He was technically a civilian employee of the National Security Agency, but he had pushed himself to make it through TALON Force qualification, with some help from Jack DuBois, his buddy and the only other "city boy" on Eagle Team. He had earned a special commission as an army captain and had held up his end on missions before. And he was a commo wizard like nobody Travis had ever seen. Putting him on an airplane headed east probably was part of the plan, a decision made in the NSC war room. Travis knew he would be briefed on it when the time was right, but he could make an educated guess. If he was right, it would be one more complication on a mission that already had the earmarks of a real rodeo.

By the time the TALON Force came together for their final briefing before taking a chopper ride and boarding the C-17 Globemaster that would take them into harm's way, Stan Powczuk had stopped bitching about Hunter Blake, who had flown out earlier after being briefed by Travis. Sarah Greene had written a letter to her folks at home, to be delivered in the event of—just in case. And Jack DuBois had withdrawn into a cool silence. They had been up and down the mountain and tested themselves and their gear.

They had their game faces on.

1900 hours
Camp Jihad, northern Iraq

Mustafa sat on a rock at the edge of the camp in the twilight and scanned the mountain slopes that surrounded him. His faith was like the rock upon which he sat, solid and sure. He had risen from his fifth prayer of the day only moments before, and his heart was at peace for this life and the next. But for the moment, he was disquieted by the sound he had heard as he knelt in the mud of this miserable wilderness.

Last night's storm had brought a torrent of rain and a mud slide that left the camp a sodden mire in its defile among the mountains. The slopes above were stones and straggly trees, most of the soil having long ago washed down into the valley. What was left must have descended on them in the night. The rain had transformed the valley floor into a bog that was impassable for even their rugged vehicles.

Allah be praised, the Prophet's experiment had been a success. The machine of the Russian had performed its magic and plucked the Great Satan's mighty jet from the sky. They had all seen it on the radar screen, the blip that was the fighter plane tumbling down into the mountains like a stone. And they had heard it, the roar of the engine overhead suddenly silent, then the scream of its fall and even the thunder of its crash in the mountains.

But the Prophet in his wisdom had not been so quick to rejoice. He did not trust the instruments of the Russian and warned that what they heard must have been no more than thunder itself as the storm came on. He demanded proof, and so had sent out the Iranians to search for the wreckage of the American plane.

Mustafa cursed the Iranians. They were cowards, trembling at every sound, afraid of being discovered by their enemies so far from home. He would have liked to go himself to search for the wreckage of the plane, but the Prophet in his wisdom had insisted Mustafa and the rest of his bodyguard stay near him. And that was wise,

Mustafa knew. There were many dangers in these mountains and the two Russians were not to be trusted.

Mustafa's devotion to the Prophet was complete. He even emulated his leader's long beard and his clothing. People told him they looked like brothers, so much alike. It was proof of his devotion that he understood that by doing so he put himself at risk of being taken for the Prophet by infidels who would kill him for the price on his head. So be it, Mustafa said when he thought of that. It is in Allah's hands.

Mustafa worried that the Iranians would not dare to go far from the camp and might never find the proof the Prophet sought of the power of the Russian's machine. He had prayed for the proof to be found and for the valley floor to dry so they could be on their way. The Prophet in his wisdom had prophesied that by the use of the Russian's machine they would provoke another war between the American devils and the Iraqis. This time, Saddam Hussein would not withstand the onslaught and Iraq would fall. This was the will of Allah, for the holy republic of the ayatollahs of Iran to take its place as the rightful power in the region and silence dissent from reformists at home.

But even such a desired fulfillment of prophecy would put the Prophet and his party at great risk if they remained in these mountains. When he thought of what they might do with the Russian's machine, Mustafa prayed silently again that Allah would see them safely out of this accursed place to use the machine against the American Satan. He imagined what could be done if, as the Prophet in his wisdom had suggested, they had two or three or a dozen such machines.

Imagining striking at the American Satan with such an arsenal filled Mustafa's heart with joy. But he could not shake the uneasy feeling that had come over him at the sound he had heard while at his prayers.

It was not unusual in these parts to hear gunfire in the distance. The Iraqis patrolled this rough country and bands of Kurds called it home. Whether it was Iraqis and Kurds or rival Kurdish bands doing the shooting,

Mustafa had on more than one occasion heard firing, once even what might have been rocket grenades or light mortars.

But as he knelt in prayer moments before, Mustafa had heard a single gunshot down the valley, in the direction the Russian had gone early that morning with his accursed rifle. Now the valley was still, and the mountains that surrounded the camp.

Mustafa sat on his rock and wished that Allah had seen fit to give him the power to see in the oncoming darkness.

1100 hours EDT
The White House War Room, Washington, D.C.

Tom Burgess loosened his tie and opened the button-down collar of his blue broadcloth shirt. He leaned back in his high-backed chair, a cup of coffee in his hand, and surveyed the layout.

The cup was embossed with the presidential seal and the layout was the White House War Room. The members of the National Security Council had stepped out to attend to other matters. The national security advisor and the Director of Central Intelligence were in the Oval Office briefing the president. The others were canceling social plans for the evening or wrapping up things at their respective agencies.

It was the lull before the storm, in a manner of speaking, and Burgess was taking advantage of the opportunity to conduct a mental review. There were checklists aplenty for these situations, and they had all been checked and double-checked. But he liked to do a little private inventory for his own peace of mind.

Burgess knew something of TALON Force and General Krauss and his command system, if only enough to do his job. Enough to know that this evening's business was being handled a little differently than was customary. Krauss, who had priority on all the satellite intelligence

on his unit's operations, had chosen this time to patch
the War Room directly into the transmission stream
rather than relaying the information. Burgess supposed
it was because the thing tonight involved a downed air
force pilot and Krauss meant it as a courtesy. Whatever
the reasons, it was none of Burgess's business and he did
not concern himself about that part of it. They all had
their jobs to do.

Burgess had served a stint in the army after graduating
from a respectable third-tier university and found himself
assigned to a series of intelligence posts, the last in the
Pentagon. Too young for Vietnam and discharged long
before the Gulf War, he had been one of thousands of
junior officers who did their duty satisfactorily if not with
particular distinction. It was no fault of his that he had
missed his country's wars.

After the army he had considered joining the CIA but
he was married by then and thought better of it. Instead,
he had gone to work for the Department of Defense,
where his background in army intelligence and Pentagon
contacts helped him work his way up the civil service
ladder until finally he landed a job as an assistant deputy
on the NSC staff. When operations were afoot, it was
his job to supervise the support personnel assigned to
the War Room. And so he found himself, a man of respectable if modest accomplishment, a witness to stories
that could never be told.

Burgess was one of the faceless functionaries that
every government department relied upon to get things
done. And he was okay with that. At forty-three, he had
a comfortable life in the Virginia suburbs with his wife
and daughter, a high school freshman who had inherited
her mother's good looks.

The only thing that ever really bothered him was these
occasional stints in the War Room. It bothered him that
he was a privileged spectator with a ringside seat in the
safety and comfort of the War Room, while better men—
and women, he had learned—risked their lives in highly
sensitive and dangerous operations around the world.
For him, they were only voices and in some cases grainy

images relayed by satellite. And sometimes they did not come back. Sometimes the voices stopped, the images dissolved. Sometimes the men and women out there died.

Burgess sipped his coffee and ran over his redundant mental checklist again. And he offered up a silent prayer that this would not be one of those times.

Chapter Five

The Black Hawk helicopter came for TALON Force Eagle Team on their mountaintop and whisked them away into the gathering darkness.

Only Travis knew where they were or where they were going. The others did not ask and he did not tell them. It didn't matter. All they cared about now was the mission, and they had all the mission-critical information they could handle. There was no time for extraneous details.

It was the kind of mission guaranteed to spook any seasoned specwar operator.

Off the top, it was a hybrid, a combination of two mission types, CSAR and direct action. A straight combat search and rescue mission was tough enough but relatively straightforward. You went in hot and heavy, located your boy, made the snatch, and got the hell out. There were a lot of things that could go wrong. You had to plan and configure your assets to counter them—AAA defense and suppression, air cover, a ground security force to throw up a perimeter and deal with any local resistance. But it was straightforward—one objective, in and out. Travis had run CSAR ops in the Gulf War and again in Kosovo. He knew they were hairy as hell but doable.

Direct action missions—going after a specific target—were something else. There were a lot of variables, and the type of target dictated the mission profile. Taking out something stationary—a bridge, an ammo dump, even a command-and-control bunker, was one thing. Mobile targets were tougher and the smaller the target the tougher it got. Going after a specific individual—a kill was difficult, a snatch even more so—was the toughest thing of all. It could be done, but the risk/reward ratio could get all skewed as hell.

Special recon missions were another kettle of fish, but recon was not going to be part of this operation, except as a tactical component of the overall scheme.

CSAR and direct action missions challenged the best of operators working with all the support the U.S. military machine could offer. Travis knew TALON Force couldn't always call on full support because their missions were too sensitive. But he had dealt with that problem before and he had confidence in his team.

It was when you mixed things up, tasked a team with multiple objectives, that you exponentially increased the risk of bad luck or a mistake.

That was what Travis was thinking as the Black Hawk set him and his team down alongside a runway in an undisclosed location far from any signs of life. His people offloaded the helicopter and made their way without any unnecessary conversation to the waiting C-17.

The massive McDonnell Douglas/Boeing Globemaster III sat ready in the moonless darkness at the end of the runway, its four Pratt & Whitney turbofan engines idling and its cargo hatch open to form a ramp beneath its tail, waiting for them. With a wing span over half the length of a football field and a fuselage even longer, the C-17 was the air force's top-of-the-line intra-theater heavy cargo transport. The cargo bay could be configured to accommodate 100 passengers on seating pallets, 48 stretcher patients, or 102 paratroopers with all their gear.

This particular bird, one of two out of the air force's fleet of eighty that was designated with a code word priority as on-call for TALON Force along with its carefully selected crew of three—pilot, copilot, and loadmaster—would be traveling light tonight. But that was the whole point of TALON Force when you got right down to it—

small, highly trained, and specially equipped teams that could move like a squad and hit like a battalion.

The Eagle Team members went up the C-17's ramp, each carrying a duffle bag crammed with personal equipment and supplies. They made a second trip to bring the rest of their gear onboard, and then Travis called Sarah aside.

They stood on the tarmac at the foot of the ramp and Travis looked down at her.

"I guess you know we're going into hostile country," he said.

She shrugged. "We always do."

"More hostile for you than the rest of us, I mean."

She knew he didn't mean because she was a woman. They knew each other too well and had been through too much together for that.

"Arab country, you mean."

"Yeah." Travis smiled a crooked smile and added, "No place for a nice Jewish girl like you."

"I'll take my chances," she said.

"I know you've got grit, more than your share. That's not the point. But if you want to take a pass on this one, I'll understand."

"If Jews took passes, there'd be no Israel."

"Reckon you've got a point there."

"Is that it, Boss?"

"That's it."

"Then let's get this show on the road."

Travis nodded and smiled. They walked up the ramp to join the rest of the team and he signaled the loadmaster they were good to go.

The cargo ramp closed silently at the rear of the aircraft as the team got busy with the pre-mission ritual of making themselves and their equipment ready.

Travis was still thinking about the mission that lay ahead as he made his way forward.

They were to make a nighttime insertion into rugged terrain occupied by hostile forces—Iraqi line units and Kurdish guerillas would almost certainly be in the area. And there might also be Turkish units there. The Turkish officer who had briefed Travis at Adana had made it clear that the Turks were not squeamish about crossing their border with Iraq in pursuit of the PKK and its supporters. They had done it before.

The whole thing with the PKK being up in arms over their leader's death sentence in a Turkish court had made for headaches Travis didn't need. For one thing, it meant the Turks couldn't guarantee the security of any forward staging areas on PKK turf in southeastern Turkey near the Iraqi border. It was the nearest friendly ground to the area of operations in the Iraqi mountains, and it would have been nice to stage a heavy helicopter reaction force there, just in case. For another, it meant the Kurds in the area of operations would be on the move, on the alert, and spoiling for a fight. They would shoot first and ask questions later, operating on the assumption that anybody they came across was either an Iraqi or a Turk.

Even if they know we're Americans, there's no guarantee they won't open up on us, Travis thought. There were several factions among the Kurds, often as interested in fighting each other as their common enemies. If the team tangled with a group that supported the PKK, they could expect no favors. The PKK blamed American intelligence for leading the Turks to their leader Ocalan in the first place.

Travis knew there might be a fourth hostile force, if whoever had authored the minority opinion about Osama bin Laden was right.

Once they were in the area of operations, the team had several objectives and that was where it got complicated. They were to locate the pilot, dead or alive. If he was alive, they were to bring him out. That was where Captain Sarah Greene, M.D., came in. She was one of the best in the world at practicing medicine under primitive conditions.

They were also tasked to find and destroy the weapon, whatever it was, that had brought down the F-16. Ideally, the brass in the War Room would prefer that they capture the gizmo and bring it out with them too. But that was asking too much, even for them.

While they were at it, they were also supposed to find what was left of the F-16, get photographs or transmit satellite imagery for analysis, and destroy the plane's armaments if they could be located to keep them from falling into enemy hands.

They had offered no guidance on which of the mission's objectives took precedence—the pilot or the gizmo. And Travis had not asked, because he knew it would be his decision to make when the time came. He just hoped it wouldn't come to that, that he would not have to face the question of one or the other. There was always the possibility that whoever had the gizmo had hauled ass after downing the F-16.

Nothing had been said in the intel briefing from NSC about bin Laden other than the minority opinion that he might be involved. Nothing had to be said. Travis knew that if bin Laden was there, they were to neutralize him one way or the other. Like the gizmo, the preferable option would be to capture him and bring him out. But that was hardly likely.

Forward of the cargo bay, Travis found Sam hunched over a control panel, dialing in data from a geosynchronous satellite on station over the Middle East.

When he sensed Travis looming over him, Sam looked up and smiled.

"I whipped this together on the flight over. Pretty hot, huh?"

"Jim Dandy," Travis drawled. "What is it?"

"A miniature commo center, as much like mine back at NSA as I could manage with the equipment available."

"If you say so."

"Did you know General Krauss is sharing the satcom feed with the suits in the War Room?"

"Nope."

"He is. Usually he gets the stream direct at TF Command and relays what he figures they need to know, but he's cutting them in on the whole shebang this time. I was wondering why."

"The general's got his reasons, I reckon."

Travis was not worried about the satcom stream. His command link was direct to General Krauss, and that was all he needed to know. He figured he had enough to worry about.

"I can monitor just about everything from here. I'll be in contact with you every step of the way, Boss."

"I reckon you will, hoss, but not from here."

"Not from here?"

"Nope."

"What do you mean?"

"I mean you're going along on this one, Sam."

"Do you think that's a good idea?" Sam asked.

"Not especially. But I've got my orders. Come with me."

Sam followed Travis back to the cargo hold where the team was checking their equipment one last time.

"Look, guys, it's the waiter," Stan boomed, grinning broadly. "I'll have the wonton soup and sweet 'n' sour pork with fried rice."

"Eat my—" Sam protested, but Travis cut him off.

"Okay, y'all simmer down. I'm going to run through this one more time for Sam's benefit so hear me good. If anybody has any questions I want to hear them now."

One thing they all wanted to know about was the RF gizmo they were going after. Each of the TALON Force operators wore a wristband RF field generator. It was a small device aimed by pointing your arm at the target and activated by voice command. One of them could fry the ignition in a troop truck or kill a computer-aimed weapon at a range of up to 200 meters. The team members had seen them work, had used them before. It didn't take much explaining for them to understand the power of a similar, larger machine that could knock out an F-16 at 15,000 feet.

Travis had studied the intel brief relayed via satellite from the War Room and he told the team what he had learned about Dr. Fensterman's theories.

"These wristband generators are as good as it gets with our technology, as far as making the things portable. With what we know about RF, it would take a generator the size of the Ft. Worth stockyards to generate enough energy to reach out and disable a jet at 15,000 feet. But somebody out there has figured out a way to do it with a machine portable enough to take it up into rough mountain country. That means it will probably fit in the back of a pickup truck. Which means you could get one within range of an airport—or a military airfield—without being detected."

Jack cursed softly and Sam shook his head, frowning. They all knew what that meant. A terrorist with a weapon like that could wreak havoc on civilian air traffic or vital installations like the air bases in Adana or Aviano.

"Near as our people can figure," Travis continued, "this thing is highly directional, like a laser beam. It has a radar component for target acquisition. And it is obviously capable of playing pure hell on anything computerized. I can't say I'm clear on that, why it works on computer systems but not old-fashioned analog systems with wires and tubes. But that's what they tell me, something about modulation or calibration, something in the nature of solid-state digital systems. That's about all we know, except that whatever this thing is, it's years ahead of the best we've got."

"That's why we're going to go in there and grab it," Stan said, grinning.

"A secret weapon," Sarah said softly. "A death ray, like in *Flash Gordon*."

" 'Wars may be fought with weapons, but they are won by men,' " Jack said. "George S. Patton."

"The Soviets were working on RF for years before the wall came down in eighty-nine," Sam said. "I've read about it."

"Well, I reckon somebody bought themselves a smart Russian," Travis said.

1115 hours EDT
The Pentagon, Washington, D.C.

In the SCIF in the bowels of the Pentagon, Mac, the
CIA man, was chewing a stick of gum he had bummed
off the kid Bob and was on the phone to his team out
at Langley. The man on the phone there pointed out
that it had only been twenty minutes since Mac called
the last time.

"I know what time it is," Mac growled. "So what's
the word?"

"Nothing so far that looks like our boy."

"He's tricky and he can afford the best," Mac said.
"He might be transmitting in microbursts to avoid
intercept."

"The sigint guys are all over it, Mac. If bin Laden's
transmitting from the target area, we'll pick him up."

"I hope you're right."

"Are you sure it's him, whatever this thing is you're
working on?"

"Let's say I have a hunch."

Mac heard the other man laugh softly.

"That's a hell of a hunch, man—a couple million dollars' worth. You know what it costs to fiddle with these
birds."

"They can take it out of the reward money," Mac
joked.

The U.S. government had put a five million dollar reward on bin Laden's head. Of course, a government
hump like Mac wouldn't be eligible for the payoff, but
it put things in perspective if you thought about it. If
Mac could help finger the bastard it would save Uncle
Sam the reward. Of course, to the suits in the front office
five million was peanuts anyway.

"I'll page you if we get anything," the man at Langley promised.

"I don't think you can reach me. I'm in a tin can here."

"So call back. I got nothing better to do."

1130 hours EDT
The White House War Room

The heavy hitters of the NSC were huddled at their table, where they had a clear view of all the monitors and digital status readouts. At the other end of the room, their senior staff was in a huddle of their own. Like the crew in the SCIF, they represented a cross section of the nation's military and intelligence community.

"How's the clock running?" one of the men asked.

"On schedule, just over an hour to insertion," another answered.

"You comfortable with the plan?" asked the first.

"If I wasn't, I would have said so before it was too late."

"I know. I'm just thinking out loud."

"You have a problem with the plan?"

Tom Burgess stood in the background, scanning the satellite feeds and displays. There was nothing to see on any of the monitors yet, and the radio traffic relayed by satellite from the C-17 sounded routine, the pilot calling off his checkpoints in coded transmissions.

"Pretty skimpy on support, wouldn't you say?" asked the first man.

"Between the PKK thing in Turkey and the RF threat in the target area there's not much we can do."

Conventional SAR had been pulled out of the area where Daniels's F-16 went down because of the RF threat. Nobody could be sure the targeting radar on the device was similar enough to the kind used by traditional SAMs to enable air cover to lock on and acquire a target. Daniels's wingman had reported an anomaly and the scientists' examination of the telemetry from the aircraft involved left them divided on the subject. So the decision was made to pull out the helicopters and their fighter air cover, just in case. They did not want to risk littering the Iraqi landscape with helicopters and their crews. One thing was certain. Anything that could take down an F-16 from 15,000 feet could wreak havoc on helicopters hovering a few hundred feet off the deck trying to home in on a downed pilot's beacon signal. The risk was too great.

Especially since everyone agreed there was little chance the pilot had survived. Nobody had reported picking up a signal from his beacon and the weather and terrain were against him, not to mention hostile forces. They knew there was a chance he was still alive, that he had activated his beacon but the signal just hadn't made it out of the rough country. That was why they had tasked the specwar operators—whoever they were—to locate him in addition to dealing with the RF threat.

The first man was navy. He had flown jets off carriers back in his day, and he couldn't get Daniels out of his mind. He remembered O'Grady in Bosnia, scrambling around in the woods and eating ants with search parties tromping all over him for five days before he was rescued. It was O'Grady's good luck that a pilot from his squadron stayed on station a little longer than he was supposed to, stuck with the search when there was little reason to believe O'Grady was still alive. But nobody was out there looking for Daniels, not yet.

The other thing bothering the former naval aviator was the end game, like he had said.

"How are they supposed to get out of there when they've done the job?" he asked.

"You heard the plan," the second man said.

"Yeah. That's what bothers me."

Chapter Six

Travis had thought about how to get in and get out. Insertion and extraction were fundamental to any spec-ops plan, always the base you built on. And he didn't want another exfiltration like on their last mission—a disaster that had them fighting their way to the Persian Gulf through Kazakhstan, Turkmenistan, and Iran. Like everything else about this mission, though, it was complicated by the RF threat and the PKK. The RF angle in particular trimmed their list of options.

Eagle Team had used gliders on their previous two missions and had recently been working with a high-tech craft that was basically a glider, but it could do things no normal glider could touch. It could be launched from a land base or a C-17 mother ship at altitude and Hunter could do wonders with it. He could fly it halfway across the United States and land it in a particular shopping center parking lot in front of the store of your choice. Whatever Stan might think of Hunter, Travis knew the "surfer dude" was a hell of a pilot. But the experimental glider prototype was loaded with computerized systems. It was unlikely the motorless craft with its stealthlike signature would be detected by radar. But it was a chance they couldn't take. If they were wrong and the RF weapon system spotted them, the mission would be over before it got started, the glider destroyed, and all of them with it in one neat package. Besides, the downside with the glider was that, while it could take them almost anywhere, it did not yet have self-launch capability and would be of no use in getting them out. It was strictly a one-way ride.

Another technique that had proved effective in the past was a SAR stay-behind. You put SAR helicopters in the target area and had a couple of them set down and off-load their ground security force. Stir up a bunch of dust, then reboard and take off. In all the confusion, your team stays put until the choppers are gone and nobody's the wiser. The RF threat made that approach too risky, too.

The same thing went for using the team's new V-22 Super Ospreys. An airplane that could convert to a helicopter in flight by swinging its rotors from vertical to horizontal, the Osprey had all the advantages of a helicopter for landing a team in a tight spot without the downside of a chopper, particularly limited range and low airspeed. The Osprey would be ideal if it weren't for the risk of having its computer systems fried by the RF gizmo.

Travis hoped the gizmo was still there. With all the hoops they were jumping through to accommodate it as a potential risk, it would be a shame if whoever was operating it had already pulled it out. Its being there would complicate the mission but he had already allowed for that. He had factored it into the series of calculated risks that made up an operation like this. And he didn't want to come up empty.

So that left them with one viable option—a jump. Parachutes, even the sophisticated models TALON Force used, were relatively low-tech gadgets with no computers to worry about. With the exception of Sam Wong, Travis knew the people on his team were some of the finest parachutists in the world. If anybody could pull off a HALO—High Altitude Low Opening—jump into rough terrain on a moonless night, it was them. Sam had qualified on conventional jumps as part of his team qualification, and even daytime HALO jumps, but night-time HALO was another matter.

The decision had been made up the chain that the enemy's RF capabilities might pose a threat to the team's

communications equipment. The thinking was that anything that could generate a directional beam strong
enough to knock out an F-16 at high altitude might very
well be capable of creating something along the lines
of an EMP—Electro Magnetic Pulse—that would disable
their radio and straight-up satcom systems. That was
something not even a commo wizard like Sam could fix
remotely from his cubbyhole at NSA or a C-17 orbiting
the area of operations. He would have to be hands-on
to make the fix, and that meant he went in with the team.

So insertion would be by parachute. Travis didn't mind
that. He liked a jump to kick off a mission. It got the
team's adrenaline pumping and focused their minds.
There was the weather to consider. A new storm cell
was moving in from the coast and Travis could only hope
the window of clear air over the drop zone would hold.
From the latest reports, it would be close.

Getting out was still iffy. If they were successful in
capturing or destroying the RF weapon, it would be safe
for choppers to come in and pick them up. The problem
there was the situation with the Kurds in Turkey. It
meant there would likely be no forward staging area for
a reaction force to stand by for the call. The only option
was to have them already airborne and orbiting somewhere close, refueling as needed. But that was not practical because there was no way to know when they would
be needed. TALON Force's special equipment was designed for a seventy-two-hour operation before recharg-
ing, and Travis figured it would likely take most of that
to get the job done. You couldn't keep choppers in the
air for seventy-two hours. Besides the practical problem,
there was the secrecy thing. The brass did not like for
anybody to find out about TALON Force, and that even
included friendly forces. The preference was for the team
to rely on their own resources and the handpicked C-17
crews assigned to them. Outside help was to be called
on only as a last resort.

So a plan had been devised that Travis didn't care for
at all. It was too complicated and contingent, and there
were too many chances for it to misfire. But he had not

been able to come up with anything better, so they were stuck with it. A conventional reaction force from Adana was the fallback option. It would require a lot of lead time and that might mean a long wait in a hot LZ for help to arrive, but there was nothing Travis could do about that.

It's like hunting bobcats with a lariat rope, he told himself with a wry smile. You knew the job was dangerous when you took it.

1500 hours EDT
The White House War Room, Washington, D.C.

"What's the latest on the weather at the target?" the Director of Central Intelligence asked Tom Burgess.

Burgess, who was the answer man for the head table in the White House War Room, checked his notes.

"Last word I had a few minutes ago, the window was holding. The storm front is moving in from the Med, but it is still clear over the target."

"Double-check that for me, will you?"

"Yes, sir."

Burgess turned and made his way down the row of technicians manning monitors and consoles to the airman who was the War Room's link to meteorology.

"How's it looking?" he asked.

"Not good." The baby-faced airman looked up at Burgess. "Do we know what the critical time period is exactly, sir?"

Burgess checked his watch.

"Less than an hour."

"Radar shows the front still moving in. It's going to be close."

"Thanks."

Burgess left the young airman at his work and reported to the DCI. Weather was marginal.

He wondered how marginal it would have to be for the men at the head table to abort the mission.

1500 hours EDT
The Pentagon, Washington, D.C.

When the bird colonel in the golf togs finished his briefing, Mac spat out his gum and swore under his breath.

"What?" Bob the young techno-wizard asked.

Bob and Dr. Fensterman had become pals in the hours they had spent cooped up together in the SCIF. He and the wild-haired doctor had been going over the data from the aircraft telemetry again and comparing notes. Bob was doing most of the talking. Dr. Fensterman had been handed a hamburger from the commissary and was devouring it like a wolf.

Bob was as baffled by military briefings as Mac had been by what he called Fensterman's technobabble.

"What was that all about?" Bob asked again.

"That was about show time."

"Pardon?"

"He was telling us it's show time. They're about to go in."

"Who's about to go in?"

"I don't know," Mac said. "And if I did, I wouldn't tell you."

The audio components of the wall-mounted monitors crackled to life with a voice that Mac guessed was the pilot of the plane taking the operators in. The voice was laconic the way pilots' voices almost always are, whether they're pointing out the sights for passengers on a commercial airliner or counting down a missile launch over Belgrade. Whatever this pilot was reporting was in code, but Mac figured he was telling somebody he had reached a checkpoint and was making his run.

Mac knew nothing about TALON Force, but he had been through this before. He knew a mission was underway and that it wouldn't be long before they started getting real-time intelligence from the area of operations. The pilot's coded message meant the operators were about to be inserted. Mac guessed it would be by parachute.

It was almost midnight in the mountains of northeastern Iraq now, and there was a storm blowing in. Mac tried to picture it, a crew of specwar badasses waiting in the belly of their plane for the signal to step out into the dark and stormy night.

He grabbed the phone on the desk in front of him and dialed Langley again.

"Come on, you pricks," he muttered. "Have some news for me this time."

**2320 hours
Airborne over the Turkey/Iraq border**

Travis had told his people everything he knew about what waited for them on the other side of the cargo hatch that would be lowering in a couple of minutes. They were all volunteers and that gave each one of them the right to refuse to jump. It was a formality. Travis knew his people and they had been through this before. None of them would opt out at this point, not even if a vision had come to them that they weren't coming back this time. None of them would step back from the door this late in the game—not even Sam Wong.

Sam was no snake-eater. He had busted his hump to qualify for missions because he knew there were times when the team needed him on the ground instead of at his computer console. But extreme heights bothered him and he knew he would never have made it through jump qualifying without Jack DuBois's help. He was a geek at heart and had never pretended otherwise. It was asking a lot of a geek to strap on the gear and duckwalk off the end of a lowered cargo ramp into the black night sky at 20,000 feet over what the Turkish officer had called Indian Country.

Sam would be strapped into a double harness with Jack DuBois. Since he wasn't night HALO qualified, he would have to ride down with somebody who was. And Jack was the jump master of their crew. He had more jumps under his belt than any of the rest of them.

"Come to me, little brother," Jack said with a broad smile, holding the straps of the harness that would secure Sam to his chest in his big hands. "Like in the bosom of Abraham."

"Bosom of Abraham? What is that, Old Testament?" Sam asked nervously.

"You know it."

"No I don't. I'm Buddhist."

Sam made no secret that the prospect of a night HALO jump—never mind all the rest of it—scared him to death. But when it came right down to it, he looked into the eyes of the rest of the members of the team and said he was good to go. His mouth was so dry he had to swallow a couple of times to get the words out, but he did it. He volunteered.

As he stepped into the harness and Jack buckled him in, the big marine leaned over and whispered in his ear.

"Remember the first rule of cool, Sammy," Jack said. "Never let the rednecks see you sweat."

2330 hours
Camp Jihad, northern Iraq

Osama bin Laden sat with his legs crossed on the blanket that served as the makeshift floor of his tent. The tent itself was a tattered and nondescript military castoff that might have been used by any of the forces that inhabited these mountains. The only furnishings were straw pallets and blankets rolled up in a corner. The mud that had come down the mountain in the heavy rain the night before had worked its way under the walls of the tent to spread over everything inside.

The Saudi's men, the cadre of faithful followers who served as his bodyguard, had made an effort that day to clean up the mess because they could not bear to see their Prophet so indisposed. For himself, bin Laden welcomed the imposition. He was a serious man, a man of purpose, and it satisfied his ascetic nature to suffer hardship in the service of his cause. He was engaged in a *jihad*, a holy war against the Great Satan, and if Allah chose to make his way hard, so much the better.

In sharp contrast to the primitive setting of the tent itself, the electronics array unfolded on tripods inside the tent to keep the machinery clear of mud and dirt was state of the art, top-of-the-line stuff. Osama bin Laden knew the value of technology and that instant, global communications were essential to the enterprise he had undertaken. In his travels, he had availed himself of some of the best technical minds in the world in designing and assembling equipment that was compact, portable, and yet powerful enough to reach around the world.

If Allah had seen fit to make him the son of a decadent betrayer of the true faith, he had also granted him the enormous wealth of a Saudi prince in the bargain. It was Osama bin Laden's duty to make use of that wealth for the high purpose Allah intended.

At the moment, he was making use of the technology his inherited wealth had provided him by watching CNN's international newscast down-linked from a satellite by the powerful satcom transceiver that was part of his ever-present travel package.

The American infidels were clever in their manipulation of what they called the news, but Osama bin Laden had long ago learned to read between the lines to garner important information. It was the arrogance of the Western devils that their technology ruled the world, and the wisdom bestowed by Allah that allowed bin Laden to garner grains of truth from their propaganda to keep abreast of events around the world, even from this rude camp in the Iraqi mountains.

He was still brooding over an earlier reference to him by a news anchor. The infidel had called bin Laden a terrorist in reporting that the CIA had been unable to locate him since he had abandoned his camps in Afghanistan.

It is, like beauty, in the eye of the beholder, bin Laden mused. The West was in some ways still a mystery to him, but he had concluded after much prayerful thought that the Americans in particular defined terrorism as much in terms of technology as in terms of their own political agenda. If one had jet aircraft at his disposal to rain down bombs upon a sovereign nation with which you are not at war, as the Americans did in Tripoli in 1986, you are a statesman. But if one must resort to delivering the same blow by means of a truck bomb as the faithful did at the American marine barracks in Lebanon, you are condemned as a terrorist. The marines were foreign troops occupying Muslim lands as the Western imperialists had done for centuries. What threat was Libya to the mighty United States compared to such an impudent aggression?

"O Great Prophet."

It was Mustafa, the captain of his bodyguard. The man could not bring himself to enter without bin Laden's permission, and he insisted on addressing him in that way. It had been all bin Laden could do to dissuade the man from calling him *mahdi*. The literal meaning of the word was "he who is guided," and it was the title to be given the spiritual and temporal ruler many Muslims believed was destined to establish a righteous reign throughout the world. Mustafa meant well by this, but bin Laden would not permit it. It would be viewed as blasphemy by some, as a sign of vain ambition by others. There had been claimants to the title in the past, and bin Laden knew the story of the most famous of these, Muhammed Ahmed of nineteenth-century Sudan. He was the *mahdi* of Kitchener and Khartoum, and a fine legend for the faithful. But he had not prevailed against the British Empire in the end, and bin Laden had no intention of joining the list of martyrs who had wrung moral victories from the infidels. His aim was real victory, and if Allah saw fit for his *jihad* to make the way clear for him or another to someday ascend to the role of true *mahdi*, so be it. It was in Allah's hands.

"Come."

Mustafa's head appeared beneath the tent flap, his eyes catching the light from the kerosene lantern hung from the tent pole, its yellow glow offset by the flickering blue light from the television monitor.

"O Prophet."

"What is it, Mustafa?"

"The Russian with the long rifle. He is coming back down the mountain."

"It's about time. I thought he might have gotten lost out there."

"And he's carrying something over his shoulder, O Prophet. It looks like a body."

"What's that you say?"

"It appears the Russian has made a kill, O Prophet."

Chapter Seven

Hunter Blake checked his instruments. From the pilot's seat of the ancient DC-3, he looked down past the original instrument panel with its primitive analog dials and gauges at the high-tech LANTIRN—Low Altitude Navigation and Targeting Infra-Red, Night—package. He and a couple of technicians at the air base in Adana had lashed it together hurriedly before he took off and so far it was working fine. Flying was fun and always had been, no matter what kind of ship it was. Navigation, on the other hand, was work. He couldn't imagine how the original crews of these old "gooney birds" had found their way from point to point back in World War II.

The old bird was a dinosaur, but Hunter had to hand it to the old-timers who drew it up and put it together. It was a tough and durable ship. He knew that after the war the DC-3, known as the C-47 by the military, had been a workhorse all over the world. Some third-world countries were still flying them on regularly scheduled routes into the 1960s.

As a backup to the LANTIRN system, Hunter could dial up Merlin, the Boeing E-3 AWACS plane circling thousands of feet above him to track air traffic along the Turkey-Iraq border. Another AWACS, designated Magic, was performing the same role farther south over the Iraqi No-fly Zone.

If Hunter had any problems with his improvised on-board navigational system, Merlin could talk him in to his target.

Hunter prided himself on his skill as a seat-of-the-pants pilot when the occasion demanded, but he knew his target would be easy to miss at night, especially if the weather developing to the west overtook him before he got where he was going. This was one time he did not mind having a little extra help available.

With the confidence bordering on arrogance of a natural pilot, he felt sure of his ability to find what he was looking for and set his old crate down without doing too much damage, even as primitive as the landing site was supposed to be according to the reports. He was already thinking ahead to the role-playing and sleight of hand it would take to pull off their cover story. A key part of that would be hiding the high-tech electronics package he was using to get there and the extra fuel cells he would need for the next leg of his trip so that nobody would find them. The old DC-3 had to look like the real thing, an authentic relic that was just barely airworthy.

Hunter knew the old bird would look the part from the outside anyway. He remembered his first look at her in a hangar back at Adana.

"Where the hell did you dig up that thing?" was his first question.

That was a long story, but the main thing was that it was perfect for his part of TALON Force's mission. Perfect right down to the faded Turkish lettering on the fuselage above the wings. He had been assured the lettering spelled out "Ankara Studios, Ltd."

In the co-pilot's seat, Lieutenant Jennifer Margaret Olsen, USN Office of Naval Intelligence, sat calmly applying theatrical makeup, ignoring the bumpy ride of the underpowered little gooney bird as it lurched along in the updrafts from the Taurus Mountains a couple of thousand feet below them.

Jen, a blue-eyed blonde Scandinavian-American bombshell from International Falls, Minnesota, was focused on transforming herself. She was in the process of becoming an aging brunette, a French film star who had seen better days but was still big in the backwaters of the region

where state-run television programming had failed to dim
the allure of French New Wave films from the 1960s.

She was guided in her efforts by publicity photographs
of the old star as she had been in her glory days and a
couple of candid snapshots as she was now. According
to the info package from the NSC, the actress now lived
as a recluse in the south of France. She would never
know that she was about to make a comeback in the
Turkish hinterlands.

2330 hours
Airborne over eastern Turkey

The C-17 Globemaster had flown a similar route to the
one Hunter was following in his old DC-3 thousands of
feet below, eastward through friendly Turkish airspace.
But while Hunter's flight—if it went according to plan—
would terminate at a little-used airstrip in the boonies
somewhere east of Mardin in southeastern Turkey near
the Iraq border, the C-17 had turned south toward the
target area, descending to an altitude of 20,000 feet for
its final approach.

Aft in the cargo hold, TALON Force operators
watched the cargo hatch lower and felt the big ship buf-
feted by high winds. That was to be expected at this
altitude, especially with a storm front moving in. With
the exception of Sam, they had all jumped HALO before
under conditions this bad or worse.

Travis waited for the signal from the loadmaster, who
was plugged into the ship's internal communications system and taking his cues from the pilot, who was monitoring their position on a pinpoint GPS SatNav system.
Travis felt his pre-mission butterflies give way to a deep
sense of inner calm. He had done all he could and they
knew all they were going to know about what awaited
them in the dark mountains below. This was what they
trained for and it was why they had been chosen, a handful from among thousands. It was time to go to work.

The only worry Travis had was that there would be a last-minute call from the War Room to abort the mission. You never knew what they were thinking back at the NSC, or what information they were factoring into the mix. Maybe they would get skittish about the weather. There were a lot of maybes in a deal like this. But that was the nature of the beast. Travis knew his team was ready. Their mission was virtually suicidal, but their missions always were. If it was easy, they'd send somebody else.

"Go! Go! Go!"

The loadmaster gave them the hand signal and the magic words. The five figures, Jack and Sam moving as one, waddled out onto the cargo ramp under the weight of their gear and parachutes and stepped out into the slipstream in the wake of the big ship and the cold darkness. There was no turning back now.

1530 hours EDT
The Pentagon, Washington, D.C.

Mac thought he might have imagined it, but the pilot's voice sounded a little different this time over the speakers in the SCIF. His last transmission had been in code like the rest of them, but there was something extra in the way he said it.

"That's it," Mac muttered.

"That's what?" Bob asked.

"Insertion." Mac looked up from the phone in his hand into the kid's eyes behind the thick glasses. "They're going in."

"Who's going in? How?"

"If they told me they'd have to kill me," Mac groused dryly. "But I'm guessing they jumped."

"It's the middle of the night over there."

"That's right."

"And there's a storm front moving in."

"Right again."

"Are they nuts?"

"Yeah. Thank God they're on *our* side."

1530 hours EDT
The White House War Room, Washington, D.C.

The monitors had come to life and they were getting
images from satellites. One was a wide-angle view of the
area of operations, a black-and-white picture with the
effect of a relief map that showed the rugged mountain
elevations. Another was a closer look, maybe a dozen
square miles that made the situation they were monitoring seem much more real than it had before. In the closer
view, Tom Burgess could make out the features of individual mountains and ridges. He could see large boulders
strewn down the slope of one mountain toward the valley
floor below.

Burgess was no technician, but he knew what he was
looking at. It was the product of a sophisticated "eye in
space" surveillance system that had some light-gathering
capability. It wasn't night vision exactly, like the goggles
used by specwar operators and the chopper pilots of the
elite 160th Special Operations Aviation Regiment. But it
could obviously pull together images in low light.

It was midnight in northern Iraq on a night with no
moon and the storm front was only minutes away from
all but obliterating the scene. So far, the images were
less than optimal but still useful.

Too bad the satellites couldn't find Captain Daniels or
even pinpoint the location of the wreckage of his F-16
with a high level of certainty. The weather had been
against them. Even during the daylight hours over there,
when there had been a break in the weather at ground
level, there had been a problem with clouds aloft that
had complicated a search by satellite.

Burgess knew there were satellites up there that could
zoom in on an individual car's license plate, but it was
never a simple matter to have the one you needed where

and when you needed it. Some of them were in geosyn-chronous orbit, basically hovering over a given spot on 'the earth's surface twenty-four hours a day. Others were in orbits designed to maximize their coverage, tracing a path over areas of interest on different continents with every revolution. He knew the people at NSA were working on bringing their satellite assets to bear on the situation with Captain Daniels. But his wasn't the only crisis in the world. With "situations" working simultane-ously in the Balkans, North Korea, and the India-Pakistan border region, there were a lot of legitimate demands being made on resources that were impressive but not infinite.

"Geronimo."

Burgess turned toward the sound of the voice. It was one of the staffers seated around the second table, a newly minted commander fresh from a SEAL team and assigned to the chief of Naval Operations' staff. He had been sent over from the Pentagon as part of the group that presented the original ops plan from the JCS. Bur-gess remembered his name was Greeley.

Burgess went over to him. "Excuse me. What did you say?"

"Geronimo. Isn't that what you say when you jump out of an airplane?"

"In the old days, I understand."

"Well, somebody just did that."

"We have insertion, sir," one of the men at the con-soles monitoring communications reported.

"What do you think?" Burgess asked, looking up at the satellite images. He could tell by the look on Gree-ley's face that he would rather be with the team going in than sitting here in the war room.

"HALO from twenty thousand feet into a sky with no moon. Thirty-mile-an-hour crosswinds on the leading edge of a hellacious storm front that's racing them to the drop zone. Which is a flat spot the size of a football field on a rocky ridge with vertical slopes falling away on three sides. In a no-man's-land where every son of a bitch within two hundred miles has a Kalishnikov, a bad attitude, and more ammo than he can fucking carry." Greeley leaned back in his chair and locked his fingers behind his head. He looked up at Burgess and smiled tightly. "Piece of cake."

2335 hours
Over northern Iraq

As always, there was no sensation of falling.

Once they cleared the turbulent wake of the C-17, there was only the whistling wind and the dark sky that shrouded the earth far below. It felt like flying—or hanging suspended from some great celestial ceiling.

Almost all the members of the team used their BSDs to orient themselves. The exception was Sam, who kept his eyes shut tight and tried to fight back a wave of nausea at the thought of somehow slipping out of the harness that strapped him to Jack's chest and kept him from plunging to his death.

The team's helmets were marvels of modern technology, custom fitted and made of lightweight ballistic microfiber materials. In addition to providing protection against small-arms fire, they were engineered to provide local and global communications and even a minicomputer workstation. Embedded micro bio-chips inserted underneath each team member's skin near the right ear served as transceivers. Linked with the helmets, they enabled team members to communicate with each other and "straight up" via satellite to almost anywhere in the world. Without the helmets, the chips alone were good for up to 1,000 meters, line of sight.

The BSD folded down from each helmet like a monocle. It could be used to generate a laser pathway that painted images onto the wearer's retina, a form of holograph. Each team member could activate his or her BSD to view a display of status reports, maps, or telemetry. Linked as they were now by the systems in their helmets to a satellite, they could call up images of what the satellite was seeing in real time. The BSD could also be used as a laser range finder or to designate targets out to 3,000 meters for precision munitions. Or, as in a night HALO jump, to serve as a guidance system zeroed in on the team's drop zone. A handy added feature was the BSD's thermal viewing capability, effective up to 2,000 meters in low light, smoke, or fog.

The members of TALON Force were almost all outstanding operators, impressive physical specimens who had the benefit of some of the finest training in the world and had been chosen from among thousands of candidates from elite military units. They were righteously confident in their own abilities and the cohesive strength of the team.

But even the proud and competent operators of TALON Force would have readily admitted that the cutting-edge weapons and equipment they were issued played a key role in the edge they held over any competition. The helmets with their BSDs were only part of the ensemble.

The free fall from 20,000 feet to a low-altitude opening is a hell of a ride under any conditions, and the combination of the elements at play this time made it beautiful in a wild and dangerous way that could not help but impose itself on the most focused professional.

The team was practically flying down the sky, holding their bodies in aerodynamic position, their backs arched, legs and arms spread like wings and rudders they could maneuver to change direction and control their rate of descent. They were winging in from the heavens like dark angels and there was no more thrilling feeling to be had by mortal man.

To the west, lightning played in bold flashes and jagged veins across the towering dark clouds of the storm front. It was very close now and coming fast. If they were going to beat the storm to the landing zone, it wouldn't be by much. It was a race and the stakes were high. If the leading edge of the storm overtook them, it could scatter them like chaff, driving their opened chutes miles from their target to land in a scattered array that would make it all put impossible for them to ever join up and proceed with their mission. That was if they were lucky. If they weren't, they would fall to their deaths in the mountains waiting below, their chutes shredded and trailing behind them like tails on kites.

Even with their high-tech instruments providing heads-up readouts on location and altitude, it was a dicey proposition, falling that far and then pulling the ripcord at exactly the right moment. Pull too soon and you were at the mercy of the wind too long and, even with the highly steerable TALON Force chutes, you might be driven off course and land on a killer cliff face. Pull too late and you would come in too fast, the weight of your gear your enemy then, and land hard on the rocky height at a speed that guaranteed at least a broken leg or busted ankle. And that was no way to start a mission.

But four of the five would not have traded places with anybody in the world. The storm was like a Wagnerian stage setting that perfectly complemented the deep inner thrill of defying death on a mission no one else would even attempt, against odds no one else would dare to face—for an objective that was worth everything they had to give.

Jack shifted his focus from his BSD to take in the scene unfolding around him, the towering thunderhead looming over him, racing him to the hostile earth below.

"Can't believe they pay me for this," he muttered.

"Copy that," Travis answered from somewhere off in the dark sky, having picked up Jack's remark on his helmet commo system.

"It's a warning from God," Stan chimed in. "To the ragheads down there."

Even Sam made a contribution to the crude tributes offered by operators who were more eloquent in their actions than their words.

Finally daring a look around him, the techie opened his eyes just in time to see a bolt of lightning fire off so close he thought he could have reached out and touched it. As the accompanying thunderclap boomed around them like artillery, he moaned and tried to pray.

"Oh, shit," was all that came out.

Chapter Eight

Hunter stole a peek in his mirror as Jen stepped out of her flight suit behind him in the passenger cabin of the old DC-3.

It wasn't much of a passenger compartment. Most of the seats had been taken out long ago. Hunter and the two technicians had taken a stab at trying to rig it up like what they thought an over-the-hill French movie star would be traveling in if she happened to be traveling in this part of the world. They thought about some kind of boudoir setup back there, but there wasn't time to get fancy. They had spent most of the time they had patching in the LANTIRN package and loading the extra fuel. The best they could come up with was a brightly colored but mismatched pair of shower curtains from the Base Exchange. They had strung them on a wire to divide the cabin in two. Behind the curtain, there were bunks that folded down out of the bulkhead. On this side of it, a few seats remained in the forward half of the cabin. It looked tacky as hell, but maybe that was appropriate. She was supposed to be a has-been.

Hunter, like all the other men and some of the women who had ever caught sight of her, wanted desperately to see Jen naked. As far as he knew, in her natural state she was a buxom blonde with dazzling blue eyes and a perfect smile, like a billboard for the Swedish bikini team. But he could not be sure. For all he knew, the blonde blue-eyed thing was a disguise too, just a role she played.

He had seen her in a dozen different guises, from a fresh-faced farm girl with freckles to a lethally seductive *femme fatale* in black leather with hair and eyes to match. He had even seen her as a convincingly frumpy septuagenarian, complete with varicose veins and cataracts.

He had imagined what she must really look like under all that and he had set himself the goal of getting to know her well enough to be sure, to satisfy his curiosity once and for all. And he had given it his best shot.

Hunter was not vain to excess, but he was male-model handsome with his blond hair, chiseled features, and killer smile. Women had always flocked to him—but not Lieutenant Jennifer Margaret Olsen, USN. She had been nice about it, so sensitive and skillful in deflecting his advances that he could tell she'd had a lot of practice. He admired the way she had handled it, just a simple no. She hadn't gone into a lot of stuff about mixing business and pleasure, the need for team cohesion, or how important it was to keep relationships on a professional level. It was just no, without explanation. It left him thinking she didn't figure he needed to know anything more than that she wasn't interested. He had to respect her for that.

But he was still curious. So he took his eyes off the instruments as the old gooney bird pounded through turbulence and darkness and sneaked a peak at her as she stepped out of her flight suit.

"Damn," he muttered under his breath as he caught sight of her, the discarded flight suit an olive drab heap at her feet.

To his surprise and heartfelt disappointment, the body that emerged matched the face she had so artfully constructed while sitting beside him in the copilot's seat. She had totally reconstructed her own face to give it the bags and sags of a woman thirty years older. Even her teeth were different, the perfect white pearls gone beneath a dingy cigarette-stained set that featured the French star's trademark overbite. The effect was so convincing that she had actually seemed to become the woman she was going to impersonate.

Hunter hadn't realized that Jen had already donned the bodysuit that went along with the face. She turned and smiled at his reflection in the mirror as if to let him know she had been on to him all along.

Of course she knew I was watching, Hunter chided himself. Otherwise she would have stepped behind the curtain to change. He waved a hand and smiled back in his mirror. Okay, he was saying without words. Joke's on me.

Then he shook his head to clear the image of Jen Olsen in the bodysuit with its fat hips and thighs and drooping breasts. And that butt. It was as big as a footlocker!

2345 hours
The drop zone, northern Iraq

They almost beat the storm, but not quite. The high winds and lightning at its leading edge engulfed them just as they popped their chutes, seemingly in unison. Streak lightning illuminated the drop zone a few hundred feet below them just as a tailwind racing ahead of the storm caught them up and hurled them forward, threatening to send them careening beyond the flat DZ and into the dark chasm beyond.

Jack DuBois, with the added weight of Sam Wong strapped to his chest, fought his shroud lines hard and spotted the DZ coming up fast. The drop zone was a flat, rocky space at the crown of a ridgeline where it made a right angle to follow the course of the river in the valley below. It was 150 meters long and a little more than half that wide. It was bigger than a football field, but not by much.

The big marine drove himself and his piggyback partner toward the rocky flat, then worked the shrouds on his aerodynamic chute to soften the landing as much as he could in the last few meters before impact.

If any of them was going to overshoot the DZ it should have been Sarah Greene. She was the lightest in body weight and the mixed combat/medical load she carried weighed less than the others' full combat loads. But she was okay. She landed closer to the edge of the little plateau than she would have liked and had to fight the billowing chute like a wildcat to keep it from dragging her over the brink, but she got it done. After a bumpy roll, she came to rest within two or three meters of the edge, bruised from the rocks but okay.

Travis got down in good shape and spilled his chute without any major problems. He saw Stan nearby, getting to his feet and peeling off his harness. He accounted for Sarah, too.

"Where are Jack and Sam?" he asked, looking around the rocky flat.

A flash of lightning stabbed out of the sky, lighting the DZ like a strobe. A gust of wind brought the first of the rain, angling down in sheets that dropped visibility with the naked eye to almost zero. Travis, Stan, and Sarah used their BSDs for thermal viewing, scanning the DZ.

"Barrett to DuBois," he called out over his helmet commo system. "Do you read me?"

There was no answer and the three operators set to work. With the efficiency that comes with practice, they secured their chutes and broke out their weapons and equipment. Each of them carried enough firepower to rival a conventional platoon, and there was a lot of equipment to be removed from protective casings and reconfigured for comfortable carry and easy access. They were done with that in less than a minute, their speed the product of efficiency learned in the hundreds of blindfolded repetitions that was part of their training.

"Travis to Jack. Do you read me?"

Still no answer.

1545 hours EDT
The White House War Room, Washington, D.C.

"They're down," one of the men at the consoles in the back of the room announced. "On the DZ."

There was no backslapping or shouts of joy, but the DCI—head of the CIA and charter member of the NSC's inner circle—let out a long sigh and asked if there was any fresh coffee. There was always plenty of coffee in the White House War Room, but it was the DCI's style to ask rather than order a cup or go get it himself.

The president's national security advisor showed no reaction to the news that the team had made it to the DZ. It was his style to always be thinking a couple of steps ahead. At the moment, he was wondering if TALON Force—he was one of the few men in the war room who knew all about TALON Force—would find the RF weapon itself or only signs that it had been there. It seemed logic would dictate that Saddam Hussein would have pulled the thing out of there immediately after taking down the F-16. He was bound to know that leaving it in the area meant exposing it to a counterattack in one form or another. And such a weapon was too valuable to risk.

The president's man pondered that. He remembered all too well the problem Saddam's mobile SCUD launchers had given them. He hadn't been the president's man then; that was the Bush Administration. He had been a general at the time, in charge of G-2—Intelligence—on the staff of an army corps. He knew plenty about Saddam's wizardry at sleight of hand. So he wasn't expecting TALON Force to find the RF weapon, really.

And that left the pilot. The president's man thought that was a long shot, too. There had been no confirmation that the pilot had even been able to eject, much less any sign of a chute opening. The terrain was brutal and the weather had been very bad—though not as bad as it was going to be over there tonight, according to their weather information. It was twenty-four hours and counting since the F-16 had gone down. And no one had reported any sign to indicate the pilot had survived the crash, not the AWACS crew aboard Magic or the satellite tenders at NSA. The air force was still flying Deny Flight missions, but they had bumped up the minimum altitude to 30,000 feet. The F-16 pilots from Daniels's own squadron had put in a lot of "vul" time in the last twenty-four hours and they hadn't picked up anything either.

Of course, he might have tried to radio out or activated his beacon and the signal just didn't get through. But the odds were he hadn't survived.

So why send in TALON Force? Because they couldn't take the chance that the RF weapon was in there somewhere, possibly vulnerable to the kind of high-risk strike the enemy would never expect. They couldn't take the chance one of their pilots was still alive in those mountains and not do anything about it. You never abandoned one of your own. That was policy and there were good, practical reasons for it. You could not ask the next man to risk his neck if he knew you might not come for him if he got into trouble. But beyond that, it was a matter of honor. The president's man was decidedly old school on that score. It was the right thing to do. And it was too dangerous for anyone else, which was why they sent in TALON Force.

But that did not mean they were expendable. Far from it. And that was why the president's man put his head in his hands and rubbed his temples when they got the report that two of the TALON Force members were unaccounted for at the DZ.

1545 hours EDT
The Pentagon, Washington, D.C.

Mac stood up and took a deep breath. He was going out for some air. Under the circumstances, that only meant walking out the door of the SCIF and down the corridor about fifty feet to the men's room, escorted there and back by one of the armed guards stationed outside. Nobody was allowed to leave the building and nobody went anywhere without an escort until the operation was secured.

But they were a long way from that. They were just

getting started, and already there was bad news. Of the five operators who had jumped, only three were accounted for at the drop zone. Nobody had told the men in the SCIF that in so many words, but Mac could decipher most of what he heard over the speakers. They were getting satellite imagery on the monitors now, but there was not much to see because of the weather.

Like a couple of bodies at the bottom of a ravine, Mac thought.

He was having a bit of a flashback to that night a long time ago and the carnage at Desert One. It wasn't that bad this time. Not yet. This mission was still a Go, and he knew that whatever five men had been tasked to do, the three remaining could probably get done. But it was a hell of a way to start, and he was tired of hearing updates on the storm that had closed in, how bad it was going to be and how long it was going to last.

He had a sick feeling in the pit of his stomach. There had still been no report of a sigint intercept from the target area, no sign of Osama bin Laden. It was a hell of a way to start an operation.

Chapter Nine

Mustafa hurried back from making his rounds to check the tent's perimeter. The rain was cascading down like the wrath of God, and Mustafa stood ankle deep in a sea of mud outside the Prophet's tent with his head tucked down into his shoulders against the deluge, waiting for permission to go inside.

"Come."

Mustafa ducked under the tent flap and buttoned it up behind him. He saw in the light of the kerosene lamp overhead and the flickering blue light from the Prophet's monitor perched on its tripod that there must still be enough soil left on the accursed mountain to make mud. It was seeping into the tent again, undoing all the work Mustafa and the rest of the Prophet's bodyguards had done that day to clean up inside the tent and brace the uphill wall against just such a thing.

The Prophet sat cross-legged on a doubled blanket, ignoring the rain and the mud. He was watching something on the monitor.

Mustafa paid no attention to the electronic marvels. To his mind, they were the work of Satan and only a man such as the Prophet had the strength to deal with them without losing his soul. He did note with satisfaction that two of his men were there, on either side of the Prophet, to ensure his safety as Mustafa had ordered must always be the case whenever the Russians were in the Prophet's tent.

Pretsky was a fat devil with an unhealthy pallor and a

face like an unclean pig, with puffy cheeks and a short snout. The other one, Mikhail, was a cold-eyed infidel whose face never let down its hard mask except when he was caressing his precious rifle, as he was now. The Russians sat opposite the Prophet, Pretsky staring at the monitor and Mikhail cleaning his Dragunov rifle.

"The perimeter is secure?" the Prophet asked.

"All the devices are in place and activated, O Prophet."

In such a storm, it was no use to put the Iranians out as sentries, which was their duty. They would only curl up under the rocks out of the rain. A man could hardly see his hand at arm's length anyway. The electronic devices were more reliable. Even in the storm, they would detect motion and activate an alarm in the tents of the camp. Mustafa did not know how the devices worked and had no interest in learning. He had been shown by the Prophet himself how to set them out around the camp and what to do if there was an alarm. It was all he needed to know.

"We could have done without more of this damned rain," Pretsky muttered in English. It was the only language bin Laden's men, the Russians, and the Iranians had in common. The Iranians' English was very poor, but it sufficed for their purposes. "We are held prisoner here by this damned mud."

"It is the will of Allah," the Prophet said calmly.

"Of course it is," Pretsky said sarcastically.

Pretsky had no desire to stay any longer in this wilderness. Truth be told, he had never wanted to come here in the first place. He was a scientist, not a soldier. The smell of bin Laden's millions had brought him here. The fat Russian didn't see why he had to risk his life on this fool's errand in the first place. It had been his intention to simply demonstrate his device and collect his fee. What he had in mind was a show in some safe, dry place. His client would furnish an aircraft, a drone or whatever, to fly over and he would prove that his machine could do what he said it could do. He was confident in the technology. It had been developed by some of the best minds in Russia. It didn't matter that Pretsky himself had played only a small role in the process. But it was he who had managed to smuggle the necessary data out of the country. Communism had failed. It was a capitalist world now, and he meant to have his share of the wealth.

Bin Laden had insisted to the point that Pretsky felt he was little more than a hostage in this madman's camp. Who knew what kind of a devil's bargain bin Laden had struck with the Iranians? That was none of Pretsky's concern. In spite of everything, he had proven that his machine was all he claimed it was. He was due his pay now and safe conduct out of these mountains. He would be out already if bin Laden were not a maniac who insisted on a souvenir from the American jet Pretsky's machine had destroyed.

Well, he had a souvenir now. But this damned rain made travel impossible, unless they left Pretsky's machine behind and trekked out on foot. Pretsky had suggested they do exactly that. He could build another machine, and they could destroy this one to make sure it didn't fall into the hands of an enemy. That made sense. It was the logical thing to do.

But bin Laden operated on a logic all his own. Pretsky had learned that to his grief. His vision of millions of U.S. dollars tumbling into his Swiss bank account in payment for the prototype of the machine he had delivered to the terrorist buried in a new avalanche of dollars for the production models he would build seemed like a dream now. How can bin Laden be so stupid? Destroy the prototype and get me out of here. I'll make you as many of the bloody machines as you want once I'm safely out of this damned place.

But all Pretsky said aloud was, "Perhaps we should reconsider leaving the machine and the vehicles and walking out."

Sitting beside Pretsky with his Dragunov sniper rifle broken down into its components on a dry rug beside him, Mikhail went about the task of cleaning his weapon. When he was done cleaning it, he would replace the regular scope with a night-vision model from his kit. He saw that bin Laden seemed not to hear Pretsky and he almost smiled. The fat technician who called himself a scientist was as yellow as he was fat and soft.

For Mikhail, it had been a good day. He had waited patiently in his hide for his prey to make a mistake and his patience had paid off.

Underneath the blanket spread along the rear wall of bin Laden's tent lay the American, asleep or unconscious—it was hard to say. It would have been a good shot to kill him outright, but Mikhail had made a great shot and brought him down alive. How much longer he would stay that way was anybody's guess. But that was not Mikhail's problem. He had done his job. It had been a good day.

And it might be a good night as well. Mikhail had baited a trap for any Americans who happened to come looking for their lost pilot. He didn't think their helicopters would be flying in this weather, but they hadn't been flying earlier either. That was curious, Mikhail thought. But Mikhail thought the *Spetsnatz* way, and that meant to expect the unexpected. What would Alpha Group do in a situation like this?

Yes, he told himself as he began reassembling his clean rifle. He thought of how the trap would look through the eyepiece of his night-vision scope. This might be a very good night indeed.

2355 hours
The drop zone

Jack's eyes snapped open and he blinked through the fog in his head. It took a few seconds to get his bearings and then it all came back to him. He and Sam had been the last in on the DZ, battling the gusty wind to keep from overshooting it. Everything had looked okay until the last second when Jack saw Sarah, struggling with the wind in her chute, being dragged across the rocky flat directly into his path. An instinctive reaction on the shrouds had lifted Jack and Sam enough to clear her, averting a crash that would have put all three of them out of action.

But Jack paid a price for his lightning reflexes, the maneuver carrying him too fast toward the edge of the DZ. He shut down fast and hit hard, within a couple meters of the rim. But he landed off-balance and couldn't hold it. The wind took him and Sam sprawling over the lip and into the darkness beyond. He didn't remember what happened after that, and he knew he had caught a knockout blow on the rocks.

"Thank you, whoever designed the Battle Sensor Helmet," he muttered. If not for the special high-tech helmet, he knew he would not have survived the impact.

Jack felt Sam's weight shift in the harness on his chest.

"Are we down yet?" Sam asked, reaching out with one foot in a futile search for solid ground. "I can't—"

"Be cool," Jack said calmly. "Open your eyes and take a deep breath."

Moving slowly and gently, Jack punched up the HUD readout from the Auto Trauma Med Pack that was engineered into his camo suit. It was a built-in system that served two functions. Its bio-chip health status sensors monitored his vital signs, body functions, and injuries. In addition to feeding this data via satellite to the ops center in the White House War Room, it would execute first aid measures and activate drugs and fluids from the ATMP in case of an injury or a wound. It could also seal wounds if it came to that.

Jack was relieved to see the readout showed no injuries beyond a possible mild concussion. He could live with that.

Sam was wiggling in the harness now. Jack knew the kid was reaching out for the ground, trying to feel something solid under his feet.

"Sammy, please be cool," Jack repeated. "Breathe deep and be still."

"Where are we, Jack?"

"We're in a bit of a situation."

"We're hung up, aren't we?"

"Yes, but it's not a problem."

"The hell it's not! We—"

Sam's voice died in his throat as both men heard fabric rip and felt themselves dropped two feet then brought up with a jolt as the snagged shrouds strained against their combined weight.

"It's like Nietzsche said," Jack whispered. "What does not kill us makes us stronger."

"Neitzsche," Sam muttered. "Bet you he never jumped out of a perfectly good airplane."

Jack had no way of knowing how long he had been out, but he knew what the drill was for the rest of his team. They would gear up, stash their chutes under the rocks on the DZ, and move out. The storm was really raging now, and they wouldn't go far. They would get off the flat ridge-back and set up a defensive perimeter somewhere nearby to wait out the worst of the storm. All of which meant they weren't far away.

Jack had a pretty good idea where he was, but knowing was little comfort. He knew he had been headed for the northeast corner of the DZ where it dropped off into a vertical slope that fell a couple of hundred meters to a jumble of rocks at the base of the ridge. He looked up to see how far they had fallen from the DZ, but the rain blinded him. When he looked down, all he could see was the rain falling into blackness.

His chute had snagged something, a ledge or an out-cropping of rock, in the slope face and stopped their fall. Now he and Sam were suspended in midair and he could feel the rock of the cliff at his back as they twisted in the wind.

"Anybody out there?" he whispered into his helmet commo system. He wasn't sure why he was whispering. Maybe he sensed that any disturbance, even a loud voice, might undo their tenuous hold on the cliff face and send them hurtling down to the rocks below. "This is Jack calling."

2355 hours
Airborne over southern Turkey

Jen, her transformation complete, was back in the co-pilot's seat and strapped in tight.

Hunter stole a sideways glance at her and shook his head. She was a totally different person now, as authentic an aging French movie star as he ever wanted to see.

"It's a little bumpy," she said in English with a convincing French accent.

"Yeah, the storm's traveling faster than we are. But we're almost there."

"Storm's a good thing, if you think about it," Jen offered, still with the accent.

Hunter knew she was getting into her character. He also knew the turbulence bothered her more than she wanted him to see. Hell, it would bother anybody, he thought, especially in this flying boxcar.

"Yeah? How so?" he asked, keeping his voice calm and steady. He didn't want her to know that the turbulence and limited visibility were getting on his nerves, too.

"Our cover story. We're supposed to be having trouble with ze plane, looking for a place to set down and make repairs. Ze storm makes it more convincing."

"Yeah, you're right."

The storm made it convincing as hell, as far as Hunter was concerned. They wouldn't have to bother with the smoke bomb he had rigged under one of the old gooney bird's two engines to simulate a problem. The weather was problem enough. He only hoped the old crate held together until he could get her on the ground in one piece. And he hoped the weather over the target would be better than this when the call came for him and his French costar to fly in and pick up the team.

According to LANTIRN, their destination was dead ahead and closing fast. Hunter eased the old ship's nose over and took her down for a look. If the Turkish officer back at Adana had done his job, somebody down there

would be expecting them. But that didn't mean that whoever it was would be much help with the landing. Their
arrival had to look like a surprise to everybody in the
place. And that meant no landing lights, even if there
were any still in working condition. Which meant the
landing was going to be a lot trickier than Hunter would
have liked. It was one thing to set the old bird down and
live to tell about it. He had to make sure it was still in
flying condition for the next leg.

They broke out of the cloud cover at less than a thousand feet and Hunter could make out terrain features
beneath him. The LANTIRN system had done its job,
he was relieved to see, and brought them into a narrow
valley surrounded by mountains. Hunter lined up on a
sparse nest of lights dead ahead that he knew would be
the little village whose name he couldn't remember. Just
short of the village itself lay the rocky airfield the Turks
had used for air supply and even some passenger flights
in the past but abandoned long ago. If they were lucky,
the abandoned strip would be long enough and flat
enough for the old DC-3 to set down.

It should work, Hunter told himself. The airstrip and
the plane he was flying were of the same vintage.

He made one pass over what looked to be the airstrip
and dropped a flare out his window. Banking into a
climbing turn to bring himself around into the wind, he
saw the flare floating earthward. Its pendulous arc of
light showed him the airstrip and he groaned. It was as
bad as he had been told, little more than the width of
an interstate highway and just long enough to land on
with very little margin for error.

"How does it look?" Jen asked, still sounding authen-
tically French.

"No problem," Hunter answered her with a smile.
"Lucky for us I happen to be the world's greatest pilot.
Relax, mademoiselle, your life is in my hands."

Chapter Ten

Tom Burgess watched the monitors come on-line. The telemetry looked good, so the experts told him who were paid to know about such things. Vital signs in the normal range, slightly elevated as you would expect under the circumstances. No significant trauma, only the bumps and bruises that were part of a night HALO jump into rough country. And there were five of them.

Burgess made his report to the head table, then went to the staff table to let the men there know, too.

"They got them," he said.

"Who?" Commander Greeley asked.

"The ones who went missing at the drop zone. We have a voice link via satellite now. It's choppy because of the weather, but they're down and talking. And they're healthy, all five of them."

"Excellent." Greeley grinned broadly. "Where were the other two?"

"They went over the side but their chute hung up on a ledge. They were just hanging there. The others found them and lowered lines and pulled them up."

"Two on a chute, buddy-jumping?"

"Apparently."

"That's odd."

"They were lucky," Burgess said. He didn't care if there were two of them on one chute. He figured they had their reasons.

"Damned straight," Greeley said. "Lucky as hell."

"Maybe it's a good omen."
"Let's hope so."

1600 hours EDT
The Pentagon, Washington, D.C.

Mac was back from his walk to the men's room when monitors in the SCIF started picking up reports from the team at the DZ. All accounted for now and no casualties.

What they got at the SCIF was patched through on relay from the White House War Room, and Mac knew they were getting an edited version. Only the inner circle at the NSC was cleared for the raw feed. The men in the SCIF had security clearances, but not high enough for everything. Mac would never know who those people were out there, those five operators who had survived the jump and were now probably holed up in the rocks somewhere to wait out the storm.

He didn't mind that. He was an old hand at this stuff and he understood the whole need-to-know thing. It was enough for him just to know that they had people out there, whoever they were, who could pull off this kind of operation. It made him proud.

Mac ran it all down for Bob and the professor, explained to them what the stuff they were hearing and seeing on the monitors meant. They were excited, too, and gave each other uncoordinated high fives.

Enough celebration, Mac told himself. Let's see if we have anything to contribute.

He called Langley again and this time there was news.

"I paged you," the man on the other end of the line said.

"I told you, you can't reach me in here. It's a dome of silence."

"We have something."

"Talk to me." Mac held his breath.

"An intercept."

"Our boy?"

"Looks like. It's from the target area. A microburst, just like you said."

"In code?"

"Naturally. We're working on it now. It's similar to one bin Laden's used in the past."

"Son of a bitch," Mac growled. "It's him. I was right."

"Looks that way."

"We're going to nail that bastard this time."

"From your lips to God's ear, Mac."

Monday, June 12, 0030 hours
Çukurca, Turkey

Hunter reversed both engines and leaned on the brakes as the gooney bird finally settled onto the rocky strip bulldozed along the side of a mountain after a couple of hard bounces. He brought the old crate to a wheezing stop with all of thirty meters to spare. Another couple of seconds and they would have gone off the end of the runway into a patch of boulders that would have gutted the DC-3.

"What did I tell you?" Hunter gave Jen his best movie star grin. "Nothing to it."

"I'm no expert," Jen murmured, her knuckles white from her death grip on the frame of the copilot's seat. "But I'd say zat was a nice bit of flying."

"You're too kind."

"I had no idea you're almost as good as you think you are."

"Yeah, well—huh?"

"But enough small talk, monsieur. It is show time."

She was looking out the cockpit window on her side when she said that last part, and Hunter looked past her out of curiosity. There would be time enough later, if they were lucky, to continue their conversation about how good he was.

What he saw startled him. He wasn't sure what kind of reception he had been expecting, but it hadn't included torches. There were people coming their way from the direction of the village and they were carrying honest-to-God torches.

"Looks like that scene in *Frankenstein,* where the villagers storm the castle."

"That's not the script we're playing, Blake." Jen's accent was gone.

"We know that, but do they know that?"

"It's your job to go out there and tell them."

"Pardon?"

"Get out there and set up the bit. I've got to make an entrance."

"I'll see what I can do."

By the time Hunter worked his way out of the cockpit and opened the forward cabin door to lower the steps to the ground, the first of the villagers or whatever they were had reached the plane.

Hunter ambled down the steps, bathed in the light of torches held aloft by a motley crew that might have been anybody—Turks, Kurds, the PKK steering committee for all he knew. There were more than a dozen of them, with more still coming.

Hunter's costume for his role in the little play they were going to try to pull off was hardly a costume at all. He was wearing a battered leather bomber jacket over a T-shirt and faded blue jeans, and Swiss hiking shoes. It was an American look, but he hoped it would be taken for a bogus one, like he had seen a lot in Europe. He was hoping he looked like a Frenchman who might be in the movie business in a small way. The downside was that he didn't really speak French. He didn't speak any foreign languages. It occurred to him that his insistence that English was the only language that mattered because it was the international language of aviation might have been a bit off the mark.

The earpiece that was his remote link to the satcom relay package hidden aboard the DC-3 would pass for a hearing aid, and Hunter planned to pretend he was very hard of hearing if he got too deep into a French conversation.

"Hallo," he offered, trying to affect a French accent. *"Q'est qua'ce?"*

It was as close as he could get to one of the phrases Jen had tried to teach him during the flight. But he had been busy flying the airplane and had not paid her much attention. He thought what it meant was either "How's it going?" or "What's up?" He couldn't be sure.

A big man emerged from the pack, the rest of the figures content to stand just beyond the right wingtip of the DC-3 and gawk.

The big man was bareheaded. He wore what looked like a military tunic over his shoulders and his pants were stuffed into high-top boots. This guy's in the army, Hunter thought, but whose?

The man said something in what Hunter hoped was Turkish. All he knew about the Kurds' language was that it was supposed to sound like the Farsi spoken by Iranians. Hunter didn't have much of an ear for languages, so he didn't worry about it. It was whatever it was, and he would just have to work with it.

Hunter shrugged in his best French style to show that he didn't *comprendez-vous*.

The big man pointed at the lettering on the plane's fuselage and said something else. Hunter thought he heard "Ankara" in there somewhere and guessed that the big man was asking what the hell a beat-up old Ankara Studios airplane was doing way the hell out in the boonies in this kind of weather, something along that line.

The stragglers were arriving now, more figures trudging out in the bad weather, guided by torches. At the fringe of the little crowd, Hunter spotted men carrying rifles. They didn't appear to be in uniform. Maybe they were Turkish soldiers who had been off-duty when the sound of the DC-3 and the light of the flare roused them from whatever they were doing. Hunter hoped they were Turkish soldiers. If they were Kurdish partisans, Jen's little show could have the shortest run in show business history.

The big man repeated his question. Hunter was

stumped. Not knowing what else to do, he drew himself up and delivered the one line he had in the production.

"Monsieurs y madames," he said. *"Je present Yvette!"*

On cue, Jen appeared in the doorway of the DC-3. She struck a pose and waved, then blew a kiss toward the torch-bearing crowd standing there in the rain.

There was a moment of stunned silence.

And then the rocky little airstrip exploded in a chorus of rough voices.

"Yvette! Yvette!" they cried.

Hunter took a deep breath and let it out slowly as the big man strode to the bottom of the steps from the airplane and bowed deeply from the waist, the cries of "Yvette!" ringing out behind him.

I'll be damned, Hunter thought. This just might work.

0100 hours
The mountains of northern Iraq

The rain seemed to ease a bit and Travis gave the order to move out from their defensive perimeter among the rocks on the slope two hundred meters below the DZ. TALON Force was an all-weather crew, thanks to their space-age Battle Ensembles. With their helmet-mounted BSDs, they could see through the dark of night, the falling rain, or just about anything else that came their way. As long as they could latch onto a satellite with their helmet commo systems, they could download real-time imagery that was better than any map and pinpoint their location anywhere on the planet to within a few meters.

And that wasn't all. They called the suits they wore "chameleon" suits because they had the same effect as the background-blending reptile. The real name for it was LOCS—Low Observable Camouflage Suit—and it was a wonder. Micro-sensors woven into the ballistic fabric of the whole ensemble—suit, gloves, helmet, and boots—"read" the visual background and actually copied it. Like a chameleon that changes color to match the rock he's lying on, an operator wearing the LOCS was literally transformed visually into an exact match of his environment. Watching with the naked eye, all you could see was a shimmer with motion. Other than that, the wearer was, for all practical purposes, invisible.

If there was a downside to the ensemble, it was its appetite for power. The ensemble was charged before each mission, and a charge was good for seventy-two hours of normal operations. The LOCS feature was the most power-hungry component and could only be used intermittently for brief periods. It was limited to a max of six hours continuous use.

There was no way of knowing how long the mission would take, so they would conserve power by using the LOCS feature sparingly. For the time being, given the conditions, they would rely on stealth and the cover of darkness.

Each of the operators wore a belt fitted out with charge cells to supply additional power to the ensemble in an emergency—if an ensemble were somehow disabled or the seventy-two-hour charge was depleted. The belts carried enough power to run the whole system for about two hours or the LOCS for thirty minutes.

In addition to the ensemble, the team was armed with some prototype weapons that gave them incredible firepower. Since their missions were highly classified, they often brought along conventional weapons, too. On this mission, each operator was carrying as backup a carbine version of the ubiquitous AK-47 with a folding stock. Leaving AK-47 brass behind wouldn't give anybody reason to suspect a crew of space-age super-operators had been on the scene. But they had their prototypes too, in case they needed the firepower they offered.

With their all-weather technology in good working order, the only reason for waiting out the worst of the storm was the footing on the treacherous mountain terrain. Technology could only go so far. As yet, it couldn't keep you from losing your footing on wet rocks and loose gravel and taking a tumble.

Now that the rain was slackening, they were good to go.

They moved in a staggered file at twenty-meter intervals. Jack, fully recovered from the blow to his head, took the point. Travis came next, followed by Sam and Sarah. Stan brought up the rear, responsible for monitoring their back trail.

While waiting out the storm, Travis had lost contact with the satellite for a time. Now he was back in touch and there was news. One of the orbiting satellites, a recent model tricked out with all the high-tech options, was coming on station over their area of operations and sending back better intel than they had been getting from the geosynchronous bird. They had a possible fix on the crashed F-16, and Travis was moving the team that way. It was as good a place as any to start.

Chapter Eleven

Hunter Blake thought things were going about as well as could be expected.

Whoever the big man was who seemed to be the leader of the village, he had certainly recognized Yvette when he saw her and so had the rest of his torch-bearers. They had swarmed around Jen in her costume and makeup like she was the real thing and literally carried her on their shoulders back to the village, Hunter tagging along in the wake of the crowd like an afterthought.

They had taken "Yvette" to the largest structure in the village, a stone hut near the center of the place that might have been a police station or army barracks at one time, or maybe what passed for a city hall in this part of the world.

Once inside out of the rain, they had deposited Jen on a table in the center of a big room and every man in the crowd had made it a point to press close enough to touch her. Many of them insisted on kissing her and she offered them her hand.

The best news of all, the way Hunter saw it, was that none of the villagers spoke French. They only spoke their native language, whatever that was, and a little bit of English. That suited the hell out of Hunter.

Jen was disappointed. She was fluent in French, Swedish, and Finnish, and knew some Danish, and she wanted to play her character in her native tongue. She was a French film star, for Christ's sake! Where was the challenge in faking an accent? Even Hunter could do that.

She thought Hunter was taking this all pretty calmly. Was he so dense about languages that he just didn't understand the situation? That was a possibility, but she decided to give him the benefit of the doubt.

The crowd fluttered around Jen with a great deal of hand waving and shouting, and somebody produced a bottle and started a fire in the fireplace at one end of the big room.

"We wish you be comfortable in humble village," the big man told her, holding himself erect. "You dream to us. We see many your film."

"We have your films," one of the others put in. He was a little man and obviously not a soldier. "We watch them here."

"How nice," Jen purred. "You are loyal fans."

"Indeed," said the little man, doffing his rough woolen cap. "I am Abdul, the projector."

"Pardon?"

"I mean, I operate projector. My name is Abdul."

"Go and get one of Yvette's films, you little man," the big man said, with a sweep of his hand. "You know the one. My favorite."

Abdul tried to explain that there was a problem with the projector. He had been working on it but it only cooperated when it wanted to, like a woman. He smiled sheepishly at having let that slip out and tipped his cap to Jen.

Abdul was sent to get the projector and came back in a few minutes with a machine that was probably as old as the DC-3 sitting on the airstrip outside. He had a couple of reels of film from the 1960s, Yvette in a French sex farce that was widely condemned by puritanical Muslims in the region.

But Hunter was glad to see they had not fallen in with Puritans. These were men starved for entertainment, and they could not believe their luck that Yvette herself had been delivered into their village. It must be the will of God, one of them told him.

He couldn't help noticing that this function was strictly stag. There were no women in sight, and Hunter assumed they must be waiting in their houses for word that it was safe to come out. An airplane landing at their little abandoned strip was cause for alarm to say the least. The men had gone out to investigate and left the women and children in the relative safety of the village.

The thing was, none of the men seemed in any hurry to tear themselves away from the fabulous Yvette to go and tell the women it was safe to come out now.

When Abdul, after several minutes of fumbling with the projector and hooking it up to a crank operated generator, ruefully announced that he was unable to make the thing work, there were angry shouts of disappointment from the others. Abdul assured them he would take the accursed machine home and make the necessary repairs. The little man hurried out with the projector under his arm, pelted by more shouts and curses.

But the men's disappointed soon faded. What did it matter if the fool Abdul could not make the pictures on the wall when they had Yvette in the flesh here among them?

Hunter made his excuses to the big man and said he needed to go and check on his airplane. The big man—Hunter belatedly learned that his name was Kamil—made a halfhearted offer to go with him and help but it was clear where he wanted to be.

Hunter thanked him anyway and made his way to the door. He looked back at Jen, the center of attention in a room awash with testosterone and the smell of goats. Anybody else, he would have worried about leaving her with that roomful of rough villagers. But he knew Jen could take care of herself.

0100 hours
The mountains of northern Iraq

Now that he had survived the night HALO jump, Sam had convinced himself the worst was over. As he followed Travis through the rain over the rough, broken terrain, he felt like his pulse rate was almost back to normal now. Unlike the other members of the team, he was not hauling a full load because he had not jumped his own chute. What he had been able to bring along, tucked in with the rest of Jack's gear, was a laptop computer with a satellite uplink/downlink component from his improvised commo station aboard the C-17.

Sam's normal role on missions like this was to coordinate communications—sometimes from his station at the national security agency. There, he could easily query any of the constellation of thirty-six satellites available to TALON Force and relay data to the team in the field. Lately, he had been operating in the field more often than not. This time, he was a lot closer to the action than he would have preferred, but he figured that was no reason to slack off on his job. What made TALON Force work was everybody doing what he or she did best. For Sam, that was communications. And Travis was happy to hand off that chore so he could focus on his responsibilities as team leader.

The laptop gave Sam capabilities beyond even the "straight-up" satcom functions of the helmet commo system. He could target different satellites and download real-time data and even access computer systems back at NSA for additional information.

He figured if he had come this far, he might as well make a contribution to the mission. He knew that having him along could be a burden on the others because they were inclined to look after him as well as themselves.

Wearing the battle ensemble was always a wild experience for him. He had been fitted for one of the outfits just like everybody else, and he had been through the familiarization drills. This was his fourth field mission. By the time they worked their way down the mountain to semilevel terrain only a hundred meters or so above the valley floor, Sam had reacquainted himself with the BSD's thermal viewing feature and was beginning to feel like an operator himself.

While the others scanned their respective zones of responsibility for any hint of trouble, Sam made his way along with one eye on the ground at his feet and the other on the screen of his laptop. He had figured out a way to remotely task the flyby satellite with all the bells and whistles to sweep the area for any signals that might be a radio message or a pilot's rescue beacon.

**0100 hours
Camp Jihad, northern Iraq**

Osama bin Laden weighed his options.

As much as he despised the porcine Russian Pretsky, the man had a point. Mikhail's capture of the American pilot was all the proof he needed that the RF generator had performed as advertised. It had snatched an American F-16 out of the air at 15,000 feet. Allah be praised.

It worried bin Laden that the Americans had not reacted immediately. He knew it was their policy to launch missile strikes on Iraqi anti-aircraft installations that targeted American planes with their radar. He had hoped they would respond in kind this time. That they had not done so was troubling. Did they not realize what happened to their airplane? Surely they did not believe it had simply malfunctioned.

No, certainly not. If so, they would have swarmed all over these mountains with their rescue helicopters until they found the wreckage and their pilot. They had responded in such a way immediately after the downing, their helicopters passing within a few kilometers of bin Laden's camp. It was due to a shortcoming in the RF generator that he had not struck against the rescue force itself. It took time to recharge the machine after its strike against the F-16, Pretsky had claimed.

The man Mustafa called the Prophet distrusted Pretsky intensely. He suspected that the fat, soft Russian had been unwilling to use his machine a second time for fear of a retaliatory strike by the Americans.

In any event, bin Laden had to admit Pretsky was right about one thing. They had proven the machine could do the impossible. And he had done it in such a way, in such a place, that the Americans almost certainly would blame Saddam Hussein for it. This was the hope of bin Laden and the Iranian ayatollahs. They wanted nothing more than for the American Satan to destroy the usurper Saddam and leave them as the power in the region. This was the will of Allah, bin Laden knew, to have a holy power on earth.

The thing now was to get out of these mountains and get to work producing more such machines. He had plans for such machines. He could wreak havoc with them and make himself a power to be reckoned with among nations—in the name of Allah, of course. With his Iranian allies at his side and the multitude of the faithful in every corner of the world, the day of the *mahdi* might very well be at hand.

But there had been nothing on CNN about the Americans losing an aircraft over Iraq. That was curious and troublesome. What were the Americans waiting for? They must be up to something.

What to do with the American pilot? That was another question. Alive, he made a good hostage. If he died, which he almost certainly would from the hole the Russian *Spetsnatz* had put in his leg with his long rifle, it was the will of Allah. He would still have value as a trophy—proof of what bin Laden had accomplished.

The capture of the pilot was a coup, no question about it. It was such a coup that he had taken the calculated risk of informing his associates of it by satellite transmission. There was little to fear from such a small boldness. He had the latest and best technology, encrypted microburst communications the Americans were not likely to intercept, or to decipher even if they did.

There was no getting around the fact that the contemptible Pretsky had a point. The reaction of the Americans—seemingly no reaction at all—was most troubling. And bin Laden had urgent business elsewhere. It made sense to destroy the prototype RF generator and make haste back to Iran.

There was just one thing that argued against that course

of action—bin Laden's deep desire to find the wreckage of the American plane. He knew from watching CNN that when a suicidal American had flown his A-10 Warthog into a mountain in Colorado, its ordnance had not detonated. He also knew that F-16s on Deny Flight missions over Iraq were heavily armed with missiles. How amusing it would be to retrieve the American's missiles and use them against some unsuspecting enemy—the Chinese perhaps. CNN had offered extensive coverage of the reaction in China to the accidental bombing of their embassy in Belgrade. Imagine if American missiles were to strike even closer to home.

The fantasy of sparking a confrontation between the Americans and the Chinese was so delicious that bin Laden found it impossible to resist.

0420 hours
The mountains of northern Iraq

"Boss."

"Yeah."

"It's me, Sam."

"You got something?"

"I think so. Yeah, I got it."

"What?"

"Satellite downlink from the flyby. I got a hit on a query."

"Give me the *Reader's Digest* version."

"I got a fix on the beacon. Captain Daniels's rescue beacon. And it's not far."

Chapter Twelve

The wind shifted from the west to the north sometime in the very early morning and the storm cell moved with it, finally spending itself in a rainy front that reached Tikrit on the Tigris and south to beyond Samarra, moving toward Baghdad before it finally petered out.

The morning's first light hinted at a clearing sky as Colonel Harim of the Iraqi army alit from his staff car and presented himself at the headquarters of the Republican Guard regiment stationed west and a little north of Kirkuk. The regimental headquarters was set up in a commandeered farmhouse in the foothills. Harim remembered from his flying days that the village of Qal'a Sharqat was almost due west across the Tigris.

Naturally, the colonel commanding the regiment was still asleep at that hour and the major on duty had to send someone to wake him. Colonel Harim waited patiently for him and accepted a cup of tea offered by an orderly.

When the regimental commander arrived, Harim presented his credentials and explained his business. Harim was assigned to Army Intelligence and had been sent from Baghdad with orders from high authority. The commander was to show him every consideration.

"It's about the American plane," Harim said as a beginning.

"We see a lot of American planes up here," the commander said ruefully.

"This particular one crashed in the mountains north of here night before last. Perhaps you heard?"

"There were reports. With the storm, we could not be certain."

"Radar confirmed it. I was assured that we were not responsible."

"There was no American retaliation."

"None," Harim agreed.

"Perhaps it was a mechanical problem."

"Perhaps. But we were wondering why the Americans launched no search and rescue operation other than a quick reaction force immediately after the plane went down."

"We?"

"In Baghdad."

"Oh, I see."

"Don't you find that interesting?" Harim asked.

"I find quite a lot to be interested in right here," the commander said.

"Yes, I've seen your reports. I take it the Kurds are making a nuisance of themselves over the PKK business."

"Yes, a nuisance."

"I would have thought they'd all go over into Turkey to make trouble." Harim studied the man carefully. "It's the Turks that mean to hang their leader."

"It's been my experience that logic does not always apply when it comes to the Kurds, Colonel."

"Perhaps not. In any event, I have my orders, as you can see."

"Indeed."

"I am to go into the mountains to investigate the American airplane."

"I'm not sure I follow you, Colonel. I understood you to say we had nothing to do with downing the plane."

"Exactly. And we don't want the Americans to claim we did, do we?"

"Ah. You're to find the plane and determine the cause of the crash."

"Yes, and I will need an infantry escort from your regiment."

"I take it you know a good deal about airplanes then."

"I used to fly them." Harim indicated the black patch he wore over his left eye. "Before I was reassigned to Intelligence."

"I see."

Harim was mildly disappointed that the commander did not ask about the patch. It was the result of an injury suffered in a crash after his Mirage was shot up on a mission over Iran in the last year of that war. He had not seen any action in the war with the Americans and their allies, beyond hiding in bunkers in Baghdad from their smart bombs. Harim called that one the Oil War. But that was another story, and the commander gave no indication that he was interested in Harim's stories.

"How large an escort did you have in mind?" the commander asked.

"A platoon, I should think. With trucks."

"Of course." It was the commander's turn to study Harim for a moment. "Are you sure that will be enough?"

"Yes."

"You wouldn't like a full company, perhaps with a bit of armor support?"

"It's an investigation, not an invasion. A platoon will do. With trucks."

"If you will excuse me, Colonel, I will see to it."

Harim walked outside to instruct his driver to wait here for him with the staff car. Harim would ride in one of the trucks with the infantrymen as far as the roads were passable after the rains and they would walk the rest of the way. He told his driver he expected to be back that evening, the next morning at the latest.

Inside the headquarters, the regimental commander was in conference with his adjutant.

"The man is a fool," the commander whispered. "He is going up into the mountains and wants to take a platoon. In trucks."

"Too bad we can't send him in a helicopter. It would be easier."

"And he might come back alive. Except for the Americans and their No-fly Zone. I wouldn't want the good colonel from Baghdad shot out of the sky. I understand they are flying higher now, but I am sure they would still swoop down on one of our helicopters."

"What difference does it make," the adjutant asked, "if he's going into those mountains with only a handful of infantry?"

"And it will be green infantry at that. Detail a platoon of our newest replacements. No sense wasting experienced men on a fool's errand."

"Doesn't he know the mood the Kurds are in up there?"

"He's seen my reports."

"Did you tell him what he's in for?"

"He didn't ask." The commander lit a cigarette and blew the smoke out through his nose. "Colonels don't come from Baghdad to ask questions. They come with all the answers already."

"Well, he's either a brave man or he's mad."

"That's his concern," the commander said.

"And if he is ambushed and calls for help?"

"That—is my concern."

0530 hours
The mountains of northern Iraq

Travis had made his decision based on the fact that the information relayed from the flyby satellite by Sam indicated that the pilot's rescue beacon was stationary, emitting signals at constant, regular intervals. That meant it was operating on its own, signaling automatically on a preset cycle. Which meant the pilot was probably either dead or incapacitated. At the very least, it meant he was stationary and not operating the beacon manually. It was possible he had set it up on auto mode and then relocated, but Travis discounted that scenario. The whole idea of the beacon was to give SAR a fix on your position. It didn't make sense to set it and then wander off. There was another possibility, but Travis put that one on hold for the time being. He didn't want to think about that one until he had to.

Sam also reported that the flyby satellite had confirmed the earlier estimate of the location of the crashed F-16. They were on course to the crash site and it was not far.

It was decision time for Travis. Like in a tabletop exercise at West Point, he had all the data input he was going to get. It was up to him to make the right inferences from what he knew and make the call. Except this was the real deal—this was life and death. It never got easy, but Travis had been in this situation many times before. He had been either lucky or good so far. And he didn't like to think it was luck.

He split up the team.

They had leads on the location of the wreckage and the possible location of the pilot. Both were on their list of objectives, and either might provide a lead to the RF gizmo. And bin Laden, if he happened to be part of the mix.

Travis, Jack, and Sarah would check out the pilot's rescue beacon. Stan and Sam would proceed on their current course to the wreckage. Travis split them up that way for a couple of reasons. Sarah went with him because she was the doctor and the pilot was her responsibility if they found him alive. Jack went because, if Travis's suspicions were correct, it would take at least three people to do the job. And he wanted Jack with him because if he was right his section of the team was going to face the higher risk.

Stan caught the split because he was senior. As a Navy Lt. Commander, he was equal in rank to Travis and was his second in command on TALON Force. If he was going to split the team, Travis wanted Stan as senior man in charge of the second unit. Jack was a hell of an operator, but it wouldn't be fair to him or Stan to do it the other way.

Travis sent Sam with Stan because he didn't want Stan to have to operate solo. As good as they all were, it was always best to work as a team covering each other's backs. Sam was an extra pair of eyes and ears and Stan might need him. Sam could still relay any new info he came up with to Travis by satellite relay. And he would come in handy directing Stan to the wreckage over some rough terrain.

There wasn't much time. Both units had a lot of ground to cover and it was best to travel as much as they could under the cover of the darkness and weather, since they were leaving their LOCS systems turned off to conserve energy. Travis made quick but thorough work of explaining his plan. He laid out the responsibilities, the objectives, and the most likely contingencies. There were no questions.

The two units moved out.

0600 hours
The crash site

Stan and Sam found the crash site about the time the rain stopped.

After scouring the terrain 360 degrees with their BSD night-vision systems, they moved in slow and easy— ready to switch on their LOCS systems at the first sign they had company. Stan made sure they moved as a team, one moving while the other covered. But the place was isolated and it was easy to understand why. Captain Daniels' F-16 had come screaming to earth in a steep dive that ended against a high ridge. It was a tough climb to get there, and searchers without help from satellites or aircraft were unlikely to have looked there. The F-16 was more intact than they had expected to find it, and Stan figured the low fuel load was why. He remembered that Daniels and his wingman were almost due to refuel when he went down. Nevertheless, he was impressed with the satellite technology that had picked up a heat signature from the debris.

It had taken a flotilla of search aircraft and a small army of mountain SAR specialists weeks to find what was left of the A-10 its pilot had flown into a mountain in the Colorado Rockies in an apparent suicide a few years back. Daniels's F-16 had come in at a less catastrophic angle, but still it was a piece of work spotting it through the weather.

According to the NSC briefing, the General Dynamics Fighting Falcon had been armed with two AIM-120 AMRAAMs, or Advanced Medium-Range Anti-Aircraft Missiles, mounted on wingtip pylons and a pair of AGM-88 HARM air-to-ground missiles on hardpoints under the wings, in addition to its M61A1 Vulcan 20mm rotary cannon. The F-16's left wing was broken off and curled back alongside the fuselage, the HARM missile still mounted on its hardpoint and the wingtip AIM-120 jutting up like a spear. The right wing was missing but a quick search located a chunk of it, including the tip, wedged against a rocky outcropping forward of the wrecked fuselage. The AIM-120 was still attached to its pylon, but there was no sign of the second HARM air-to-ground missile that had been carried under the wing.

"Not bad," Stan muttered. "We got three out of four and the other HARM's probably buried under the plane."

It was better luck than they had any right to expect.

Nobody had thought to bring a camera on the mission to take photos of the wreckage using the special high-speed low-light film that didn't require a flash. But there was a reason. Why take snapshots when you've got all this high-tech stuff?

Stan told Sam to fire up the "straight-up" satcom link from his helmet commo system to feed images of the wreckage back to the White House War Room. He had Sam do a walk-around of the wreckage, pumping images up into space. Neither man knew what he was looking at in any detailed sense, as far as what had made the

plane crash. They would have needed Hunter Blake for
that. But they could see that the canopy and the pilot's
seat were gone, which meant that Daniels had managed
to eject. They passed that information along to Travis by
satellite relay and made sure the people in the White
House War Room got the message as well.

Then the two of them dragged the AIM-120 from the
right wingtip over to the main body of the wreckage.
While Sam nervously stood watch, Stan rigged the wreckage with an improvised demolition charge using det-cord
and C-4 plastic explosives. He wired the det-cord into an
electronic detonator that could be triggered remotely. He
added a second device that would set off the explosives
if the ordnance was tampered with. Anyone who found
the wreckage would be safe as long as they did not try
to remove one of the missiles.

So far so good, Stan thought. That was one item they
could check off the team's to-do list, but they had plenty
yet to do. It would be getting light before long and he
and Sam had some ground to cover.

0600 hours
Çukurca, Turkey

Hunter was thinking it would be light soon and maybe
he had dozed off for a couple of minutes after finishing
his work on the DC-3.

There had been plenty to do for an ace pilot unused
to being hands-on with manual labor. He had to double-
check to make sure the dismantled LANTIRN system
was out of sight in the wiring crawl space beneath the
floor of the cockpit, then break the extra fuel cells out
of their hiding places beneath the cabin floor and manually pump the fuel into the tanks. When he was done
with that, he was beat. He'd had a long day, from his
bitchfest with Stan at Camp Secret that morning to the
chopper ride to Base Secret to catch a ride on a C-17 to
Adana. There, he had busted his hump working with the

technicians to get the gooney bird ready for all-weather flying.

And then there had been the flight in the bad weather all the way from Adana to whatever little podunk goat-herding village this was in the Turkish version of hillbilly country. Yup, it had been a long day.

So he didn't exactly blame himself if he happened to nod off for a couple of minutes. But he would have gone back to check on Jen if it hadn't been for that. As it was, he awoke to the sound of voices underneath the co-pilot's window and looked out to see Jen at the foot of the steps. She was having an animated conversation with Kamil, the big man who seemed to run things around here. And he had brought some friends with him.

Hunter made his way to the cabin door at the head of the steps and tried to assess the situation.

Kamil was holding Jen's right hand and she was smiling up at him, rattling off a lot of French Kamil didn't understand, then using English with a heavy French accent as if she were having trouble translating.

Hunter could tell from the body language that it was the kind of trouble you would have to expect in an operation like this. Kamil was hitting on Jen and she was trying to get out of it without resorting to kicking him in the balls, a maneuver of which she was perfectly capable. Kamil's friends were apparently just interested bystanders, but Hunter noticed they had blankets over their shoulders and rifles in their hands.

At last she seemed to have gotten through to the big man and he shrugged and threw up his hands as if to say okay, for now. He doffed his cap, put his big hands on her shoulders, and kissed her on both cheeks, then bowed from the waist as he had done before. Jen turned and made her way up the steps, the big man watching her every move until she disappeared from his view inside the DC-3.

Hunter smiled and waved, but Kamil paid him no attention. Kamil spoke briefly in hushed tones with his associates and then turned his back on the DC-3 and started back toward the village.

Kamil's friends did not follow him. They threw their blankets on the ground under the DC-3's right wing and sat down, their rifles beside them.

"Looks like they're going to stay," Hunter offered.

"Kamil told them to keep an eye on us. He's afraid we may leave without saying good-bye."

"They're going to shoot us if we try?"

"The guns are to protect us. Kamil says this is a dangerous place these days."

"What was that all about with the French and the kissing?"

"Kamil wanted me to spend the night in his house but I insisted on sleeping on the plane."

"He's got the hots for you."

"He's had a crush on Yvette since the sixties. And thanks for coming back to give me a hand. Your concern is touching."

"I had a lot of stuff to do here. I knew you could handle those guys."

"Right." She pulled up the steps and closed the cabin door.

"How did you talk your way out of a pajama party with King Turk?"

"I convinced him I needed my beauty sleep and I didn't want him to see me in the morning without my makeup on and all my stuff was on the plane. I told him I didn't want to shatter his romantic illusions."

"And that worked?"

"Sure it worked." She pulled off the brunette wig and stepped through the shower curtains to change. "Men are pretty much the same all over."

"I guess he's jealous of me, though."

"I told him you were gay."

"What?! And he believed you?"

"Said he knew it the minute he laid eyes on you."

"I hope you're kidding." Hunter decided to change the subject. "So we're okay here for a while, you think?"

"Depends on what you call okay," she said through the closed curtains. "I had to promise we'd stay at least until tomorrow night, even if you got the airplane ready to go before then. I'm going to be the guest of honor at a film festival if Abdul can get the projector working."

"Really?"

"Yeah. Abdul, the little guy, is going to hook up his projector and show that old film of mine, I mean Yvette's."

"Sounds good."

"Easy for you to say. You didn't have Kamil's big mitts on your butt all evening."

"I take it he's not disappointed that you, Yvette, has put on a few pounds."

"He likes it, says I look better than ever." She stuck her head out from between the shower curtains. "It seems Kurds like their women with a little meat on their bones."

"Well, a lot of men do. The—who?"

"Kurds."

"Those guys are Kurds?"

"Duh. I thought you said you prepped this mission with somebody in Adana."

"I did, the Turkish liaison officer at the air base. He said he would get word to a contact up here to be expecting us."

"If he did, his contact is playing it pretty close to the vest. Can't say I blame him."

"I got the distinct impression from my Turkish pal that he was sending us in among friendlies," Hunter said. "I figured they'd be Turks, civilians, or maybe one of their militia outfits."

"You figured wrong. Maybe you should stick to flying and let me handle the cloak-and-dagger stuff."

"Well, there are all kinds of Kurds," Hunter offered defensively. "They're not all on the warpath."

"Yeah, Kamil and I were talking about that."

"He calls the shots around here, I guess."

"Literally. He's a district chief with the PKK."

Chapter Thirteen

Mikhail tried to be philosophical about it.

He had lain in his hide all day the day before and it had paid off with a shot at the American pilot. With the skill of a true *Spetsnatz* professional, he had made his shot count, bringing down the pilot without killing him. That should earn him a bonus from his employer, the Saudi crazy man with his millions and his holy war.

It was perhaps too much to ask for another success so soon.

After lying in ambush all day and bagging the pilot, then carrying him back to camp after twilight, Mikhail had carefully cleaned his Dragunov sniper rifle, outfitted it with a night-vision scope, and returned to his hide. Having located the pilot's rescue beacon in the rocks where he had lain hidden almost all day, but not quite all day, or he might still be on the loose, Mikhail had set a trap. He had programmed the beacon to transmit at intervals throughout the night in hopes of drawing more victims to his killing ground.

The others in the camp were perplexed that the Americans had not mounted their usual SAR efforts on behalf of the downed flier. To them it was a mystery. But Mikhail was not like them. He had been trained to expect the unexpected. Putting himself in the place of the Americans, he had considered the possibility that they might try a different approach to locating their comrade. Perhaps they had some idea of the kind of weapon that had brought down their plane. You had to give the

Americans credit—they were very good at the technolog-
ical side of things.

If so, then it made sense to Mikhail's way of thinking
that perhaps they would send, not a fleet of helicopters
with air cover, but a small team of operators to conduct
the search on the ground. He had himself been a part of
similar operations and he knew what such men were capable of doing. He prided himself on being such a man.

And the Americans had many resources of this kind.
Mikhail had studied them when he was with the KGB's
Alpha Group, the elite of *Spetsnatz*. You had to know
your enemy as well as yourself, his trainers had told him.
The Americans had their SEAL teams and Special
Forces, their Delta Force. Mikhail knew they prided
themselves on what they called specwar operations, and
that combat search and rescue was one of their
specialties.

Who would they send? he had wondered as he set out
from camp in the dead of night with the storm howling
around him. He would like very much to have one of
their green berets for a souvenir, or perhaps a black
beret with that big gaudy SEAL emblem pinned on the
front. An American beret would make a fine trophy,
perhaps with a bit of blood on it from the massive head
wound his Dragunov's 7.62mm slug would make.

They wouldn't come in daylight, he knew. They would
prefer the night, when their night-vision goggles gave
them the tactical advantage. The darker the better and
a moonless night with a storm raging would be best. They
would come then, he thought, because they would be
sure no one else would be about. Ordinary men, ordinary
soldiers, would be huddled in their shelters to wait out
the storm, leaving the field to elite operators like the
American specwar teams.

And so Mikhail had lain in his hide throughout the
night, waiting for a chance to spring his trap and win his
trophy beret. He fought off the effects of going without
sleep through the exercise of his disciplined will and he
remained alert, watching from his hide on the rocky
slope across the valley where the American pilot had left

his hiding place a few minutes too soon the evening before.

The memory of that shot, playing over in his mind like a videotape on a closed loop, kept him awake and ready to strike again as the storm pounded down around him. Finally the rain slackened and then moved away to the south and left him alone in the stillness of the very early morning when the sky was still inky black.

But the night had not been good like the day. He had seen nothing from his place of concealment, no stealthy Americans with berets green or black. Oh well, Mikhail thought with a sigh as he prepared to leave his hide and make his way back to the camp, perhaps it was too much to ask.

The sky had lightened some time ago and the figures of the rocks and trees and mountain slopes were emerging from the darkness around him. It would still be a while before the sun rose over the horizon, but the day was upon him. Mikhail relaxed and let the fatigue of the sleepless night register for the first time. They will not come in daylight, he told himself. They will hole up under cover until it is night again. Maybe then they will come.

Mikhail was already thinking of getting back to the camp and lying down to rest. Now that he had resigned himself to disappointment, he felt very tired and looked forward to crawling into his blankets in the tent. He thought about making his way over to the place across the valley where the American's beacon sat atop a boulder, sending its signals into the sky. He had originally planned to go over there and turn it off if nobody came. But it would be a long hike down the slope on his side of the valley and then up the opposite slope, difficult steps he would have to retrace before setting off for camp.

To hell with it, he thought. Let it beep all day. Maybe the Americans haven't located it yet. Even if they do, they won't come to check it out before tonight. And I will be waiting for them.

With a groan at the stiffness in his joints, Mikhail carefully backed out of his hide and rose to his knees. He remained motionless for a time, surveying the shadowy predawn landscape before he rose to his feet and started back to camp.

0600 hours
Near the sniper's hide

"Bingo," Jack whispered over his helmet commo system to the rest of the team. "I got a dead man walking."

"Confirm," Sarah said from her position. She was nearest Jack and put out the description, leaving the marine free to track the target in his sights. "Walking west on the south slope, twenty meters below the crest. One man wearing a Ghillie suit."

The camouflage Mikhail wore over his clothes looked like a tattered cloak that covered him from head to foot, strips of cloth in varying shades of the colors found in the rocky mountains cut in different lengths to break up his silhouette.

"This guy's slick as boiled okra," Travis muttered. He could just make out the sniper from his more distant position, now that Jack and Sarah had fingered him. "Must have been invisible in his hide."

"Yeah, but he's out of it now," Jack said softly. "And he's all mine."

Jack sighted in on the figure picking its way among the rocks on the steep slope. The aiming device nestled underneath the barrel of his XM-29 Smart Rifle along with a four-round grenade launcher automatically computed the range. The XM-29 carried a base load of 85 of its 5.66mm smart bullets with combustible cartridges that eliminated the need for heavy brass in a box magazine forward of the trigger group housing. The bullets could be directed in flight by a millimeter wave sensor linked with the aiming device. They were armor-piercing rounds and Jack meant to feed the sniper a short burst of three.

"Hold your fire, Jack," Travis ordered tersely. "We need him alive for a little bit longer."

"Copy that," Jack confirmed the order.

But he didn't like it. Jack had dealt with snipers before and he knew a clear shot at one was a rare thing indeed. You didn't want to pass up an opportunity to kill a dangerous man you might never see again. There was no guarantee you'd get a second chance.

Travis was thinking more strategically.

His gamble had paid off. He had suspected a trap and the team had moved into position in time to spot it. Thinking like the enemy, Travis had worked off of a couple of assumptions. First, the fact that the beacon was operating in automated mode suggested that the pilot was either incapacitated or that he had been taken. You always proceed on the more dangerous of the possibilities, so Travis had approached the situation like it was a trap. Thanks to Stan and Sam, they knew Captain Daniels had been able to eject before the crash. At least that meant they probably weren't dealing with a phony beacon, and Daniels was out there somewhere.

Assuming the beacon was a trap had meant hustling his unit of the divided team to the area where the beacon's signal had been detected. But they wouldn't move in on the signal itself. Instead, they would form a loose perimeter around it, in a three-point diamond pattern, on the lookout for anybody lying in wait to spring a trap.

Travis had gambled that the ambush party would have been in position all night and would pull out at first light to rest and regroup. And his gamble had paid off. Now they had a lead to the location of the enemy camp. All they had to do was follow the sniper.

"Y'all hold your position," Travis told his team. "Let's make sure he doesn't have any amigos out here with him."

It stood to reason that anybody laying a trap for a rescue team would likely be set up to spring their trap at night, when a rescue was most likely to be attempted. Given the conditions in the area, it would be extremely high-risk to try it in the daytime. TALON Force, with its LOCS units, was better equipped to operate in day-time than anybody else in the world, but nobody outside the team knew that.

They had gone in after O'Grady in Bosnia in daylight with choppers and air cover, but that was a different situation. There was no RF weapon hiding in the Bosnian woods to knock them all down.

Which made Travis think that this sniper, whoever he was, had been expecting a specops CSAR operation in-stead. As he watched the camouflaged figure moving away down the slope to the west, Travis's lips curled into a tight, angry smile.

He's a lone wolf, Travis thought. Figured we'd come in with a small team looking for that beacon he set up and pick us off one by one.

Satisfied the sniper was working alone, Travis issued instructions for the rest of his three-person team to fol-low. Jack was nearest the sniper so he would take point. Sarah would fall in behind Jack, and Travis would check their six o'clock as they went.

As they were preparing to move out, Sam came up on Travis's helmet commo system. He reported that he and Stan were leaving the wreckage and were en route to rendezvous with the rest of the team. He also passed along the latest intel relayed by satellite from the White House War Room. Sam's buddies at NSA had inter-cepted a satcom transmission tentatively identified as coming from Osama bin Laden. The point of origin was not far away, only a couple of kilometers to the west, the direction their sniper was heading.

The sun was working its way up over the horizon be-hind them as they prepared to move out. Travis gave the word to Jack and Sarah to activate their LOCSs. He didn't want to take any chances on the lone wolf sniper checking his back trail and spotting them following him to his lair.

0630 hours
Camp Jihad

Captain Mike Daniels could not be sure if he was awake
or asleep and having some kind of nightmare. His left
leg below the knee alternated between throbbing like
mad and seeming to disappear.

Daniels lay on his right side on something hard that
smelled of straw, like on the farm in Virginia where he
had gone to meet his girlfriend Stephanie's mom and
dad. Some of the time the smell of straw made him think
he was back there again, that he and Stephanie had
driven down from Washington to tell her parents the
good news—they were engaged.

Some of the time, he forgot about the straw and
thought he was back in his hiding place among the rocks.
That would explain the pain in my leg, he told himself
at one point. It's a cramp from lying still in these rocks
all day. It will be night soon and I can get up and stretch.

Finally, he awoke. It was hunger that woke him as
much as his raging fever. His throat was dry and his
mouth felt like it was full of cottonballs. I'd kill for a
drink, he thought, and tried to remember where he had
left his canteen. Did he have a canteen? He racked his
brain but couldn't for the life of him remember if his
survival kit included a canteen.

After a few minutes of lying awake on his right side,
he realized that he was really awake this time and he
was in a lot of pain. His left leg was on fire and when
he put his hand to his face it was burning up, too.

Before the memory of being shot finally worked its
way into his consciousness, he realized that the blanket
covering his face was not his pilot's survival blanket. His
blanket was government-issue camouflage on one side
and bright orange for signaling rescue aircraft on the
other. And he had lined it on the inside with the heat-
retaining silver-colored sheet that looked like aluminum
foil.

The blanket that covered him now was neither camouflage nor signal orange. And it certainly wasn't aluminum foil. It was coarse gray wool with a faded pattern he couldn't make out, and he was lying on a rough pallet stuffed with straw.

And then he remembered being shot.

He remembered having no idea where it came from, just as he crawled out of his hiding place in the rocks on his way to the stand of scrubby cedars only a few feet away. He remembered his left leg buckling with the terrible impact a beat before he heard the gunshot echoing off the valley walls. Ridiculous as it seemed now, he hadn't even connected the two at first in his mind. His leg buckled and then he heard a shot. It wasn't until he had looked down at his mangled leg, twisted at an impossible angle below his knee, that he knew it was he who had been shot.

Daniels remembered trying to crawl to the cover of the trees, but he had not made it very far before he heard footsteps and looked up to find a weird creature standing over him. It was some kind of boogeyman, his face painted in brown stripes and covered from head to toe with a tattered outfit that Daniels at first took for shaggy hair. He was some kind of shaggy-haired boogeyman—with a long rifle in his hand.

That was the last Daniels remembered except being jostled along on the back of the shaggy-haired creature for what seemed like hours. And then there were the dreams.

Awake now at last, Daniels tugged the wool blanket down off his face. Where was he? That was the first question on his mind. He was afraid to ask the second one—How badly am I hurt?

As the blanket came down, Daniels saw a muddy rug and the wall of a tent. Then he saw a pair of boots and he followed them up to the face of the man standing over him. Oddly enough, the face looked familiar.

Ah shit, Daniels thought as the face finally registered. If this guy's not Osama bin Laden, he's close enough to be his stand-in.

"So, you are finally back among the living," the man said with a satisfied nod.

Mustafa turned and went outside to tell the Prophet the American had regained consciousness.

Left alone in the tent, Daniels closed his eyes and took a deep breath.

"Lord, I hate to keep bothering you like this . . ."

Chapter Fourteen

Mikhail felt the hairs rise on the back of his neck.

He couldn't shake the feeling he was being watched.

For the third time in a hundred meters, he stopped and eased behind the cover of the rocks and sat watching his back trail.

"Easy does it," Jack whispered. "He's doing it again."

Jack didn't have to worry about being overheard. With the embedded micro-chip nestled under his skin near his right ear, he could transmit clearly with a whisper so soft it hardly made a sound. And he was giving the sniper plenty of room.

Travis and Sarah knew what to do. They froze in place. It took a lot of training and discipline to stand stock-still out in the open, knowing an enemy sniper was looking your way. It had not been easy to learn to trust the technology. But they had all seen it from both sides, using the LOCS and playing aggressors and trying to spot their fellow team members. The stuff worked. It made you invisible.

The only giveaway, and it was a slight one, was that when you moved if the enemy was looking right at you he could see a shimmer—nothing more than that. As long as you were motionless, he saw nothing. Their helmets had small field generators built in that projected "virtual face shields" that blended in with the rest of the suit. There were sheaths for their weapons that plugged into the LOCS system, and gloves for their hands.

The other thing you had to remember was your footing. You might be invisible, but if you tripped over a rock or slid down-slope on loose gravel, there was nothing to keep the sound from giving you away. The enemy might not know what made the noise, but he would know something was out there.

So they all froze in place until Jack gave the word that the sniper was on the move again.

0630 hours
Indian Country

The two Kurds slouched leisurely among the rocks high on a bluff overlooking the long ridge that ran from the foothills into the mountains. They were situated well below the skyline of the cliff and knew the soldiers in the trucks lumbering up the road on top of the ridge could not see them.

There were only three trucks, and the Kurds passed a pair of binoculars back and forth between them, certain they would see more soldiers following these. But all they saw behind the trucks was the dust their tires raised, the high road already dry after the rains that morning. The rains had been heavier up in the mountains, and the Kurds knew that if the soldiers meant to go much farther they would have to leave the trucks behind. The ridge road only went so far and then you had to work your way either up and down mountains or along the valleys. The mountains were too steep for the trucks and the valleys still too muddy.

"They will leave some of the soldiers to guard the trucks," one of the Kurds said.

"Yes, and the rest will go on foot."

They both knew there would be no Iraqi helicopters or airplanes coming, thanks to the Americans who forbade the Iraqis to fly this far north.

"Why would they provoke us like this, sending so few into our mountains?"

The second man, studying the trucks through the binoculars, smiled. "Allah is good," he said.

0630 hours
Mountain ridge road

Colonel Harim cursed as the trucks groaned and strained up the steepening grade of the ridge road. He had already determined, by interrogating the driver of the lead truck, that these were new replacements fresh from the shops and farms of Karbala and An Najaf, villages located southwest of Baghdad in the flat plains of the Euphrates. As far as he could determine, these were the first mountains the recruits had ever seen and none of them had been even this close to them before.

I suppose the bastard gave me the worst of his trucks, as well, Harim thought as he studied his map.

He had noticed that the soldiers had loaded the trucks with extra rations, at least three days' worth. That was excessive, he thought, but he had to admit that his investigation might take longer than he had planned, and he wished he had brought his overcoat along. He knew the nights could be cold in the high country.

Sunday, June 11, 2230 hours EDT
The White House War Room, Washington, D.C.

"What do you make of it?" Burgess asked Commander Greeley.

They were studying the images Sam had sent back from northern Iraq by satellite, the wreckage of Daniels's F-16.

"It's a tore-up airplane all right," Greeley mused. "Afraid I'm not qualified to tell much more than that. If it was a boat, I might have a more detailed opinion."

"The gearheads are bitching," Burgess confided.

"What about?"

"They wish the man who sent these images had worked in a little closer to the cockpit, from what I can tell. Say they need close-ups of the instrument panel."

"Screw 'em," Greeley said. "They're never satisfied

and they have no idea what it took to get those pictures in the first place."

"Can't argue with you there."

"But I would like to know a little more about this right here."

"What?" Burgess asked.

In one of the images, a shadowy figure was visible in the background dressed all in black. Greeley pointed at Stan's helmet.

"I don't believe I've seen one like that before," he said.

"I wouldn't know about that."

"Looks like something new to me. The rest of the outfit, too. Who the hell are these guys?"

"Like I said," Burgess offered, getting up to go check the people working the consoles, "I wouldn't know about that."

2230 hours EDT
The Pentagon, Washington, D.C.

"See," Mac said, showing Bob a photograph of Osama bin Laden. "This is him, the guy we're after."

"Really?" Bob said. "He looks familiar."

"He was in all the papers," Mac said dryly.

Dr. Fensterman was looking over Bob's shoulder at the photograph and munching potato chips.

Guy hasn't stopped eating since he got here, Mac thought. He's gonna bust out of those pants.

"I know," Bob said, brightening. "He's that dude on *Mork and Mindy,* the crazy prophet guy."

"You're kidding me," Mac said, exasperated. How can a kid be so smart about all this technical crap and not know anything about what's going on in the world?

"That's him, right?"

"What the hell do you know about *Mork and Mindy*? You weren't even born when that was on TV."

"Nick at Nite, Mac. Don't you ever watch cable?"

Monday, June 12, 0900 hours
Çukurca, Turkey

Hunter couldn't think of anything else to do. The gooney
bird was ready to go and he was hooked up with the
satellite relay by way of his earpiece. When the team
called for extraction, he could be airborne in a matter
of minutes.

He didn't need to look at the maps again. He had
memorized them. The coordinates of the rocky basin
were seared into his brain and he had visualized the
whole thing a thousand times since his briefing in Adana.
In his mind, he saw himself at the controls of the old DC-
3, coming in low over the mountain peaks and setting her
down smooth as glass in the basin. Studying the satellite
photos, he had convinced himself the rocks scattered
around the flat basin were all small, nothing that would
damage the old bird's undercarriage so badly he couldn't
take off again.

That was Extraction Plan A. Extraction Plan B, which
they would use if the team couldn't make it to the basin,
would be a bit hairier for them but actually easier for
him. All he had to do was make a low pass over some
high ground, line up on the signal balloon and hit the
noose suspended from the balloon with the hook the guys
in Adana had rigged up to be swung out of the cabin
door. The team would all be hooked up on a modified
STABO rig and zoom—they were out of there. Jen
would fire up the motorized winch and reel them in.

Piece of cake, Hunter told himself.

What worried him most was that the call might come
that night. Jen would be the guest of honor at the PKK's
French film festival. Getting her out of there might be a
little tricky.

The team had jumped in around midnight and it was
getting on toward mid-morning now. Their ensembles
were good for seventy-two hours before they needed re-
charging, which usually couldn't be done in the field.
Seventy-two hours would be up the third midnight from

now. Hunter hoped they would make quick work of a tough mission and give him the call. He didn't fancy spending that much time partying with the PKK.

He heard the sleeping sounds Jen was making from the other side of the curtain. Hunter had to laugh. She even snored sexy.

0900 hours
The mountains of northern Iraq

Mikhail turned for the last time to look back the way he had come. He was nearly to the camp. It was just around the next shoulder in the ridge, tucked away in a defile. This was his last chance to shake the feeling that somebody was out there. The feeling had been on him since shortly after leaving his hide, but as often as he had turned and sat watching his back trail, he had seen nothing. A couple of times there was a shimmer off the rocks, but he put that down to the heat of the sun warming the stones wet from the rain. Once he thought he heard something and he froze, listening. But it may have only been loose rock sliding down the hill. That happens after a heavy rain, he told himself.

Enough of this, he thought finally. There's nothing out there and I'm tired and hungry. That's why I'm imagining things. I haven't slept all night and fatigue is playing tricks with my mind.

With that, he turned back toward the camp and trudged on. Where are those worthless Iranians? he wondered. They're supposed to be standing watch.

0915 hours
Near Camp Jihad, northern Iraq

Jack lost sight of the man in the Ghillie suit as the sniper picked his way along the rocky slope where the ridge made a bend around a protruding shoulder of rock. He passed the word for the others to hold their positions and he moved ahead stealthily. Planting one foot flat and solid before he lifted the other to avoid a misstep, he slowly made his way to a point where he could look down and see where the man had gone.

Jack had become so accustomed to the sniper's frequent stops that he fully expected to see him lurking behind the rocks. Instead, he saw the man, walking at a normal pace now, heading into a shadowy defile.

"This is it," Jack whispered as he watched the man peel off the camouflage suit and sling his rifle over his shoulder. "He's home."

And Jack knew that meant he had better be on the lookout for the sniper's friends. He was bound to have some, and if this was their camp it stood to reason they had sentries posted.

With Travis and Sarah waiting in position behind him, Jack worked his way up the slope carefully, paying special attention to his footing and making sure there were none of those little jingles or clinks your gear can make when you're moving. They are small sounds and you can get so used to them you don't hear them yourself. But the enemy does.

Like all the team members, Jack was packed tight and battened down. His weapons and equipment were stripped to the bare necessities and configured for soundless motion. But you can't be too careful this close to a hostile base camp.

And that was what it was. Jack could see the tents and the vehicles under camouflage netting in the defile. Counting the tents, he made a quick estimate of the size of the force they were up against and he knew he wasn't looking at all of them. Some of them might still be in their tents, but he could see men settling down to a cold breakfast. Guess they don't want to risk the smoke from a fire, Jack thought. Must not have the self-heating packs Uncle Sam hands out. Tough shit.

Travis had been waiting longer than he liked when he heard Jack again on his headset, reporting in.

This was it, the hostile's camp. They were on target

and a lot sooner than Travis had expected. The thing to do now was to post somebody to keep an eye on the place and wait for Stan and Sam to rejoin the team. For the next phase of the mission, Travis knew he was going to need everybody.

Travis went forward to hook up with Jack. Jack would brief him on the layout and he would find a good spot to hunker down and keep an eye on the hostiles. Preferably a spot with good cover so he could shut down his LOCS and conserve energy. Then Jack and Sarah would find a good position nearby to rest and regroup while they waited for Stan and Sam to find them. When the team was reunited, Travis would rejoin them and they would hammer out a plan of attack.

Nestled in a shadowy crevice among the rocks that gave him a good view of the camp below, Travis switched off his LOCS to save energy and linked up with the satellite and scanned the camp, streaming real-time images up to the bird to be relayed to the War Room.

He couldn't help worrying about their luck. They were less than ten hours into the mission and they had already taken care of the wreckage of the F-16 and located the hostile camp. It stood to reason the RF gizmo was in the camp and Daniels was probably there too, if he was still alive.

They were catching the breaks this time out and that worried him. Luck had a way of evening itself out and good luck early almost always meant bad luck later, when it mattered most.

Chapter Fifteen

"What's that? Is that it?"

The question came from one of the members of the inner circle. They were seeing Travis's images on their monitors, the camp hidden in the side of a mountain. There were tents that looked like army surplus—one larger than the rest, a canvas square with a dimpled roof under camouflage netting, and several smaller tents arranged in a rough semicircle with a path cleared through the middle of them.

The imagery stream continued as Travis panned to show the rest of it, the jeeplike vehicles parked beyond the tents, also camouflaged. In the back of one of the vehicles, an odd-shaped object was hidden under a tarp.

"Is that the gizmo?" the same man asked again, triggering a laser pointer to place a red dot on the tarp-covered object.

"I don't think we know yet," the DCI said calmly. "Our analysts are getting this right now, just as we are."

"Our people are equipped to laser-designate targets for guided munitions, aren't they?" the same man asked.

"Yes, they are," the president's national security advisor assured him.

"Then let's scramble some planes, paint that thing up, and blow it to smithereens," the man said.

"There is still the matter of the pilot," the national security advisor reminded him.

"Oh—of course. Yes, of course."

1100 hours
Camp Jihad, northern Iraq

Osama bin Laden sat on a blanket on the floor of his tent, his attention divided between CNN on his satellite monitor and the wounded American lying on the straw pallet.

He had awakened early and assembled the Iranians he had been provided as an escort by his friends in Tehran. Invoking the name of Allah and the spirit of the *jihad,* he had berated them most severely. He had called them cowards and worse. Time is running out, he told them. You must find the American jet fighter and you must find it today—this morning.

When their leader had protested that they had searched almost the whole length of the valley, bin Laden cursed him and all his men.

"You must not search where you think it is safe to search," he had admonished them. "You must search where you are most likely to find the accursed plane. Don't hide in the valley, climb to the high ground. The infernal machine fell from the sky, my brothers. Look in the high places. Our comrade Pretsky has given you coordinates from his radar on the great weapon. Make yourselves ready and leave at first light. Follow Pretsky's course and climb. Climb to the top of the highest mountain if you have to. But you must find the airplane. And when you do, don't waste time coming back here to tell me. Use your radios to send me the glad tidings."

When he was sure he had made himself clear, he reminded them that he would report to the ayatollahs in Tehran upon their return. They all knew what an unsatisfactory report would mean.

And then he had led them in a prayer before hurrying them out of camp in the grayness just before dawn.

Osama bin Laden wanted the ordnance from the American plane very badly. He knew the Iranians were afraid of Iraqi patrols in these mountains, and even more afraid of the Kurds. If they fell into the hands of the

Iraqis they might find themselves cruelly treated as prisoners. If the Kurds got their hands on them, they would all be martyrs.

But if bin Laden condemned them to their masters in Tehran, they would be just as dead, and they and their families for generations would be disgraced as well.

It was in Allah's hands.

In the absence of the Iranians, Mustafa and his bodyguard would be responsible for keeping watch. The loyal Mustafa had roused himself that morning already when the motion detectors alarmed. But that was only the Iranians calling in their sentries and leaving the camp. And the Russian shortly after, returning empty-handed from his all-night ambush.

The weather had played havoc with the motion detectors, too. All the rain and wind had plagued them with false alarms. No more than I deserve for buying Eastern European devices, bin Laden chastised himself. From now on, I buy strictly American, the good stuff. What does it matter? They're all infidels.

Now the Russian sniper was asleep in his tent and the other one, Pretsky, was being a nuisance again. The pig-man had been squealing about pulling out almost since the moment the American plane went down. He had a point, but bin Laden was sick of his whining. Pretsky was a fat white pig who could hardly catch his breath after hiking off into the rocks to relieve himself, yet he wanted to walk out, all the way to the Iranian border! Somebody would have to carry him. His whining had aggravated bin Laden's extreme distaste for the man, and bin Laden had taken to wondering if there weren't other scientists who could duplicate his machine for a price. He thought of the Japanese. They are geniuses at reverse engineering, he had been told.

The American amused and interested him. He was a potential source of intelligence, of course, if he lived. There was a great deal of value in that. Beyond that, it amused bin Laden no end to watch him suffer. The great American super-warrior, raining destruction from the sky like a god. Look at him, a little man, and so frail when you took him out of his great machine.

As a hostage, of course, the American had considerable value. But beyond the intelligence potential and his utility as a hostage, bin Laden saw in his prisoner the potential for an enormous propaganda coup. If only the accursed Iranians would find the wreckage of his aircraft and they could salvage even one of his missiles, there would be a way to use the two, the missile and the pilot, to embarrass the Americans and turn the whole Third World against them. If he could manage to embroil the Americans in another war, so much the better. He still had hopes that the work of Pretsky's machine might bring America and Iraq to the brink.

There would be time to think on all that later, though. Having sent his Iranians out with the fear of Allah in them, he was distracted now by the news on CNN. They had shown the same photograph of him they always used and referred to him as they always did, as a terrorist. They even mentioned the $5-million reward on his head.

But what disturbed him was the report of donations to his cause by Saudi and Persian Gulf businessmen in the amount of $50 million in the form of alms. All good Muslims were required to give alms, one of the Five Pillars of Islam, but the Saudis had stopped the transfers. Strictly speaking, alms were to be given to the poor, but clerics in Iran and elsewhere had made it clear they could also go to Islamic causes. The Saudis were in league with the Americans, who had tried to freeze all his funds in foreign bank accounts. The Americans were taking similar measures against the Taliban, the religious militia who had been his hosts in Afghanistan.

The talk of money disturbed him greatly. His wealth was a gift from Allah and his to do with as he pleased.

"With the Americans, it's always about money," he muttered, turning from the monitor to look down at Captain Mike Daniels, who lay on a straw pallet on the floor of bin Laden's tent, racked by chills and fever from the infection in his wound.

0300 hours EDT
The White House War Room, Washington, D.C.

There was a problem.

The president's national security advisor had taken a call on the president's direct line and called a huddle of the inner circle. Then he, the Director of Central Intelligence, and the rest of them had straightened their ties, put on their suit coats, and hurried out of the room.

They had left Tom Burgess with instructions to call if there were any new developments.

"What's the flap?" Commander Greeley asked.

Burgess and Greeley were at the coffeepot getting refills.

"Word's out about Captain Daniels and the F-16."

"It was bound to happen," Greeley offered.

"Yeah, but they were hoping to sit on it until we got some results."

"I'd say our people are getting results ahead of schedule."

"No question about that," Burgess agreed. "But I'm afraid the president is getting pressure to do more."

"Like what?"

"Retaliate. I don't think it's gotten any more specific than that."

"Retaliate against who, uh, whom?" Greeley asked, newly careful of his grammar since his promotion and staff assignment. "The NSA intercept indicates Osama bin Laden's mixed up in it."

"Acting as an agent of Saddam Hussein. That's the consensus."

"What do they want us to do, bomb Baghdad?"

"Something like that. Like I said, the president is feeling a lot of political pressure to take some kind of decisive action."

"Where's the pressure coming from?"

"I really shouldn't be talking about this, but—"

"We're on the same team here."

"I know. The way I hear it, a senator who sits on a couple of key committees is raising hell about it."

"Really?"

"Yeah. It seems there's a personal connection. Daniels, Captain Daniels, has a girlfriend named Stephanie."

"Uh-huh."

"And Stephanie's dad happens to be very tight with the senator."

"Well, kiss my ass."

"Exactly."

1100 hours
The mountains of northern Iraq

Travis, in his concealed position overlooking the camp, and Jack and Sarah in their hide nearby had no way of knowing that bin Laden's Iranians had left the camp just minutes before the three team members followed the Russian sniper there. Or that bin Laden's Iranians had marching orders to follow Pretsky's coordinates into the high country, which would take them southeast from the camp.

Several kilometers to the southeast, Stan and Sam had no way of knowing they were on a collision course with the Iranians. Both men could call up detailed maps of their area of operations through their BSDs. Both had access in the same way to real-time satellite imagery that showed them what the satellite saw as it looked down on the area. But the satellite view was not detailed enough to show them the Iranians, spread out in a ragged file as they made their way toward the wreckage of the American plane.

All the TALON Force troopers had their LOCS systems switched off to save energy. They were professionals, expert at concealment and stealth. But they were not invisible.

Chapter Sixteen

Colonel Harim had left his trucks behind with a squad of soldiers to guard them, at the point where the road played out along the spine of the ridge where it abutted one of the mountains that rose in an endless chain before him.

He called a rest stop to give the men a breather and check his course again. He took the map out of his tunic pocket and studied it carefully. There were three straight lines drawn on the map, indicating readings reported by as many Iraqi air defense radar stations. At the point where the lines intersected, he expected to find the wreckage of the American plane. Using landmarks and his compass, he satisfied himself that he was heading in the right direction and that the wreckage of the American plane was not far.

Colonel Harim wished his course were as straight as the lines on his map. To get from one point to another in these mountains one had to go up, then down, then up again. A kilometer on the map might be three on the ground, most of it vertical.

He missed his days as a pilot, when he would have soared over these accursed mountains like a great bird.

1100 hours
The crash site

The leader of the Kurdish band had decided not to ambush the Iraqi soldiers yet. He was curious why they were here and where they were going. From his position in the cliffs, he looked down through binoculars at the officer leading them. What brings you into these mountains, he asked silently. The leader decided it was worth finding out, and he passed the word to his fighters to watch the Iraqis and follow them. When they got where they were going and found what they were looking for, they still had to march back the way they had come. There would be ample opportunity then to kill them all.

1130 hours
Eagle Base Camp

It was down time for Jack and Sarah. There was never a time on a mission when you could really let your guard down, but there were relative lulls a smart operator could take advantage of to get a little rest and think things through. Jack and Sarah had been on tough missions before and they knew to rest and conserve their energy while they could. They might not get another chance.

They found a spot that offered good concealment and easy defense and set out a network of XM11 robot sensors. These were devices no bigger than cigarette cases that could detect and report movement or visual data directly to team members. They could be used to secure a position perimeter as Jack and Sarah were using them or be left behind to serve as extra eyes and ears for the team after they had left an area.

Once that was done, Jack and Sarah settled into their hide. They took up positions facing in opposite directions to maximize their coverage of the approaches and cranked up the Auto Battlefield Motion Sensor units in their helmets just in case. The ABMS was designed to detect millimeter wave changes out to 700 meters and alert the wearer with an electric tingle and a voice description of the threat. It would also feed visual data on the threat to the Battle Sensor Device that lowered from the helmet like a monocle. It was like having a sixth sense.

They checked the readouts from the bio-chip health status sensors built into their suits as a precaution against dehydration or any of the other physical problems they knew could sneak up on an operator without his realizing it. Their sensors showed normal range for vital signs and body function—no problem.

So they drank some fluids, electrolytes and water, and ate to keep up their strength. Jack had issue cold rations. Sarah opted for a high-energy granola bar.

"Still eating the sawdust, Doc?" Jack teased.

"Tastes better than that stuff."

"Couldn't taste any worse. Makes you wonder if Napoleon was right about an army traveling on its stomach."

"Guess it's a safe bet they have Captain Daniels," Greene said.

"I'd say. There's only one way our sniper friend could have got his hands on that rescue beacon."

"Maybe Daniels evaded him and lost his beacon in the process."

"Always looking on the bright side, aren't you?" Jack laughed softly. "Not much chance of that, Doc. A downed pilot might leave just about anything else behind, but not his beacon. He knows that's his only ticket out of here."

"Guess you're right. Any idea how we're going to get him out of there?"

"Shouldn't be a problem. We have the advantage."

"Really?" Sarah looked at him, puzzled. "I don't see how."

"It's like Sun Tzu says, 'When you induce others to construct a formation while you yourself are formless, then you are concentrated while the opponent is divided.' We can be invisible. You can't get more formless than that."

"Guess you've got a point there." Sarah tried to smile, but did not quite pull it off.

"You're thinking about him," Jack said, "if he's hurt or what shape he might be in."

"That's my job."

"Well, if he's hurt, I don't expect he's getting much doctoring in that camp."

"You're thinking about him too, huh?"

"Some. Mostly I'm thinking about the sniper."

"Why him?"

"That's *my* job."

1145 hours

Travis spent his time studying the camp through his BSD, the way it was laid out and how the men moved around in it. He also kept a close eye on his ABMS as a backup. He couldn't afford to get too focused on the target and let somebody walk up on him.

He had seen the men leaving the camp to take up positions as sentries and perimeter defense. He had also seen them resetting what looked like motion detectors forward of their positions among the rocks on the slope. Making careful mental note of the sensors' positions, he filed that information away for later.

It was almost noon and Stan and Sam should be joining up with Jack and Sarah within the hour. They would need time to rest and regroup, but that shouldn't be a problem, Travis was thinking. Like everything else on this mission, the end game was going to be complicated. He felt reasonably sure he was looking at the RF device in the back of that vehicle down there. It also stood to reason that the hostiles had Captain Daniels stashed in one of those tents, most likely the big one in the middle of the camp. So all he had to do was capture or destroy the RF gizmo and rescue Daniels without losing any of his team in the process. As an added bonus, the NSA satcom intercept gave him reason to believe Osama bin Laden was in the camp, too.

Except for the presence of Captain Daniels, the camp was a target-rich environment, perfect for a precision air strike. For that matter, the team could bring enough firepower to bear on the camp by itself to do the international community a world of good. But Captain Daniels was a very big exception. There was no way for Travis to know what condition he was in, even if he was still alive. For all he knew, the pilot had been killed when he bailed out and all the bad guys had found was his body. But he couldn't be sure. As long as there was a chance he was still alive, that was the way they would play it.

And that meant going in under the cover of darkness, using their LOCS invisibility and BSD night-vision to get in undetected. They would have to locate Daniels and get him out of there, then deal with the rest of the camp. Travis was trying to figure out how they could snatch Daniels, identify Osama bin Laden if he was down there and do something with him, and plant a delayed charge on the RF gizmo to take it out after they got clear. That's a damned busy plan, he told himself. Remember: KISS—Keep It Simple, Stupid.

0345 hours EDT
The White House War Room, Washington, D.C.

Back home, the situation was heating up among the politicians and diplomats.

A delegation of senators led by the man who was close friends with the father of Captain Daniels's sweetheart, Stephanie, called on the president at the White House. They blew off the two reporters who spotted them going in, but everybody knew the whole White House press corps would be assembled en masse when they came out.

It was with the understanding that the press was hovering outside that the senators and the president got down to business.

There were a couple of hawks among the senators who thought the United States had called off the Gulf War too soon to begin with. They were inclined to support firm action with Saddam generally, and shooting down one of our aircraft was provocation enough for them to urge retaliation. Others were less sure of things. They knew the president had access to information they did not and were willing to listen to what he had to say.

While key committee chairmen had been notified by the White House that an aircraft had gone down, there had been very little information forthcoming in the interim. If one of their number hadn't taken a personal interest in the matter on behalf of a friend of the family and made inquiries at Adana, they still wouldn't know anything further.

The president confided in them as fully as he thought was prudent for all their sakes. He told them it had not been a conventional missile that took down Captain Daniels's F-16. The senators all knew the pilot's name, the senator who was friends with Stephanie's dad had taken great pains to put a face to the missing pilot for his colleagues, even showing them a photograph of the lovebirds. He told them steps were being taken to determine the nature of the weapon used and the persons responsible.

The senators were in agreement that Saddam Hussein was responsible. Such an action could not have been taken without his approval. At his direction, one of them insisted. And whatever unconventional weapon had been used, it was well known that Saddam had spent a fortune on weapons technology of all kinds.

The president hinted there was evidence the attack might have been the work of terrorists and offered the theory that it might have been intended as a provocation, to spur the United States into just such a retaliation as the senators seemed to be suggesting.

That got a mixed reaction from the senators, who finally agreed among themselves that a stiff diplomatic protest should be forwarded to Saddam Hussein at once. It would have to be delivered through intermediaries since the two governments did not maintain diplomatic relations. Accuse him of involvement and see what he says in his defense.

The president promised he would give their advice careful consideration. Actually, he and his advisors had already thought of sending a note and decided against it. Saddam would protest his innocence in any case, and they would be no further along than before. And they didn't like the idea of telling the Iraqis that one of our planes had gone down and we weren't sending in SAR flights to find the pilot. They probably knew that already, but there was no point in laying it out for them. If they were behind the attack, it would only underscore our concern about the RF weapon. If they weren't, the less they knew the better.

But the president would reconsider it, now that the senators had dealt themselves in. With the military situation in the Balkans and other hot spots percolating near the boiling point around the world, he didn't want a debate on the matter that might go public. This was no time to risk being portrayed as being soft on Iraq.

The senators did not pause long in front of the microphones and cameras when they left, just long enough for the senior of them to say it had been a social call and they had no further comment.

He might have given the matter more thought.

Nothing whets reporters' curiosity more than "No comment." And the notion that senators from the opposition party, staunch political rivals of the president on everything from the economy to welfare and defense spending, had dropped by the White House on a social call was greeted with derisive eye-rolling by the jaded members of the press.

The net result was that the press went on one of their patented feeding frenzies, determined to dig up the truth of the matter. All three national newscasts that evening would carry stories about reports from anonymous sources that an American fighter had been shot down over northern Iraq. Details would vary. The stories would be largely speculation, but nearer the truth than was often the case.

1145 hours
The mountains of northern Iraq

Stan motioned for Sam to freeze in his tracks. He was
picking something up on his ABMS. The warning tingle
was followed by a woman's gentle prerecorded voice:
"Movement at eleven o'clock, five hundred meters. Multiple readings."

He looked at Sam, who nodded. He was getting it too.

Stan turned and moved quickly into the rocks beside
the trail they had been following. He motioned for Sam
to get low and stay down, but his warning was unnecessary. Sam was already as low as he could get.

Sam would have turned on his chameleon camo suit,
but Stan signaled him not to. No point in using up juice
when you have good cover and concealment already, he
was thinking. Stan had been an operator since before
they invented suits that made you invisible.

The first of bin Laden's Iranians came into view a few
minutes later. He was the point man, his rifle held ready
and his eyes scanning the rocky slopes on either side of
the little trail. Behind him came the leader of the band,
who held what looked like a map in one hand, his Kalishnikov slung over his shoulder. He stopped at one point
and consulted his map, then struck out again, motioning
for the others to pick up the pace. All of them were
wearing civilian clothes after the fashion of the region.
But they had on military-issue boots. Stan saw at least
two radios in the group, late-model ones that looked
Eastern European.

He counted twenty men as they filed by his hiding
place, each with a Kalishnikov in his hands and grenades
on his ammunition bandoleer. He recognized the way
they carried their ammo and grenades before it registered that he recognized their language, too. He didn't
speak any Farsi beyond a couple of curses he had picked
up along the way. But he knew it when he heard it.
These were Iranian assholes. What the hell were Iranian
soldiers doing this deep in Iraq? Wearing civvies, like
you couldn't spot them for grunts a mile away?

He waited until the last of them had passed, then waited a few minutes more just to be on the safe side. When he could no longer see any sign of them and his ABMS was reading negative contacts in both directions, Stan stood up. He stepped out of the rocks and back on to the trail, motioning for Sam to come on. He had to give the signal a couple of times before Sam finally showed himself. Then they moved off down the trail again in the same direction they had been headed before.

When they had covered some distance, Stan called a halt and told Sam to hook up with the bird and let them know back at the White House War Room that they had bumped into a squad of Iranian soldiers.

"Those guys were Iranians?" Sam asked, looking back the way they had come.

"Is the Pope Polish? Send the message."

While Sam was making contact with the satellite, Stan called up Travis on his helmet commo system. Travis wasn't talking because he was too close to the enemy camp, but Jack answered.

"What's up with you guys?" Jack asked. "You taking a break back there?"

"Nah," Stan answered. "We just got held up in a little traffic."

Chapter Seventeen

When Tom Burgess got the satellite relay from the team about their sighting Iranians, he knew the news qualified as what the president's national security advisor had meant by "any new developments." Tom put a call through to him in the Oval Office where he and the other NCS senior officials were still meeting with the president.

"Very interesting, Tom," the security advisor said when he heard the news. "But the identification is based on a team member's observation, you say? There are no documents or prisoners or anything, right? I'm just thinking it would be easy to mistake a Kurd for an Iranian if you're not an expert. Their languages sound very similar, I understand. Our man out there's not an expert, is he? On Iranians, I mean."

"I don't believe so, sir. Our records don't show that."

"I see." There was a thoughtful pause. "Well, you did well to call, Tom. It is very interesting news. I'll share it with the president, of course."

"Yes, sir."

Burgess wasn't an expert on Iranians either, but he was willing to take the word of the man who was out in the field. If he said they were Iranians, that was good enough for Tom Burgess.

As it happened, it was very nearly good enough for the president, too. It gave him pause about that diplomatic protest and putting the forces in the region on alert for a possible retaliatory strike. He gave orders to have everybody down the line stand by in case it became necessary to go that route. But if there were Iranians involved, that put a whole new light on things.

1300 hours
Camp Jihad, northern Iraq

As the afternoon wore on, the heat became oppressive under a cloudless sky. The sun scorched the high slopes and heated the rocks strewn everywhere. For the second day, a night of torrential rain was followed by a day of clear skies and oppressive heat. Down in the camp, Osama bin Laden had been thinking about getting out of these accursed mountains. He wondered if the searing heat of the sun might have dried the muddy valley floors enough to make them passable. With his four-wheel drive vehicles, they needn't drive on the valley floor itself. They could pick their way along the lower slopes. If necessary, they could destroy the machine to keep anyone else from using it and walk back to Iran.

It disturbed him that the Americans had not blamed Saddam Hussein and lashed out at him as they should have done. Surely they must know by now that their plane was brought down by a new secret weapon. Even the Americans must be aware of RF technology and suspect its use in all this. How could they sit idly by when they had every reason to believe Saddam Hussein had such a weapon at his disposal and had used it against them?

This result was less than he and the ayatollahs in Tehran had prayed for. He knew they would not be pleased to have supported such a venture with so little to show for it. On the other hand, they would almost certainly appreciate the significance of what bin Laden had accomplished. He had proved Pretsky's design could perform miracles, silently reaching up into the sky and plucking down an American war bird. They might have designs on such a machine themselves, and the man who built it.

For these reasons as well as his delicious fantasy of

entangling the American Satans in another war, bin
Laden wanted desperately to locate the F-16's ordnance.
It would be another card to play in the high-stakes game
he called his *jihad*.

There had been no word yet from the Iranians, and
he was tired of waiting for them to do their duty. Waiting
could be dangerous, and bin Laden had begun to suspect
that his time was running out in this place.

1330 hours
The mountains of northern Iraq

Well along in the afternoon, Travis got the word that
Stan and Sam had hooked up with Jack and Sarah at
the hide.

Good, he thought. Now we can put our heads together
and come up with a plan. He had some ideas, but he
had confidence in his team to have input of their own.
He knew there was a time to make the tough decisions
on your own and a time to listen. And he was in a mood
to listen.

The camp below was not in shadow any longer. It was
catching the full blast of the afternoon sun now, and
Travis had seen nothing moving down there for almost
an hour except for a lone sentry sitting on an overturned
supply crate in front of the big tent. And even in the
sweltering heat, the flap of that tent was closed. Otherwise, it looked like siesta time, when everybody crawled
into their tents or any spot of shade they could find and
took a nap.

That went for the sentries up in these rocks, too, Travis
figured. So this was as good a time as any to vamoose.
He reached into his pack and located what he needed
by feel, without having to look for it. It was one of his
Micro-UAVs, a hand-launched Micro-Unmanned Aerial
Vehicle. About the size of a cigarette lighter, it was used
to collect intelligence by over-flying areas of interest. It
could look over a hill, around a corner, even fly through

the rooms of a house if need be. Travis was tempted to launch the little drone and steer it by remote control down into the camp for a closer look. If the flap on the big tent had been open, he might have tried it. Besides, he figured even the sleepy sentry perched on the supply crate might notice a flying bug the size of a cigarette lighter.

Instead, Travis positioned the little drone so that its video "eye" was aimed at the camp and carefully packed sand around it before placing rocks on top of it. The drone would keep an eye on things while he was gone, its transmitted images on call through his helmet/BSD system whenever he wanted them. That done, he prepared to back out of his hide and make his way back to the reunited team.

Just to be on the safe side, he activated his LOCS before moving out of his hide. It was a good thing he did, because just as he straightened up and turned to move away, one of the sentries appeared from around a boulder and walked right into him.

The man was dressed in the long dresslike robe of an Arab, with the kind of turban Travis remembered the mujahideen wore. The man's eyes bugged out and he fell back a step. He mumbled something in Arabic. He must have thought he had bumped into a devil or an evil spirit of some kind, because he started to scream. But his eyes lighted on Travis's rifle and he lunged at Travis with his arms spread wide to grab him in a bear hug.

Travis broke the man's grip with a wrestling move and grabbed him by the throat when he saw he was about to cry out.

The two grappled silently among the rocks on the cliff overlooking the camp as seconds ticked by. There was no time or room for either to bring a weapon into play. This would be settled hand-to-hand. Travis had the obvious advantage, but the man fought with superhuman strength, his heart pumping pure adrenaline. He shoved his weight against his ghostly enemy and drove him toward the edge. If he could not beat this devil, he would take it with him over the cliff.

Travis looked down and saw his foot braced at the very brink of the drop-off, the stone crumbling under his heel and sending dust wafting in the still air toward the camp below.

The man grunted and cursed under his breath as he struggled to take the devil down with him. Travis used leverage to turn the man and got the hold he was looking for. You unlucky bastard, he thought. Another couple of feet and I'd have let you pass right by. You never would have known I was here.

But it was too late for that now, and Travis had to make sure the man gave no cry of alarm and did not live to tell of bumping into a devil on the cliff. Once he got in position, it was a simple thing to apply enough muscle to twist the man's neck until it snapped. When that was done, Travis held him, his grip tight on the man's throat to make sure he died quietly.

They'll miss him, Travis thought. I can't just leave him here.

1340 hours
Camp Jihad, northern Iraq

The dead man made a racket when he came down. He caromed off the cliff wall and tumbled end over end, landing in a heap on the valley floor, his bandoleer rattling with the impact.

There was a stirring in the tents and then shouts.

Mustafa was the first to reach him, with Mikhail close behind.

"He has no wound," Mustafa announced after examining the body. He looked up at the cliff. "He must have fallen."

"Yes," the Russian said. He too looked up. "Odd that he didn't cry out."

Still looking up at the cliff, Mikhail's shooter's eye caught something at the top, a shimmer, like the heat of the sun off the rocks.

1400 hours
Eagle Base Camp

"There's a high point about here," Stan reported, pointing to a spot on his map. "They'll be able to see the wreckage from there, but it'll take them a while to make it the rest of the way."

The team was together again, huddled in the hide Jack and Sarah had selected and prepared.

"How long till they're there?" Travis asked.

"Couple of hours maybe. They weren't exactly highballing it."

"They're scared shitless up in these mountains," Jack laughed softly. "They don't know who they're going to catch it from—the Kurds or Iraqis. But they know they're going to catch it from somebody if they stay up in here long enough."

"They're gonna catch it from that F-16 ordnance when it blows up in their freakin' faces," Stan chortled. "I wish I could be there to see it."

"I wish I could figure out how to get an NLG into that camp without them spotting it before it took effect," Travis said. The Non-Lethal Generator was the size of a small trash can and somebody carried one on almost every mission. Jack had the honor this time. When activated, the thing generated a low-frequency RF field that made everybody within 600 meters who wasn't wearing protection sick as a dog. It would be perfect for a deal like this. Get everybody in the camp puking and shitting their brains out, and the team could walk right in and snatch the pilot, blow the enemy RF generator, and grab Osama bin Laden, too, if he's there. The problem was, the effect was quick but not instantaneous. The hostiles could do a lot of shooting before they got sick, or run out of range of the NLG if they had the presence of mind.

"Exposure to an NLG might be more than Captain Daniels can take if he's injured or wounded," Sarah said. As the team's doctor, the pilot was her responsibility.

"Yeah," Travis agreed. "That's the other thing."

"I'm for going in there and lighting 'em up," Stan said. "Pick our spots, synchronize our watches, and shoot the shit out of them."

"You come up with the same plan every damned time," Jack noted.

"And it's a good plan every damned time," Stan insisted.

"Except for the pilot," Sarah pointed out.

"If we hit them fast enough, they won't have time to do anything to him," Stan said.

"They may have already done something to him," Sarah said.

"Yeah, that's a problem," Travis put in. "We don't know what shape he's in. We're not even positive he's down there. They may have killed him already and dumped his body. If that's the case, we could just hit them with all we've got."

"I've been thinking about that," Sarah said. "I want to go in and find out."

"Into the camp?" Travis frowned.

"That's crazy," Stan said.

"You guys got a better idea?"

1500 hours
Çukurca, Turkey

Hunter was in the village, drinking their crappy homemade wine and making excuses for why "Yvette" had just now made her first appearance of the day.

He had been stalling them most of the afternoon. She's putting her face on, he told the villagers. You know how women are, he said, takes them forever to get ready to go anywhere. He tried to tell them how tough it had been traveling with such a prima donna around the country on this comeback tour of hers. He told them this was the first decent place they'd stopped and he was glad the storm had blown them off course.

What he didn't tell them was how glad he was his

Turkish friend back in Adana had come up with the idea of Jen impersonating a French movie star because the PKK apparently had no bones to pick with the French.

But the natives were getting restless, especially big Kamil. He made it clear that it wasn't every day a movie star came to his village, especially one he had been in love with since he saw her for the first time in a French film at the cinema over in Bitlis when he was a young man. And he had to say, Monsieur Poof—he had taken to calling Hunter that—he didn't see any sense in wasting time sitting around drinking like this. He could sit around and drink any time he felt like it, but the woman of his dreams was over there in the airplane—so near and yet so far.

Hunter had stalled as long as he could because he knew Jen was in no hurry to put on another performance. She had been able to talk Kamil out of showing her how much he loved her last night, but she wasn't sure she could pull off the same trick a second time. She had made it clear to Hunter there were some things she would rather not do for her country. And Kamil was one of them.

Little Abdul came up in the middle of the afternoon and Kamil had asked him if he had the accursed projector fixed. Abdul said he thought it was in the mood to cooperate now and he had the film loaded and ready to go.

That was all Kamil needed to hear. The plan had been to have a big dinner in the village hall that evening and then screen Yvette's old movie. But Kamil was impatient. He wanted to see the film right now with its star at his side. They could eat later.

Abdul gave Hunter a look when nobody was watching and winked at him. It happened in a second and left Hunter a little confused. Was Abdul trying to let him know that he was his contact here in the village, the one the Turkish officer in Adana had sent word to? Or was he just flirting with Monsieur Poof?

And then Kamil would not be put off any longer. Followed by some of his men, he stomped out to the old DC-3 and banged on the fuselage.

"Yvette! Yvette, come out of there and let us adore you!"

Finally, Jen had answered the call. Kamil escorted her back to the village and showed her to the place of honor, a chair set atop a table in the same big building as the night before. Abdul was there with his projector. Someone had freshly whitewashed the wall that would serve as the movie screen for the night. The joint was packed and everybody was having a good time, throwing back their wine and ready to be entertained.

Kamil was red-faced, flush with the wine and his love for the great Yvette, and he took a seat beside her atop the table.

Hunter was pretty much ignored by the crowd. And that was just as well because, just as Abdul's ancient projector sputtered to life and the oil lamps were dimmed for the movie, he heard the signal in his ear piece that meant the team was trying to raise him by satellite relay. He eased out the door and jogged across the field from the village to the old gooney bird and waved hello to Kamil's men still camped out under its right wing. They nodded amiably enough, with their rifles on the ground beside them.

Aboard the plane, he hurried to the cockpit and slid back the control panel in the wall beside the pilot's seat and plugged into the satellite relay. He listened for a moment, acknowledged the message, and closed the panel again.

It was time to go. The team was going to move on the enemy camp soon. Allowing for the time it would take the old gooney bird to reach the rendezvous in the rocky basin, Hunter and Jen would get there at dusk if they left now. All he had to do was go back to the village hall and pry "Yvette" loose from Kamil, the lovesick PKK boss.

Chapter Eighteen

Monday, June 12, 1500 hours
A camp in the mountains of northern Iraq

Captain Sarah Greene, M.D., made her way carefully down toward the enemy camp. She had stripped down to her battle ensemble, helmet, suit, boots, and gloves, and left her field pack and weapons for Jack to carry along with his own gear. The rest of the team was deployed on the high ground above the camp. They had moved into position stealthily, their LOCS systems on and using preplanned routes that would avoid the sentries and motion detectors Travis had spotted earlier. She knew they were up there now, ready to back her up any way they could. But if they were watching her, it was not in a literal sense. They knew where she was going and with their BSDs they could pick up the shimmer effect when she moved, so by watching very closely they could tell approximately where she was at any time. But they weren't really watching her.

Like the rest of the team, she was invisible.

The micro-sensors woven into the ballistic fabric of her ensemble were reading the visual elements of her environment and mimicking them so precisely that she was literally invisible to the naked eye. It had been difficult to accept the power of the technology at first, to convince herself that people could look right at her in broad daylight and not see her. But she knew it worked. It had kept her alive before.

She and Travis and Jack had used their LOCS systems less than an hour trailing the sniper back to his camp, Travis another quarter of an hour extricating himself

from his observation post and his fight with the sentry.
Stan and Sam had preserved their full energy load, rely-
ing on stealth to locate the crashed F-16 and make their
way back to rejoin the team. There was plenty of juice
left in the systems. Even Travis's suit, which had been
used the most, had at least another four hours. And this
was the kind of situation they had been saving them for.

The second lesson Sarah had to learn in using the
LOCS was that, while the ensemble rendered her invisible, it did not eliminate any of the other properties of
the human body. She still cast a shadow. That was why
they had waited until the sun moved enough to cast the
camp below in shadows that covered the ground and
portions of the tents.

She still had weight, too. Her boots made noise with
every step and left footprints. So she willed herself to
move slowly and step carefully as she made her way
toward the camp. It seemed to take forever. And she
knew that the Iranians Stan and Sam had seen on the
trail would soon reach the wreckage of the F-16. After
that, it was only a matter of time before they triggered
Stan's explosive charges. Stan had assured them the explosion would be massive, loud enough to be heard in
the camp. That would stir them up and make it even
more difficult for her to go undiscovered, invisible or not.

After what seemed an eternity, she reached the level
ground at the edge of the camp and eased her way down
the path between the smaller tents arranged in a semicircle. The big tent was her target, and she was relieved to
see the flap that served as its door was now open. It
seemed another eternity before she eased through the
opening into the shadowy darkness of the tent.

It was all she could do to suppress a gasp. Sitting cross-
legged on a blanket and watching CNN on a satellite
television monitor was a man with a face she knew from
hundreds of photographs. It was Osama bin Laden.

It occurred to her to do something, but she had
brought no weapons with her, just syringes from her
medical kit stuffed inside the front of her suit. While she
was deciding whether to apply a silent but lethal martial

arts move, a second figure rose from the shadows at the rear of the tent. He was bin Laden too!

0700 hours EDT
The White House War Room, Washington, D.C.

Tom Burgess and Commander Greeley stared at their monitors like the others in the War Room. They had received a report by satellite relay that one of the operators was entering the enemy camp. They still had the image transmitted by the Micro-UAV that Travis had planted to keep an eye on the camp, although it was beginning to break up as the device's battery ran down. They also had fresh images of the camp from different perspectives, members of the team up-linking by satellite the views from their hiding places on the cliff overlooking it.

"He's in there now?" someone asked at the head table.

"That's what they're telling us," came the answer.

"One of them's showing stress," reported the man at the console monitoring telemetry from the health status sensors in the team's ensembles. "Elevated heart rate and blood pressure. Not bad, though."

"That'll be the one that's gone in there," Tom Burgess said softly.

"Damned right his vitals are peaking," Greeley said. "They'd better be. He's really got to be on his toes in there."

"But where the hell is he?" Burgess asked. "Do you see him?"

"No," Greeley admitted, squinting at the nearest monitor. "Whoever he is, he's damned good."

Burgess nodded, focused on the monitor.

"Burgess, who are those guys?" Greeley asked.

Burgess didn't answer, just shook his head. He still hadn't seen anything.

1500 hours
Eagle Base Camp

Travis sent his message by satellite relay to General Krauss at TALON Force command in the Pentagon for distribution to the relevant commands. It was time to prep the assets for an air strike so they could be in a position to come in fast once the team either got control of the RF machine or destroyed it. Either way, it wouldn't be a threat to the aircraft at that point and he wanted to have a strike on call with as quick a response time as possible. The air force jets could scramble from Adana and haul ass to the general area, then orbit and refuel as necessary up near the Turkish border until he called for them.

Same for the extraction backup, a conventional CSAR heavy reaction force. If they went up now, they would still have a long way to go and they'd have to refuel to get here. They couldn't be on scene until a couple of hours after Hunter's ETA at the rocky basin in his gooney bird. But Travis wanted the backup on the way in case Hunter didn't make it.

Travis had not trusted the whole "Terry and the Pirates" angle with Hunter and Jen from the first. It was a harebrained scheme as far as he was concerned, with too many ways for it to go wrong. But Hunter had said he was on his way and he would get there before anybody else could.

Travis knew that if his team didn't grab the RF gizmo or knock it out, Hunter and his DC-3 was their only way out. The ancient gooney bird was as computerless as you could get. Even if it was still in enemy hands, the gizmo wouldn't pose a threat to that old bird. That wasn't the case with the jet fighters of the air strike or the high-tech helicopters of the backup extraction team. If the hostiles still had possession of the gizmo when it came time to leave, Travis knew he could not ask those guys to fly into a trap.

Either way, Hunter was due to get there first. That

made him their best chance because whatever was going
to happen was going to happen soon, as soon as Sarah
got clear of the enemy camp with her report on Captain Daniels.

1535 hours
Çukurca, Turkey

Hunter pushed his way through the crowd in the village
hall toward the table where "Yvette" and Kamil sat above
the crowd. The room was dark except for the flickering
light of Abdul's projector. Hunter saw the black-and-white
images of Yvette's thirty-year-old French bedroom farce
playing out on the freshly whitewashed wall as he neared
the table in the center of the big room. He caught Jen's
eye and gave her a signal, pointing to his ear piece and
giving her a thumbs up to show that he had received the
call they were waiting for and it was time to go. She
nodded, but there wasn't much she could do about it.
Kamil was all over her.

All the men in the room were drinking and watching
the movie and paid Hunter no attention. He worked his
way over to Abdul. The little man looked up at him and
winked again. Hunter decided to take a chance. He drew
his finger across his throat, pointed at the projector and
raised his eyebrows to show he was asking Abdul if he
could kill the projector.

With a clatter of sprockets and loose film flapping, the
white wall went dark and the room was full of curses
and shouts.

"A small technical problem," Abdul announced, his
hands upraised. "I shall have her purring like a kitten
again in no time."

Things were thrown across the room at the little man,
but he bent over his machine and pretended to be working on it.

"Most frustrating," Kamil said to "Yvette." "Just as
we were about to be treated to your famous boudoir

scene, in which you drive the wealthy playboy mad with your irresistible striptease."

Jen put her lips to Kamil's ear and whispered something that made the big man's eyes light up. "Wouldn't you rather see ze real thing?" she asked him in English with a thick French accent. "In my boudoir?"

Hunter couldn't hear what she said, but he got the drift.

While little Abdul was still working on his projector in the light of an oil lamp, Jen and Kamil were out the door and the big man was hurrying her toward the airplane. He offered to carry her but she demurred.

"Save your strength," she told him. "You're going to need it."

He bellowed like a bull at that and practically dragged her the rest of the way to the steps of the old DC-3 and up into the cabin. He turned and glared at Hunter when he followed the two lovebirds into the cabin.

"What's he doing here?" the big man demanded.

"Don't worry about him," Jen purred. "You wait here. I'll be right back."

"No!" the big man roared. "I have waited long enough!"

He grabbed her shoulders roughly in his big paws and pulled her to him. With one arm around her waist pinning her to his chest, he ran his free hand through her hair. He cursed when the wig came off in his hand. Standing there dumbfounded, he was slow to react when Jen wriggled free of him, but he reached out for her and grabbed the front of her dress before she could get beyond his reach. The fabric tore away in his hand, and his eyes fell on "Yvette's" naked charms.

It was hardly what he had expected. Instead of the bare breasts of the woman he had loved so long, Kamil found himself ogling a mass of foam rubber with stitched seams, one of the sagging breasts having come away in his hand with the front of the dress.

"Yvette," he murmured, his eyes wide with shock and disbelief. "What have you done to yourself?"

And then he felt the cold muzzle of the pistol in Hunter's hand behind his right ear. Moments later, when

Hunter had the gooney bird's engines revved up and ready to go, Kamil stood in the open cabin doorway. "Yvette" held the pistol then, but it was still snug in his ear and he had no doubt she would shoot him.

He called down in Kurdish to his PKK compatriots camped under the wing to shoot the plane full of holes. Kill Monsieur Poof, he told them. But he knew they wouldn't shoot as long as he was in the doorway and "Yvette" held a gun to his head. When the airplane turned and started up the rocky airstrip he accepted her invitation to jump and avoid the flight back to Adana where he would surely join President Apo on Imrali Island.

That was considerate of her, he thought. Nevertheless, before he stepped out the doorway to tumble among the rocks, he looked over his shoulder at her.

"I want you to know," he said, "you have broken my heart, Yvette."

And then he jumped.

His compatriots opened fire with their rifles as soon as he was clear, but it was too late. The gooney bird was out of range by then and beginning its climb into the sky.

Chapter Nineteen

"Where is that raghead SOB?"

The voice outside startled Sarah. She was standing just inside the tent, trying to work out a way to get past the two men to the body lying in the shadows at the rear of the tent without giving herself away by passing between the man watching CNN and the television monitor.

Her problem was solved by the uproar outside, a man's voice cursing and the noise of people stirring. The two men, the two Osama bin Ladens, went to the front of the tent and stepped outside.

Sarah moved quickly. Now that her eyes had adjusted to the tent's dark interior, she was satisfied that she was alone with the man lying in the shadows. She rushed to the prone figure and knelt at his side. She checked for a pulse at his throat and felt the heat of his fever. Working quickly, she peeled away the blanket and examined his badly wounded leg. It was fractured and ugly with infection. His pulse was rapid and weak, his breathing labored. She did what she could to clean and stabilize the wound.

"Who are you?" the man mumbled weakly.

"Never mind," she whispered. "Are you Captain Daniels?"

He nodded. "Am I dreaming?" he asked.

"No. Lie still."

"Gotta be dreaming. Can't see you . . . but I can feel your hands."

"Sh-h-h."

"They're cool."

"Shut up, Captain."

"Yes, ma'am."

As she retrieved the syringes from inside her suit and prepared to give him injections of antibiotics and biomed fluids to help him fight off the shock and infection, she took an extra second to activate the "straight-up" satcom component of her helmet commo system. She had not planned to transmit for fear the signal might register on some of the equipment in the camp and alert the enemy. But she knew it was important for the men in the White House War Room to see proof that Daniels was alive. She only transmitted for the few seconds it took her to find a vein and start the first injection, then she switched off the system. If her signal had been detected, she hoped the ruckus outside, which was getting louder by the second, would distract the men in the camp and they wouldn't notice.

0740 hours EDT
The White House War Room, Washington, D.C.

"What the hell was that?"

"Who was that?"

"Was that who I thought it was?"

The questions all came at once from around the War Room at the White House. The face, haggard and drawn, had flashed on their monitor screens for only a couple of seconds.

"We're setting up playback now," Tom Burgess announced to the head table.

In short order, the face reappeared on the screens, frozen this time in a still frame.

Burgess checked his records. He had a dossier on Captain Daniels, complete with a recent photograph.

"Is that him?" the DCI asked.

"Yes, sir," Burgess said. "It'll take a minute to run a computerized comparison to confirm, but that's him, sir. See for yourself."

Burgess showed the DCI the photo in Daniels's file.

"It's him all right, but he looks like he's been through hell."

"Yes, sir."

"But he's alive, by God."

"Yes, sir."

The president's national security advisor made the call to the Oval Office and the president personally put a call through to the senator who was friends with Stephanie's dad. He told the senator that he was sure he understood the importance of secrecy but that he wanted him to know that Captain Daniels was alive. The senator appreciated the president's thoughtfulness, if not his firm refusal to reveal anything more about the matter except to say that measures were being taken to effect the captain's rescue. The senator naturally called his close friend and that was how Stephanie found out her Michael was still alive. Like the senator, she would have liked more information, but at least she knew he was alive.

0745 hours EDT
The Pentagon, Washington, D.C.

In the SCIF in the bowels of the Pentagon, Mac jumped up and danced a jig. Then he collapsed in his chair and danced another jig sitting down. One look at Bob and Dr. Fensterman told him that they hadn't understood the significance of the message that had scrolled across their monitors. Maybe they'd get it when the War Room forwarded the satellite images of Captain Daniels in a couple of minutes.

"Tell you two geeks what I'm going to do," Mac said. Bob and Dr. Fensterman both looked interested. "When this is all over, I'm going to take the two of you to a little bar I know and I'm going to get you both plastered. Maybe then I can get through to you."

"Sounds good," Bob said.

Dr. Fensterman nodded enthusiastically. "This would be one of those bars with free nuts?" the doctor asked.

1550 hours
Camp Jihad, northern Iraq

Pretsky had finally run out of patience and his temper, famous in scientific circles in Moscow where ill temper was the norm, had got the best of him.

"There you are, you raghead son of bitch!"

Pretsky stood in front of bin Laden's tent. He was weaving and might have fallen except that he leaned on a stick to keep his balance. He had found the stick along the way and used it like a cane when he hiked off into the rocks to relieve himself.

"I see you've been at the vodka again, comrade," bin Laden said calmly.

"Of course I have, you stupid camel jockey. What else is a man to do in this wilderness? And I have drunk last of it. Understand? Vodka is gone, and when vodka is gone, is time to leave. Is time to leave, I'm telling you. Right now this minute."

"I am waiting for word from our Iranian friends."

"Those gutless raghead bastards! You think they are searching? Everyday they go just far enough to be out of your sight. Then when is dark they come back and they found nothing. You're a fool if you think they finding anything out there."

Mikhail, awakened by the shouting, came out of his tent and watched but said nothing.

"I have more confidence in our Iranian brothers than you. We will wait."

"No. We don't wait another minute. We leave now."

"You seem to be forgetting who's in charge here."

"What do I care you're in charge? You going to shoot me? You can't shoot me. I have the secret of the machine in my head. Nobody else." Pretsky turned and lumbered over to the truck with the RF machine in the back. "I go now. You do what you want and please go to hell."

"You would never make it to the border," bin Laden said, his voice still calm. "Not alone."

"Then you come with me and bring your fighters. We go."

"Not just yet."

"To hell with you then."

Pretsky, who had not been able to lift his foot high enough to climb into the truck anyway, turned toward bin Laden. Grinning like an idiot, he reached into the pocket of the khaki safari suit he had bought especially for this expedition and produced a hand grenade.

"Don't be a fool, Pretsky," bin Laden said, moving away from his tent toward the Russian with Mustafa as always following behind. "Put that down before you blow yourself up with it."

"No. I blow up machine with this," Pretsky said, his piggish eyes alight. "Then you must to take me back. Because only I build another."

"Don't do that," bin Laden warned, closing the distance between them and grabbing the Russian's hand.

As clever as he might have been with complex systems, Pretsky had never bothered to learn the intricacies of Iranian hand grenades and so was having trouble arming this one. Bin Laden easily wrestled it from his hand and turned away.

"We'll wait," bin Laden said, tossing the grenade to one of his men, "a while longer."

When bin Laden looked back, the Russian was coming at him in a rage like a bull elephant, his walking stick raised over his head.

"You stupid raghead son of bitch!"

The three reports from Mustafa's pistol sounded in such quick succession that they might have been a single short burst from a submachine gun. The first slug caught the Russian in the ribs. He started to turn toward Mustafa as the next two hit, the last just below his clavicle.

Pretsky balanced for a moment on his chubby legs, staring down at the bloodstains spreading over the front of his safari jacket. He lowered his walking stick slowly as if to lean his weight on it, but he was already dead by the time the tip of the stick reached the level of his waist and he slumped to his knees. His corpse tottered there for a second or two, then toppled over on its belly, the porcine snout driving a rut in the rocky sand.

Mustafa looked to bin Laden and the Prophet nodded, a thin smile on his lips.

Mikhail had taken all this in without moving from the front of his tent.

"I hope this is not a problem for you," bin Laden said, walking over to him.

"None of my concern, really," Mikhail assured him.

"I don't suppose you have any idea what he did with the plans, the information he used to build the machine," bin Laden asked in a much lower voice so that only Mikhail could hear him.

"I'm afraid he didn't confide in me."

"That is unfortunate."

Well, bin Laden thought, this changes things. I'll have to rely on someone to reverse engineer the machine now. Poor Mustafa, he meant well. This means we'll have to take the prototype with us. We can't destroy it now or I'll never have another one. Perhaps Pretsky was right. Perhaps it is time to be going. But I hate to leave without the ordnance from the American plane.

Just then one of his bodyguards came forward with a radio in his outstretched hand. It was the Iranians reporting in. Good news at last! They had the American plane in sight. They would touch it with their hands in a matter of minutes.

"You see, Comrade Pretsky?" bin Laden said to the dead man after acknowledging the Iranians' report and returning the radio to the man who had brought it. "If you'd just been patient a little while longer."

And then he gave Mustafa the order to prepare to move out.

"Leave everything but the RF machine, the heavy weapons, and the American. Load it all on two vehicles and leave the rest. And put the American up in back beside the RF machine. Hurry, we're leaving at once."

He told the man with the radio to send a message to the Iranians.

"Tell them to retrieve any ordinance they can from the wrecked plane, but don't come back here. We're going back the way we came, east along the valley. Tell them to join up with us en route. And tell them to hurry. We're leaving."

Sarah did all she could for the American pilot and left him as she had found him, with a promise that he would be okay and a stern warning to say nothing of her having been there. He was delirious from the fever and she was afraid he would babble. But the medicine took effect quickly and he fell into a deep sleep.

Sarah was heartsick that she could not take him out of the camp with her, but it was impossible. As short as she was, she was strong enough to lift him on her back and carry him, but there was no way she could do it without being detected. Maybe on future rescue missions they could bring an extra LOCS to make the rescuee invisible, too. She made a mental note to bring that up in the mission debriefing.

It went against all her instincts, but she had to make herself leave him there.

While the attention of the camp was diverted by the scene between Pretsky and bin Laden, she left the tent and took the shortest route through the camp toward the base of the cliff and back to the team.

The sound of the three quick shots froze her in midstride just as she was about to start up the cliff. She turned slowly to look behind her and saw Pretsky tumble over.

Better you than me, comrade, she thought as she began to climb.

Chapter Twenty

The leader of bin Laden's Iranian escort signaled his men to get ready.

Since spotting the wreckage from the high ground earlier and making his report to bin Laden, he had brought his men along at a brisk pace. Bin Laden was breaking camp and starting back to Iran. That meant they had to hurry. He knew bin Laden wanted the American ordnance very badly, but he could not be sure the Prophet wanted it badly enough to wait for him and his men.

Now they were very close. From their position in the rocks, they could see the wreckage of the American plane only a few hundred meters away. Even from that distance, the leader of the Iranians could see one of the missiles sticking up like a spear. At last the prize was at hand and they could imagine going home as heroes.

But the leader did not give the signal to move forward. A movement had caught his eyes, something to his right front. He could not be sure what he had seen, but this was no time to grow careless.

His caution proved a virtue when several uniformed men appeared, coming up onto the ridge in front of them. They were moving toward the wreckage of the American plane. How many of them were there? The leader of the Iranians began to count but decided instead to see if he could tell who they were.

"Ah," he sighed when he put his binoculars on them. He didn't know whether to curse his luck for being

beaten to the prize or thank Allah for allowing him to
see them before they saw him.

"Who are they?" the man beside him asked.

"Iraqis. Accursed Republican Guards."

Colonel Hamir congratulated himself on his map reading, his navigation, his persistence, and in general. It was
not child's play to bring a reduced platoon of green recruits this far into the mountains for such a purpose when
they could hardly understand its significance. A lesser
man might have faced a mutiny before they came this
far. A lesser man might be lying dead now in a ravine,
put there by soldiers who marched back down to the
trucks with a made-up tale about a Kurdish ambush.

The green troops had done well enough. Just shows
you what a little leadership will do. Time and again they
thought they saw Kurds in the rocks and cliffs above
them as they climbed. They saw ambushes everywhere.
But they had followed him. And now look at them. They
had found the American plane.

Colonel Harim could not help thinking that if it were
not for American planes like this one, he could have
flown over these mountains in a helicopter in an hour
instead of trudging up them all day. But of course, without them there would be no need for his investigation in
the first place.

As it was, the sun was sinking behind him in the west
and they would be forced to camp here and go back
down the mountains in the morning. Pity he hadn't
thought to bring his overcoat, but that couldn't be
helped.

Before he gave any thought to setting up a defensive
perimeter and camping for the night, though, he was
eager to have a look at the airplane. He had never had
the pleasure of examining one of the American F-16s up
close before. This was hardly an ideal specimen, of
course, but still . . .

Colonel Harim led his exhausted troops forward with
little thought to formation. They had been climbing all
day in single or double file as the terrain dictated. Not

being an infantryman by training, he was inclined to let the noncommissioned officers deal with the details. His job was to provide leadership.

Among his green troops, the noncommissioned officers were young men from the same villages, enlisted at the same time as the others, who happened to have experience in their hometown militias or home guards. They were hardly veterans, and by this point were so relieved that they could finally stop climbing they gave little thought to defense. If the Kurds wanted to slaughter them, they would have done it already.

Colonel Harim was within a few meters of the wreckage when something about it caught his eye. There was something there that didn't belong. As he realized that what he was looking at was explosive fuse and plastic explosives, a young corporal passed by him on his left with a comment about wanting a souvenir.

"Stop!" Colonel Harim ordered the young man. "Don't touch anything."

"But, Colonel," the corporal said, turning to Harim with a mischievous look in his eye an instant before his head exploded.

Colonel Harim felt the warm goo spray his face and tunic from the dead corporal and his instinct told him the booby-trapped wreckage had exploded.

But that can't be, he thought. I'm still alive.

And then he finally heard the sound of the firing from the heights to his right and slugs caroming off the rocky ledge at his feet. He turned to his men and saw them falling, many of them hit while still struggling to unsling their rifles.

"Back, men!" he roared, surprised he had air in his lungs to make himself heard. "Back to the rocks. Follow me."

He turned and made for the shelter of the rocks through which they had climbed only moments before. As he went, he drew his pistol from the holster at his belt. He pointed it toward the heights where he saw the smoke of the guns that were cutting down his men. But his pistol would not fire.

Of course, you fool, he thought, remembering to draw back the slide to chamber a round. He carried the thing with an empty chamber for safety's sake as a rule and hadn't thought to do any differently today.

It's an investigation, not an invasion, he told himself. He remembered saying that to the regimental commander that morning. But nobody had told the Kurds. Why the hell weren't they all in Turkey?

He felt the impact and thought he was killed, but it was only a ricochet, a slug screaming up off the rocky ledge and burying itself in the pocket of his tunic. That will make a fine souvenir, he found himself thinking as he broke into a run to cover the last few meters to the shelter of the rocks.

He dived among the rocks and forced himself to look back up the ridge as soldiers streamed past him on both sides. Half the young men he had brought up the mountain that morning lay dead or wounded in the open between him and the wrecked airplane.

"Hold it, boys!" he cried out to the soldiers who weren't stopping at the rocks. "You'll never make it to the trucks like that. Might as well stay together and die like soldiers."

Most of them stopped running and took cover, but a few ran on and he saw one shot almost a hundred meters away. After that the rest of them stopped, too, and dropped out of sight.

The Kurds kept shooting from their high ground until there were no wounded left out in the open. All the soldiers who had fallen there were shot and shot again until they were dead.

When the shooting finally stopped, Colonel Harim told himself it would be dark before long and maybe then they could begin to work their way back down the mountain. Until then, it was best to stay where they were and take advantage of the cover. He could not call down to the regimental commander for help. The soldier carrying the radio was among the dead, and the radio was strapped to his back out there in the kill zone.

He looked back across the level top of the ridge be-

tween himself and the crashed airplane. Most of the
young men who had followed him up here weren't
going anywhere.

The Iranians watched the slaughter from their hiding
places in the rocks on the opposite side of the ledge from
the Kurds who were firing down into the Iraqis exposed
on the ledge itself.

There was no question in the Iranian leader's mind
now what kind of luck he had that day.

"Allah be praised," he whispered.

The Iranians watched as the Iraqi soldiers bolted and
ran to escape the Kurds' killing zone, few of them even
bothering to return fire. And who could blame them?

The Kurds on the high ground let out victory whoops
as they peppered the last of the Iraqis to reach the relative safety of the rocky slope that led back down from
the ledge the way they had come.

"Enough!" cried their leader. There was no use wasting ammunition. It was plentiful enough but burdensome
to carry in these mountains and they weren't through
shooting yet. The leader turned to one of his captains.
"Leave the accursed Republican Guard to hide in the
rocks and fear the coming of night. We can finish them
off at our leisure if it pleases Allah. There's only one
way out for them, the same way they came."

The captain passed the order and the shooting petered
out along the line, ending in a last long burst fired by a
Kurd with a personal score to settle.

"Now that our Iraqi friends have led us to this treasure, let us go down and see what we can find," the
leader said.

The Iranians watched from hiding as the Kurds began
to appear. In twos and threes, they descended the heights
across the way and moved out onto the ledge toward the
American plane.

They showed no fear of the Iraqis who were left in
the rocks on the downslope to the Iranians' right, and

indeed the Iraqis did not open fire on them. The Iranian leader thought maybe the Kurds were out of range, or the Iraqis were saving their ammunition. Or maybe they were still running.

In any case, the Kurds soon swarmed onto the open ledge. A few of them went to the dead Iraqi soldiers to pilfer weapons and ammunition. The others must have figured there was plenty of time for that. They often saw dead Iraqis, but the remains of an American jet fighter was a novelty.

The Iranians watched as the Kurds moved in on the airplane.

"Perhaps the American dogs who betrayed President Apo to the Turks will pay a reward," one of them said.

"Certainly so if the body of the pilot is there," said another.

"Is he in there?"

"The devil take him. They should all come to earth so," said the leader. "The treasure is the rockets. Look at that one there."

He pointed at the one sticking up like a spear from the ruined left wingtip, the wing curled back along the fuselage. There must be a way to take such a rocket and launch it from a mountaintop, he was thinking. Imagine the destruction. It would not have to fly very straight to hit a big target like an Iraqi village. Or maybe his brothers in Turkey could find a use for it.

"You," he said, pointing to one of the men. "See if you can pull that one free. If we must, we will cut the metal to get it."

Stan Powczuk's explosives went up with a roar like a volcano, triggering the F-16's missile warheads in a conflagration that shook the mountains and sent rocks the size of a man's head flying through the air and bouncing down its slopes.

The hiding Iranians were pelted with shrapnel from the plane and the gore of Kurdish entrails, twisted gun barrels, and scraps of bandoleers.

When they dared to raise their heads there was little left on the open ledge but a black, scorched scar where the wreckage of the plane had been. Debris was still raining down everywhere and all but a few of the Kurds had joined the dead Iraqis, their mangled parts and spattered fragments adding rich red splotches and running stains to the pallet of death on the high ledge.

Even before the echoes of the blast had died, while gory debris still rained down on them, the Iranian leader rose and signaled with his hands for his men, deafened by the blasts, to follow him.

He would make no report by radio to bin Laden, and he urged his men to move quickly. The blast would have been heard as far away as the camp, and the Iranian leader knew bin Laden would think he and his men had bungled the ordnance and blown themselves up. That meant he would be hurrying to leave and there was no time to waste if they didn't want to be left behind to walk out of Iraq on their own with only their rifles to defend themselves.

It would be the same if he reported what had happened. It would mean they were coming back without the ordnance and bin Laden would be equally displeased and equally inclined to leave them behind and report their failure in Tehran.

With more hand signals, the leader urged his men back down the way they had come. His task now was to choose a course that would intercept bin Laden as he made his way east along the valley.

Having seen so much death in such a short time, the Iranian leader had come to believe there were worse things than returning home in disgrace.

Colonel Harim could hardly believe his eyes.

That might have been me, he thought.

But he instantly came to his senses. Of course not, he told himself. I had already spotted the explosives. I would never have fallen prey to such a trap.

He remembered the young corporal who had wanted a souvenir. Looking down at his tunic, Colonel Harim saw the stains that were the boy's cranial blood and gray matter. With his index finger, he explored the tear in his tunic pocket that the ricochet bullet had made. Then he shook himself out of it and looked around him.

"What are you waiting for, boys?" he said to his few remaining troops. He stood up and holstered his pistol. "Let's get the hell out of here."

Colonel Harim had had quite enough of the infantry.

Chapter Twenty-one

"That's twenty Iranians we don't have to worry about any more," Stan said over the helmet commo system.

The plan had been to detonate the charges remotely when they were ready for extraction, to make sure the ordnance didn't fall into enemy hands. But if somebody went screwing around with Uncle Sam's ordnance up here in this combat zone, it was on their head. Anyone who had merely climbed up to check on the pilot or even taken a part with a serial number as proof would have been safe. To trigger the explosives, you had to be screwing around with the ordnance.

There was nobody but stone killers up in these mountains anyway. All the noncombatants had long since moved out. As far as Stan was concerned, it couldn't have happened to a nicer bunch than the Iranians.

"Copy that," Jack said.

They could still hear the echoes of the explosion reverberating off the mountains around them.

From his vantage point looking down into the camp, Travis could see that the man he took for Osama bin Laden could hear the echoes too. He was exhorting the men to get the trucks moving. Travis watched as the sentries came in, clambering down the slopes toward the two trucks that were leaving, the tents and all the rest of it to be left behind.

He saw the lead truck had the odd-shaped thing in the back, still covered with a tarp. Travis had watched the men dump Captain Daniels into the back of the truck alongside the thing, and two of the men climbed in with him, their Kalishnikovs at the ready.

Travis called for his team to pull back to their predesignated rally point and all of them answered except Sarah.

1700 hours
Camp Jihad, northern Iraq

Down in the camp, bin Laden cursed the Iranians for blowing themselves up with the ordnance from the American plane. When the crazy American pilot flew his A-10 Warthog into a mountain in Colorado his bombs had not gone off. How had the Iranians managed to do such a thing?

One thing was certain. Such an explosion was bound to attract attention. The only thing now was to get out of here, back to the friendly confines of Iran. If it would make his brothers in Tehran feel any better, bin Laden was even willing to say his Iranian escort had died the death of martyrs.

But he cursed them for destroying the American ordnance in the process.

1720 hours
Eagle Base Camp

The team checked in at the rally point and Sarah was the last to make it. She had the greatest distance to cover and a cliff to climb in the bargain. She did not switch off her LOCS system until she was with the team again.

They were gathered in a depression on the reverse side of a ridge, a spot that offered plenty of natural cover. Their LOCS systems off again to conserve energy for the next phase of the mission, they squatted in a semicircle around Travis.

"Are you okay?" Travis asked. "I've been calling you."

"I didn't hear you. I had the volume cranked way down in the camp."

Even without hearing Travis's call, she had known with the situation changing in the camp that the team would fall back to the rally point to regroup and make a new plan.

"What shape's the pilot in?" Travis asked.

"Bad leg wound. I don't know what they shot him with, but—"

"Seven point six-two by fifty-four," Jack said.

"What, a machine gun?" Stan asked.

"SVD Dragunov sniper rifle."

"That son of a bitch!" Stan growled.

"Your sniper?" Sarah asked.

"Bet you a month's pay," Jack said, nodding. "The boy's *Spetsnatz*. I could smell it on him."

"That was a Russian they killed, the fat man. There was another there who looked Russian, too. I saw bin Laden talking to him afterward. At least, I think it was bin Laden."

"What do you mean?" Travis asked.

"There were two of them, dead ringers. I don't know."

"Hell of a deal," Stan offered. He was impatient to get the show on the road. "*Spetsnatz*. Now there's a son of a bitch needs killing."

"What about Daniels?" Travis asked again.

"Wound's in his lower left leg and it's bad. Bones are mangled, he's lost a lot of blood, and the leg's badly infected. I gave him a big dose of antibiotics and biomed fluids. He was sleeping when I left him."

"Reckon he'll make it?"

"If I get my hands on him I can keep him from dying. I don't know about the leg."

Sam had nothing to say. He'd just seen a man shot to death, and he had too vivid an imagination not to have a pretty good idea what had just happened back at the wreckage of the F-16. It wasn't the first killing he had played a part in, but he wasn't as clear as Stan about who had what coming to them.

Travis unfolded a map and spread it on the ground at

the center of the little group. This was one of those times that called for improvisation, like drawing up a sandlot football play in the dirt.

"This is where we are," he said, pointing. "This is the camp. This is the valley I'm betting they're going to follow east to get back to Iran. It's the only route that makes sense. See this right here?"

He pointed to a spot on the map and checked to make sure all eyes were on it.

"This is a break in the north wall of the valley where it curves sharply. This is a wadi, an arroyo that runs through there and down this way." He traced the wadi with his finger. "Down here is the rocky basin, our primary rendezvous for extraction."

"Are we talking about the gooney bird here?" Stan asked. "Shit, not even Blake can set down an airplane that's older than he is in that rock farm and be able to fly out again."

"I've made the call," Travis said. "He and Jen are on their way."

"Trav, we're gonna kill the bad guys and grab the gizmo. Why not call for the real deal and get some choppers in here? With air cover, just in case."

"Air strike's been ordered up on standby and so have the choppers. But Hunter will get there first and I'm not going to call the choppers in if we don't have the gizmo. Any more questions?"

There were no more questions. Not even from one of the navy's hairiest SEALs.

"All right," Travis said. "Let's light out and be quick about it. We have to beat those hombres to that point in the valley opposite the break where the wadi runs down to the basin. We'll hit them from this side, the south side, and take the lead truck. It's carrying Captain Daniels and the gizmo. When we open up on them, the first shots fired have to kill the two men in the back of the truck with Daniels. Otherwise they'll let him have it. Clear? Then we grab the truck and drive the damned thing right down to the basin and hop aboard the DC-3. That's the plan. Any questions?"

Again, there were no questions.

"Okay, let's go."

They formed up in a staggered file by instinct and training as they moved out, without anything being said.

As they made their way east, traveling parallel to the valley below and bin Laden's two-truck convoy, Jack and Stan argued for the first two hundred meters over which of them was going to kill the *Spetsnatz* sniper who shot the pilot's leg off. Then Travis told them to simmer down and the team settled into silence.

They had no way of knowing about Colonel Harim or the Kurds.

They had no way of knowing that those twenty Iranians Stan had counted out were at that moment hurrying down from the high ledge and the carnage. Or that their leader was charting a course that would intersect the valley at a place just opposite the break in the wall on the other side of the valley where the wadi ran down toward the rocky basin.

0935 hours
The White House War Room, Washington, D.C.

"What the hell's going on out there?" the DCI asked to no one in particular.

The monitors showed a montage of images that included a couple of shots of a man who looked like Osama bin Laden. There appeared to be an argument between this man and another, a fat man in a safari suit. The image stream broke at that point and the next thing they saw was men scurrying around in the camp and the fat man in the safari suit lying face down and not moving. Another break, and two trucks had been pulled away from the others, the man who looked like bin Laden shouting and waving his arms. Then the screen went blank.

"I'm not sure what we're to make of this," the president's security advisor said.

"Satcom report just in," Tom Burgess announced, handing the advisor the transcription of the team's terse sitrep—situation report.

" 'TFE: Camp moving. Confirm pilot alive/bad shape. Adjusting plan to interdict. Status air? Status extract? Over.' " The president's national security advisor read the message aloud. He stood up. "Gentlemen . . ." He caught himself. Some of the staff working the consoles along the back wall of the War Room were women. ". . . and ladies, I interpret this message to mean that the mission has reached a critical juncture. In other words, the shit is about to hit the fan."

Conversations buzzed around the room.

"Everybody tighten up, listen up, and stand by to give it all you've got," the advisor went on. "The next couple of hours are going to make us or break us."

He took Tom Burgess by the arm and looked him in the eye.

"What's the status of the air strike, Tom?"

"Wheels up at Adana. They'll refuel en route and reach standby station over the Turkish border in about an hour."

"Who are we sending?"

"Daniels's squadron, sir. They volunteered."

"You bet your ass they did," the advisor said, a glint in his eye. "Good. They'll be properly motivated. What about the helicopter CSAR reaction force?"

"They're en route. They'll have to refuel also, and their ETA's pretty far out there."

"And the DC-3? Any word on that?"

"They confirmed takeoff as ordered. Nothing from them since."

"Reach out to them. Make sure that old crate is still flying. If I were a betting man, I'd say it's going to be up to them to get our people out of there."

"Yes, sir."

1750 hours
Airborne over the Turkey/Iraq border

"I'm just saying it was the shock of seeing you naked that did him in."

Hunter Blake was feeling good. The cloak-and-dagger part of the mission was behind them. From here on in it was all flying.

"He didn't see me naked," Jen corrected him.

"He thought he did, though. It's the same thing."

"He saw a padded body suit with one tit torn off. It's not the same thing at all."

"I don't know about that."

"If you'd ever seen me naked, you'd know."

"Just what I was—"

Hunter was interrupted by the satcom relay, a message from the NSC at the White House War Room.

"No sweat," he assured them. "Their lives are in my hands."

Chapter Twenty-two

Monday, June 12, 1830 hours
At the ambush point in the mountains
of northern Iraq

The team reached their ambush point and deployed on the south slope of the valley wall opposite the break where the wadi ran down toward the rocky basin.

Travis had Sam access satellite imagery and dictate a close-up of the valley to locate bin Laden's convoy. Sam had the picture in no time and it showed them just what they needed to see. They had beaten the convoy by a full kilometer. It was still grinding its way along the valley floor, hugging the lower slopes along the north side to steer clear of the mud that made a bog of the lowest points of the floor itself.

The bad news was that bin Laden was traveling heavy. In addition to the passengers in the trucks and a handful of men walking alongside them to push when they got stuck, there was what looked like a platoon of armed men escorting the trucks on foot with nothing to do but carry their Kalishnikovs and look for trouble. There was also a four-man point team moving down the valley in a line abreast well ahead of the trucks.

And there was now a weapon mounted on top of the second truck. It wasn't easy to make out from the imagery, but it looked like a Soviet PK machine gun. With a range of 1,000 meters at 700 rounds per second, it was designed by the Russians as a company support weapon, but it had been a staple of guerilla forces since Vietnam. Every member of the team except Sam had seen PKs in action and had a healthy respect for them.

Add the PK to a platoon of AK-47s and whatever else

bin Laden's bodyguard was carrying in that second truck, and it was a lot of firepower to take on, even for invisible specwar operators.

In the time they had before their target reached the ambush zone, Travis worked out the details with his team.

There were a couple of items in the TALON Force arsenal they would not be able to call on this time. The team had priority authority to call for a limited number of cruise missiles to be launched by ships at sea or air force planes when circumstances required it and targets were appropriate. With their stand-off delivery capabilities, launch aircraft could have fired their missiles from a distance that was probably out of the range of the RF machine. But the team would be working in close this time, with the safety of a hostage to consider. Even if they succeeded in capturing the truck and making it to the rocky basin rendezvous for extraction, Travis knew the odds were that they would not be able to get enough separation from the enemy to make a cruise missile strike safe.

The other thing Travis would have liked to take advantage of was the team's specially designed "arsenal boxes." These were special rocket-launched munitions packages that could be parachuted or air-landed and left in strategic locations within the team's area of operations. Any team member could laser-designate a target using his BSD and remotely trigger the package with about a thirty-second delay before firing. The configuration of each box was customized according to the team's mission profile, but the standard load was eight rounds of bomblet clusters that could take out personnel and armor over an area roughly the size of a football field.

Not only did the threat of the RF machine make it dicey for one of their designated C-17s to fly in to drop arsenal boxes, the same problem applied to them as to the cruise missiles. The good guys and bad guys would be going at each other at close quarters, too close to use an arsenal box to full effect. Ironically, another problem was that the mission had gone too well. The team had located their targets—the RF gizmo, Captain Daniels, and even Osama bin Laden, less than eighteen hours after jumping in. There had been little time to lay on a drop, even if the RF threat wasn't a factor.

What it all boiled down to was that the split team—the five of them working in unison—would have to do what had to be done themselves. The only support they could expect was a possible air strike, if they could get their hands on the RF gizmo and put enough distance between themselves and the hostiles to give the F-16s of Daniels's squadron a clear target. Men had won medals calling air strikes on their own positions in the old days, but with the ordnance those F-16s would be hauling, it was not a good idea.

With each team member's role carefully laid out, there was nothing to do but wait. They were going to have to pull this off on their own. And each one of them knew they could do it.

Each of them took what might be their last look at their teammates with their naked eyes as they switched on their LOCS systems and disappeared.

1830 hours
The mountains of northern Iraq

The Iranian leader was pushing his men, exhorting them one minute and cursing them the next. He knew the explosion would attract attention but he was willing to take the chance that there were no other forces of any size in the immediate area. The Iraqi army unit and the Kurdish band was accounted for, both of them decimated and in no condition to do anything but lick their wounds and run away. He knew the odds were against running into anyone else so soon.

He was more worried about Osama bin Laden leaving him and his men behind. He knew bin Laden was well armed, with heavy automatic weapons, rocket-propelled grenades and even shoulder-launched missiles. He had the armament to fight his way through any opposition they were likely to encounter between him and the Iranian border. But the Iranians were armed as light infantry scouts, with just their AK-47s and a few hand grenades. Anyone they tangled with was sure to be at least as well armed and likely to outnumber them in the bargain.

The Iranian leader had chosen a course that would bring him and his men to the valley at the place where it made a sharp curve and there was a break on the other side. If they got there before bin Laden, they would take cover and wait for him. If he beat them there, the Iranians would be able to tell by the fresh tracks of bin Laden's trucks and they would follow the tracks until they caught up. But he didn't like the idea of traveling far and he didn't care for taking the risk of coming up on bin Laden's rear. The Prophet's bodyguard was known for shooting first and worrying about who they were shooting at later. Much better to get there before them and avoid any confusion.

The Iranian leader had seen enough of killing for now, and he couldn't get it out of his mind that if the Kurds had not blown themselves up on the wrecked airplane then he and his men almost certainly would have done so. Allah had been kind, and he was in no mood to test His mercy.

1830 hours
Approaching the ambush point

Bin Laden's trucks were making good time with Mustafa and bin Laden riding beside the driver of the lead truck, both drivers able to stay to the lower slopes of the north valley wall. But when the slope became too steep and they had to travel the flat valley floor, the wheels of the trucks broke through the dried upper crust and sank to the axles in mud. It was all the men walking beside the two trucks could do to push them out in some places, and the little convoy had not gone far before the bodyguards of the Prophet were covered in mud to the tops of their heads.

Mikhail marveled at their loyalty to the madman.

Left to his own devices, the *Spetsnatz* sniper rode on the back of the second truck when he pleased and hopped down to walk along beside it when it suited him. He carried his Dragunov rifle in the crook of his arm, the weapon freshly cleaned and the four-power scope capped at either end to protect the lenses from the odd mixture of hot dust and flying mud the trek had become.

Always he watched the high ground as they went along, his shooter's eye scanning the places he himself would choose for an ambush.

Unlike Mustafa, Mikhail did not believe the man who came tumbling down from the cliff had simply fallen. He believed that the reason the man had not cried out was that he had been dead already and thrown off the cliff— but by whom?

Mikhail suspected it was the work of American operators spying on the camp. His futile hide the night before when he had watched the place where he had set up the American pilot's rescue beacon had not dissuaded him from his belief that a team would come. He remembered the hair rising on the back of his neck as he returned to camp that morning. He had been almost sure he was being followed, but could see nothing on his back trail except those occasional shimmerings. Just as he had seen nothing on the cliff when the dead man fell into camp except a shimmering about the rocks like the sun burning moisture off the rocks.

Mikhail had said nothing of his suspicions to bin Laden because if he was right it was he who had led the operators to the camp. He knew bin Laden was not one to accept excuses. He was also not one to credit theories about invisible American operators!

An avid hunter even as a boy, Mikhail remembered reading an American story in his youth about an intrepid hunter. The hunter in the story matched his skills against a ferocious beast whose camouflage was so perfect that the only sign of his presence was the parting of the tall grass as he moved and the tracks he left behind. Mikhail had burned the story in disgust because the beast bested the hunter in the end.

He had it in mind that he would write his own ending to the story this time. Let bin Laden and the others be the bait that drew the American beasts in for the kill. Mikhail knew what to look for now. And he would have his trophy yet.

1840 hours
The ambush point

Travis saw bin Laden's point team appear around the curve in the valley wall, working their way along, their heads always moving as they scanned the terrain on both sides. It wouldn't be long now.

Travis had moved the team down to the valley floor, taking up covered positions directly opposite the break where the wadi ran through. The valley floor was a muddy bog from the south side almost all the way across to the north. But there was a narrow strip where the slope was not too steep and the going was dry. Travis knew that was where the trucks would go and he had designated an attack position for each member of his team.

They waited behind cover along the south wall. Even though their LOCS systems were activated, they were using cover to be doubly safe. Once the point team passed by them, they would move into position to launch their attack when the trucks reached them.

Of the four men working point, the one nearest the hidden team passed so close to Travis that he could have killed him with a knife.

But Travis remained motionless, holding his breath until the man passed by.

It seemed to Travis that he could actually see the shadows lengthening in the valley after the point team had passed and he had moved his team into their final attack positions. But he had been in situations like this before and he knew it was only the heightened state of awareness that comes in the moments before the first shot is fired that brought into such clear focus the minutiae of the scene around him.

He knew the men in the War Room at the White House would have this location pinpointed and satellites trained on the scene about to play out. Even in the gathering dusk, he knew he and his team were about to perform for a select audience gathered in the inner sanctum of the nation's war-making machine. But there was nothing those powerful men could do now to influence the outcome. That was up to TALON Force alone.

The noise of the trucks' engines preceded them as they labored around the bend and finally came into sight. Hugging the north wall, they lumbered up and down the lower slopes as the main force of bin Laden's bodyguard picked their way along the valley floor in a loose skirmish formation.

Travis resisted the impulse to check his weapon a final time. He had already checked and rechecked it. He was ready and so was his team. This was what they had come for, what they had trained for, and why they had been chosen from among so many.

He watched the trucks as they came on, two men who looked like Osama bin Laden visible now in the front of the lead truck alongside the driver, the RF machine rising behind them underneath its tarp. Travis couldn't see Captain Daniels from this angle, but he saw the two men in the back of the truck and he knew their Kalishnikovs were trained on the wounded pilot.

Come on, Travis thought, willing the trucks to cover the last few meters. That's right, come to papa. Okay, this is it. Show time.

Chapter Twenty-three

Monday, June 12, 1845 hours
The Valley of Death, the mountains of northern Iraq

The Iranian leader arrived at the height overlooking the valley just as bin Laden's trucks rounded the curve. Cautious of alarming the Prophet's bodyguard, he motioned with his arms for his men to lie down out of sight while he contacted bin Laden by radio to let him know they were coming in. Praise Allah, they had made it in time, he thought as he spoke into his radio with the good news. They were safely on their way home.

1850 hours
The killing ground

Osama bin Laden, riding in the front seat of the lead truck, heard the radio nestled in Mustafa's lap crackle with a voice rambling in Farsi. He and Mustafa exchanged puzzled looks. How could it be?

As he reached for the radio, bin Laden turned his head toward Mustafa. As he did so, he saw from the corner of his eye the two men guarding the American pilot in the rear of the truck. At the same instant, as bin Laden registered what sounded like muffled gunshots, the two of them jerked queerly and went down, one bowled over off the back of the truck, the other slumping down over the American.

In the same split second, the driver beside Mustafa gave a sudden cry and disappeared. Bin Laden felt the weight shift on the seat as the driver went out and something or somebody climbed in. Fumbling for his pistol, he had a second in the slow-motion daze that came over him to wonder why Mustafa wasn't shooting the attacker who had set upon them. Then he looked past Mustafa at—nothing. There was no one there. But the driver was gone and an instant later bin Laden felt Mustafa sag against him, unconscious.

Bin Laden went out the other side of the truck, falling as much as jumping, and scrambled madly up the slope to keep from rolling underneath the wheels of the truck, which had not stopped. He looked up as the truck, Mustafa no longer visible in the front seat and the dead guard draped over the American pilot, veered sharply to the left up the slope toward the break in the valley wall. Bin Laden blinked and looked again. He could not believe his eyes. There was no one driving the truck!

The second truck ground to a halt a few feet away, its engine sputtering and dying. As he looked up at the driver to order him to restart the accursed truck and take off in pursuit of the lead truck, he heard more muffled reports and saw a neat row of holes appear in the windshield, stitching it from post to post. He saw the driver and the two men beside him slump down behind the wheel, as dead as the others. The one who manned the machine gun mounted atop the truck had disappeared.

The radio in his hand came to life again, Farsi pouring out of it as he looked across the valley floor at the men in his bodyguard. They had seen what was happening, too, and turned with their rifles raised. But they were afraid to shoot at the truck carrying the all-important RF machine and there was nothing else to shoot at. They stood transfixed, as if ghosts had descended upon them, or devils out of the wilderness.

Jack and Stan stood motionless in their positions, their XM-29 rifles sheathed and ready, as the truck approached. When it was alongside them, each man brought his weapon up and killed one of the guards in the back of the truck. At the same time, Travis shot the driver and pulled him out, then climbed into his place and hammered the man who looked like bin Laden with his fist, knocking him out cold.

Sarah went up over the side of the truck and threw herself on top of Captain Daniels and the dead guard, adding her shield of invisibility to the protection offered by the guard's body.

Sam extended his left arm toward the grille of the second truck and voice-activated his wristband RF field generator. He shook his head in happy disbelief when the device actually killed the truck's engine, his shaking head creating a shimmer that went unnoticed by all except the *Spetsnatz* sniper.

From his position a few meters up the slope and to the rear of the second truck, Mikhail saw the two guards killed in the lead truck and the driver killed and dragged out. From that distance, he could not hear the muffled reports of the gunshots, but he knew at once what he was seeing—the invisible American operators!

He uncapped the lenses of his rifle's sight and brought the big gun to his shoulder in a single motion. Shimmers over the back of the lead truck, another—there, directly in front of the second truck. Mikhail sighted quickly and squeezed off a shot, the crack of his rifle echoing in the valley.

Stan grabbed Sam by the collar and jerked him in the direction of the lead truck. It was Sam's job, once he had disabled the second truck, to jump on board the first one and relieve Travis at the wheel. That would free Travis to lay down covering fire while Stan finished off the crew of the second truck and any pursuit that was forming and made a run for the lead truck. The techno-geek could drive the truck as well as the rest of them, but they wanted Travis doing the shooting.

As he sent Sam spinning toward the truck, Stan opened up on the second truck, killing the man on the machine gun and stitching a neat pattern across the windshield with his rifle, taking out the crew.

But just as he eased off the trigger and was about to switch to the XM-29's grenade launcher to blow up the truck's cargo of automatic weapons and heavy ordnance, the sniper's bullet hit him and he went down.

"Jack!"

Stan could already feel the air bladders built into his camo suit inflating, applying pressure to stop the bleeding of his wound. He knew that in a matter of seconds the suit's bio-sensors would diagnose his condition and the Automatic Trauma Med Pack in the suit would be pumping painkillers and medicine into his system.

Jack, already in a dead sprint to catch up with the lead truck, skidded to a stop and spun around. He saw the outline of Stan's body writhing in the mud in front of the second truck and went back for him.

"It's that *Spetsnatz* son of a bitch," Stan growled as Jack lifted him in a fireman's carry. "Gotta be."

Mikhail was firing in rhythm now, certain he had scored at least one hit already. He knew the sound of a bullet hitting meat and he had heard that with his first shot.

There was more shimmering in front of the stalled second truck, but Mikhail had to sidle up the slope a bit to get a clear shot and now he was sure he had one or more of the American ghosts spotted, running in a shimmering boil after the truck. He was guessing really, trying to lead running men he couldn't see. But he knew he was on them and he smelled a kill.

Two of bin Laden's bodyguards jumped down from the rear of the second truck and ran toward the fallen Prophet. In doing so, they put themselves between Mikhail and his prey. He coolly shot them down to clear his firing lane and kept shooting until he had emptied his ten-round box magazine, his last shot a quick one in the direction of the fleeing truck itself.

"Damn that Russian bastard!" Jack groaned as he labored up the slope with Stan on his back. "Hold up, Boss. Stan's hit."

Travis, who had just relinquished the wheel to Sam and was moving to get a firing lane clear of Sarah and the RF machine, told Sam to stop. Sam hit the brakes and the truck slid sideways to a screeching halt.

Travis spied the Russian up the slope from the second truck as he fired his last shot. He heard the round whistle a few inches past his head as he opened up with his XM-29, sending a short burst of the 5.66mm combustible rounds in his direction. But he saw the Russian duck behind the second truck at the last second and the rounds scored hits on the bed of the truck instead.

"Damn!"

"Did you get him?" Jack asked as he heaved the wounded SEAL into the rear of the truck.

"He ducked."

"Damn indeed."

Travis switched triggers and fired one of the four grenades from the launcher mounted beneath his rifle's aiming device. He saw it explode to the rear of the second truck, but couldn't be sure it had accounted for the sniper.

"Floor it, Sam!" Travis yelled. "Let's hightail it!"

Bin Laden saw Mikhail firing and two of his bodyguards go down, shot by the Russian. He didn't care. At least the Russian was shooting.

The Prophet was beside himself with rage. He screamed at his men to open fire, never mind the Russian's machine. He pointed at the truck stopped on the slope.

"Kill them! Kill them! Shoot, you dogs!"

He screamed into the radio, calling the name of the leader of his Iranian escort.

"Are you there, back from the dead?" he yelled.

"We are here, O Prophet. We are not ghosts."

"Whether you are ghosts or not, open fire on that truck!" He thought about it for a second and added, "The lead truck, the one up the slope with the machine in the back. Do you understand?"

"Yes, O Prophet. But we may hit the machine."

"In the name of the prophets, you stupid Iranian cur, shoot the bloody truck. The machine is no good to me if they take it away!"

With that, the Iranians belatedly joined in the fray, pouring fire down from the south valley wall at the truck and its cargo.

When bin Laden's bodyguards finally came to their senses, they opened up a fusillade that churned the ground around the truck into a cloud of dust and hammered it with a storm of lead that sounded like hail to the team members inside. Both the self-sealing tires on the right side of the truck were hit but held up, at least for the time being.

Travis turned his rifle on the bodyguards and returned fire with short, disciplined bursts, pausing twice to launch grenades. Jack, having turned the wounded Stan over to Sarah, joined in.

At least the truck offered some cover against the fire of the bodyguards below them in the valley. But when the Iranians opened up from the heights across the way, there was no protection. Sarah let out a yell as one of their rounds found her. Travis almost went down when a slug hit his helmet a glancing blow and went whining off into the air. He regained his balance as he registered a high-pitched whine that he realized was not inside his head. The impact of the round had apparently affected the commo gear in the helmet and he was getting feedback. He quickly switched off the commo unit and noted with relief that the LOCS was not affected. He was still invisible.

The air around them was thick with lead as Travis and Jack coordinated their fire, Travis taking a toll on the bodyguards in the valley while Jack cranked out a steady tattoo against the Iranians on the high ground. He had no clear targets, but he knew the rounds would find their way close enough to keep some of the Iranians' heads down. He switched to his launcher twice to send grenades arcing up into the heights at them.

It seemed they had driven miles by the time the truck

finally reached the break and they felt themselves top a rise and then start down. Travis looked forward and saw the rugged wadi that zigzagged down the long slope. In the distance, he could see the white curve among the foothills and scrubby plants that was the near edge of the rocky basin. They could climb out of the wadi and take off cross-country to save some distance, but he figured the walls of the depression and the way it curved back and forth down the slope would give them more cover. He knew bin Laden and his men would come after them, even without the second truck.

Stan had been hit before he could finish the job on the second truck with a grenade to destroy the store of weapons he knew was in there. But that couldn't be helped. With Sam driving their truck over the washboard high points like a crazed New York cabbie and slowing to power it through the mud in the wallows, Travis turned his attention to the wounded.

Bin Laden was no longer in a rage. He was beyond that now.

When the bullet-riddled truck disappeared through the break in the valley wall, he got to his feet and began issuing orders in rapid-fire succession. He detailed men to pursue the truck on foot and made sure they had a radio. They were to keep the vehicle in sight and report on its progress.

Others he assigned to offload the weaponry from the second truck that had survived the attack of the devils. He had Russian machine guns that could reach out 1,000 meters, RPGs, and grenade launchers, even SA-7 shoulder-launched surface-to-air missiles. He would destroy the devils even if it meant destroying Pretsky's machine. There was bound to be another Russian scientist who knew the secret and needed the money and he would find him if he had to.

From among the survivors of his bodyguard and the Iranians who were coming down now from their place on the valley wall, he detailed crews to take the heavy weapons and strike out through the break on the trail of the truck. He chose three others and sent them back to the camp to bring up the trucks they had left there.

To the rest of his men, the ones who lay scattered across the valley floor dead and dying, he gave no thought. It was Allah's will and they were martyrs of the *jihad*.

Chapter Twenty-four

"That was the damnedest thing I ever saw." Commander Greeley leaned back in his chair at the table in the White House War Room and shook his head. "And I'm not even sure what I saw."

"Don't ask," Tom Burgess warned, holding up both hands. "I don't know and I couldn't tell you if I did."

"I just want to meet those guys someday," Greeley said. "You can blindfold me if you want to, I just want to shake their freakin' hands."

At the head table, the president's national security advisor wrapped up a quick check to get the consensus of the head table and called the Oval Office.

"Mr. President," he said. "They've got the pilot and the RF machine as well."

No one could hear the president's end of the conversation.

"That's right, sir. Our people have Captain Daniels and the machine, both. No, they didn't have to destroy it. They took it away from the opposition. Yes, sir, it looks like bin Laden to me. Yes, sir, they have one of them, too."

The advisor listened for a moment.

"Well, when I say one of them, sir, there appear to be two men involved in this thing who are dead ringers for bin Laden and our people have one of them. No, sir, we can't be sure at this point if he's the real one."

He listened a little longer this time.

"That may be a little premature, sir. The thing is, we're not quite out of the woods on this thing yet. I'm sure you understand that extraction is sometimes the trickiest part of these operations. Yes, sir."

More listening.

"You're absolutely correct, Mr. President. With the RF machine in our hands, we are clear to send our aircraft in there again. And we are doing that, sir. We have an air strike and a heavy reaction force inbound as we speak, sir."

The president apparently questioned the time element.

"Well, the air strike will be on target within the hour. The choppers, you see, sir, they had to come all the way from—yes, sir, I understand. The bottom line is the choppers won't be there for a while yet. Right now, our best bet is the gooney bird."

The president apparently was not familiar with gooney birds.

"It's an aircraft sir, kind of a vintage airplane that we felt would be immune to the RF threat because it has no computers. I realize the RF threat has been neutralized at this point, sir, but we couldn't make that assumption going in. Pardon? It's a gooney bird, sir, an old C-47, actually a DC-3, the civilian model. It has two propeller engines. Yes, like the one hanging from the ceiling of the Air and Space Museum. We've rigged it up with a LANTIRN system and—no sir, it's an acronym. It stands for Low-Altitude Navigation and Targeting Infra-Red, comma, Night. Yes, sir, certainly. I'll keep you posted."

The president's national security advisor laid the red phone back in its cradle and looked at his colleagues around the head table.

"I thought that went well," he said.

1855 hours
The escape route from the Valley of Death,
northern Iraq

The president's national security advisor knew TALON Force had taken some hits. The operators were invisible to him and the satellite as well as the enemy, but the real-time readouts from the bio-chip sensors and med packs in their suits made it clear some of them were wounded. And they still had a long way to go before they started worrying about extraction.

The first order of business was to secure their prisoner. They tied Mustafa's hands and feet and Travis had Sarah give him a shot of morphine to put him out for a while. That taken care of and temporarily out of range of the enemy's guns, the team switched off their LOCS systems to take inventory.

Stan had taken the sniper's 7.62mm round high on the right side of his chest. The ballistic material of his suit had prevented full penetration, but at that relatively close range the bullet had broken his collarbone near the shoulder and traumatized his shoulder joint so severely that he had lost all sensation in his arm. Sarah said he was almost certainly bleeding internally and his right lung was in danger of collapsing.

The ATMP—Automatic Trauma Med Pack—engineered into his suit had responded immediately, the imbedded bio-chip sensors "reading" his condition and prompting the ensemble to seal the wound, stop the external bleeding, and administer the appropriate fluids and bio-enhanced drugs.

Stan was resting as comfortably as possible in the back of the bouncing truck, and Sarah said she was confident he would recover fully, assuming they were extracted in one piece. But for the time being he was going to be a limited asset—one-armed, weak, and woozy.

She reported her own wound as minor, a gunshot wound to what she described as "the upper dorsal thigh."

"Got shot in the butt, Doc," Jack laughed. "That's what you did."

Like Stan, Sarah had been saved by her suit. Lying face down over Captain Daniels to protect him, she had been hit by a round probably fired by one of the Iranians on the high ground across the valley. The distance it traveled before hitting her reduced its velocity and the medical miracles built into her suit prevented a serious injury and provided immediate, automatic treatment.

She said she was good to go but admitted she wouldn't be running any marathons for a while.

"Make an interesting scar," Jack kidded her.

"You'll never know," she said.

"Maybe get you a tattoo to cover it up."

"How's Daniels?" Travis said.

After quickly examining Stan, Sarah had turned her attention to the wounded flier. She had hardly given her own wound a thought.

"The injections I gave him in the camp seem to have helped," she said. "His fever is down and his breathing sounds a lot better. Blood pressure's low and I don't like the look of his leg. I need to get to work on him and I can't do it in this truck."

"We'll be there in a little bit," Travis said, sounding reassuring.

But he hadn't convinced himself. Their lead over bin Laden's gunmen was less than he would have liked, and he knew what it meant when he heard the noise from beneath the truck.

"What was that?" Sam asked.

"We lost the tires," Travis said. "Don't worry about it, just keep on trucking."

But when Jack leaned over the side to see how bad the tires were, he raised himself back up with worse news.

"Looks like they hit the gas tank, too. We're leaking fuel pretty bad."

1900 hours

The shadows lengthened perceptibly now and the sun turned blood red as it neared the horizon.

The scouts bin Laden had sent out were hardy men accustomed to covering distance over rough ground. Once they got their stride and found a course that kept to high ground where they could see how the wadi wound down to the rocky white basin, they had little trouble keeping the truck in sight. The one with the radio called for the others to come quick with the big guns. From a foothill that was the toe of the ridgeline they had followed, the man with the radio could see the white rocky basin opening up beyond the next rise. And there was nothing there. The devils in the truck were running to nowhere.

1905 hours
The rocky basin

"You try to raise Blake?" Jack asked.

"Yeah, no luck. He's either coming or he's not," Travis shrugged. He had switched his commo system back on and found its internal diagnostics had corrected the feedback glitch caused by the impact of the bullet on his helmet and the unit was working properly again. "Air strike's inbound, but I don't know how long a wait. If Hunter doesn't make it we'll have to make a stand and hold on for the choppers."

"Yeah," Jack nodded glumly. "Like ol' Georgie Custer."

The truck finally ran out of gas fifty meters short of the basin. They could see the white rock of the flat bowl just ahead, but the truck would go no farther.

Travis and Jack tested the weight of the RF machine. They could lift it with some effort, but it was too heavy to carry the rest of the way to the basin.

Travis ordered Sam out of the truck and told Sarah to take his place beside the unconscious Mustafa. Travis, Jack, and Sam got behind the bullet-riddled vehicle and leaned into it.

"One good thing," Sam said. "At least we're out of the mud."

"That's the ticket, Sammy," Jack huffed. "Keep that sunny side up. You and the Doc."

Sarah heard her name mentioned and, stung by the notion that the men might be bitching about her getting a free ride, she climbed down and pushed too. She leaned against the side of the truck, reaching up on tiptoe to reach the steering wheel to keep the truck on course.

"Get back up there, Sarah," Travis yelled from the back of the truck.

"Yeah, Doc," Jack said. "You gonna get your butt started bleeding again."

"My upper dorsal thigh," she corrected him. "The suit will take care of it."

"Put your backs into it, ladies," Stan crowed from the back of the truck. "Don't make me have to come back there and show you how!"

"Guess the medicine's kicking in," Travis said.

"Don't know why you say that," Jack said. "He's like that all the time."

Having found another way out of the valley near their old camp, the men bin Laden had sent back for the remaining trucks roared down a long slope and angled across the broken terrain in the direction the Yankee devils had gone. In the long shadows of the high ground behind them, they overtook the men laboring on foot under the loads of bin Laden's crew-served weapons. Those men let out a whoop at the site of the trucks and clambered aboard them with their machine guns and the rest of their arsenal. With bin Laden in the lead truck, they roared off in the direction of their scouts, following the path they had taken to the rise that looked down on the white rocky basin.

1910 hours

Travis and Jack sank to their knees in the white chalky dust of the basin to catch their breath. They had made it, if just barely.

After a short blow, Travis got back to his feet.

"We're not there yet," he said. "We need to get this wreck out there where it's flat enough for Hunter to land. He'll have to pull up right next to us if we're going to get this big boy loaded on the plane."

"Hunter ain't coming," Stan howled. "And if he does, he's going to tear that old bird to pieces trying to sit her down in these rocks."

"Can it, man. You're drunk," Jack said.

"Hell I am. I'm telling you, it's the choppers for me. I'm gonna sit right here and wait for the real deal."

"I'm of a mind to throw your white ass out of there and let you wait for El Al, you don't shut the fuck up."

"Simmer down, you two," Travis said. "Let's go, Jack. It's just a lick and promise now."

They all heard the sound of the incoming round, a grenade launched by one of bin Laden's RPGs. And they all reacted out of instinct. Travis and Jack dropped to the ground in the shelter of the truck and Sam followed suit. Sarah scrambled up into the rear of the truck and draped herself over Daniels as she had before.

The grenade landed with a roar well behind them.

While the dust of the impact was still in the air, they heard the throaty rattle of a machine gun and the whine and scrape of the rounds coming in.

"They're short," Travis noted, rising to his feet.

"They'll correct," Jack said. "I got faith in them."

"What we need is some artillery," Sam said.

"What we need is that air strike," Travis said.

"Or Blake and his bird," Jack said. "Whichever comes first."

Travis passed the word to switch the LOCS systems back on. They would be invisible again from now on, until they made extraction or the power ran out in a couple of hours. The three men put their weight behind the truck with renewed energy and didn't stop pushing until they were well out on the basin where it flattened out and the rocks were much smaller, only a few of them the size of a man.

"This is it," Travis said.

"Is this where we make our stand?" Sam asked.

"Must be, little bro," Jack answered him. "There's no place to run from here."

1912 hours
Airborne over southern Turkey

"Striker Flight Leader to Basin."

The flight of F-16s was screaming south out of Turkey with their throttles open, maxing out at 1,330 mph. Their flight leader was pissed because their refueling had taken longer than he liked.

"Come in, Flight Leader."

The voice was being relayed by satellite on a special priority frequency, but the flight leader had no trouble making out the sound of gunfire and an explosion in the background.

"Striker Flight Leader to Basin, we are inbound your location. Can you confirm we are clear to descend?"

"Confirm. We have that little problem in hand."

"Copy that."

The flight leader dropped the nose of his ship and the rest of the flight followed suit.

"Basin to Flight Leader."

"Go ahead."

"We also have your boy. He's looking pretty good, considering."

"God bless you, sir." The flight leader heard the cheers from his pilots on their tactical frequency. He did not admonish them. "Now, would you be so kind as to tell us who you would like us to kill down there?"

Travis gave him the coordinates and described the targets. He told the flight leader they would also laser-designate targets if they were still able to when he got there.

As near as he could tell, bin Laden and his men were pretty well concentrated on the high ground where he had seen muzzle flashes of at least two machine guns and a couple of RPGs. But he knew they would be splitting up as soon as it got dark to flank the team's position and get them in a crossfire. One advantage of the team's location was the whiteness of the rocky terrain. They would be able to see anyone venturing that close. He knew their RPGs had a range of only about 300 meters and he had made sure they were at least 400 meters out onto the white rocky basin. But bin Laden's Russian PKs were good to 1,000 meters, and it was only a matter of time before they zeroed the machine guns in. The team had already scored some kills on dark figures advancing across the white backdrop, but Travis knew their time was running out. When it was dark, the hostiles would come in earnest and there were too many of them with too much firepower.

The sun was almost gone below the horizon, just a red crescent still showing. Travis computed the time they had left and he didn't think the air strike would get there soon enough.

"Basin to Striker Flight Leader."

"Go ahead, Basin."

"Let me give you my coordinates, too. Just in case we're not—uh, transmitting when you make your run."

"Roger, Basin."

Travis figured the flight leader understood what he was telling him, but he wanted to be sure he was clear.

"Striker Leader, I reckon what I'm saying is, if you don't get here before the Alamo falls, I'd appreciate it if you'd kill all the Mexicans dancing on the ramparts."

"Copy that. You've got my word on it, Tex."

Chapter Twenty-five

"They're running out of time," Commander Greeley whispered. "The air strike is going to get there too late."

"It's going to be close," Burgess said. "Awfully close."

"Too late by about five minutes," Greeley said.

Burgess listened to the voices of the flight leader and the operator on the ground.

You wouldn't know it to listen to them, he thought. But he knew Greeley was right. And the men behind those voices knew it too.

He looked at the imagery on the monitors, the shadows growing longer by the second across the basin, until he couldn't see the truck and the figures around it any more. There was a flash of light within a few meters of the truck, then the soundless explosion of still another rocket grenade. They were getting closer, which meant they must have found a defile or some cover to get within range without being seen.

There was no talking at the head table.

The president's national security advisor leaned on the table with his head in his hands. They were so close, he thought, so very close.

In the SCIF, Mac drummed his fingers nervously on the table as he watched the scene play out on the monitors suspended from the ceiling, the voices and images relayed with a few seconds' delay from the White House War Room.

Where are they? he was thinking. Where're the birds? Choppers to get them out of there, air cover to strafe the bastards that are shooting at them, something. Where's the freakin' birds?

"Jesus Christ!" he said as he saw the darkening landscape swallowing up the truck and the operators he couldn't see. "Son of a bitch!"

It was going to be Desert One all over again.

1950 hours
The rocky basin

The roar of the engines followed so closely the roar of the last rocket grenade that the team didn't hear it at first. At first, they thought it was another rocket grenade, even closer than the last.

But Stan, propped up in the rear of the truck so he could fire his rifle with his left hand when the end came, looked up and saw the form pass overhead.

"What the hell was that?" he bellowed. "Look, you guys. What the hell was that?"

"It's our ride home," Jack said. "What do you think of Hunter now?"

"He ain't down yet," Stan muttered.

Travis popped a green flare. It was the fail-safe signal for Hunter to land, and Travis figured it would give him something to go by. Then he turned back to launch his last grenade in the direction of the figures crowding around the edge of the basin. He was rewarded with the sound of a scream that carried across the rocky flats as the grenade detonated.

"You got some more of those flares?" Jack asked.

"A few. What do you have in mind."

"Light'em up over there. Screw up their night vision when Hunter comes taxiing up here."

"Good idea."

"But save one."

"I will. Why?"

"I want one more shot at that *Spetsnatz* mother-fucker," Jack said, scanning the terrain to their front. He had been looking since they got to the basin and he thought he might have seen something.

"You'll never spot him out there."

"Bet I do. Bet he won't pass up one last try at us."

"Fuckin' marines," Travis muttered.

"What did I tell you?" Hunter smiled at Jen. If she wasn't dazzled by his charm, maybe she'd be impressed with his flying. "Right on the button."

"You aren't down yet."

"Girl, when will you ever learn?"

He stood the old bird on one wing and brought her around for a landing. He saw the flare fire off in the distance and what looked like a vehicle of some kind in its light.

"How about those guys?" he said. "They hitched a ride out."

Since the check-in call from the War Room, an electrical problem had developed with his satellite relay system on the flight down from Kamil's film festival, so he had been out of the loop. Truth be told, in his haste to get everything put back together and get in the air, he might not have tightened all the nuts and bolts. But it didn't matter. He'd be talking to the guys in person in a minute. Besides, he was going to come to this place anyway, no matter what he heard by satellite. The only thing that would have kept him from landing here was if Travis hadn't fired that flare. All the rest was atmosphere as far as he was concerned.

The gooney bird hit hard and caught one of the larger rocks the first time. She bounced but settled in nicely after that, and Travis went to work on the flares then, sending them way off to Hunter's right toward a low rise and bathing the place in light. He lit it up bright enough that Hunter could pick his way across the rocky flat in the excess. He taxied straight to the truck and braked the old bird hard, swinging her around to put the cabin door as near as possible to the truck.

Jen went aft to help with the loading and Hunter kept the engines revving.

"I need a hand with these two," Sarah called up to the opening door.

Jen dropped the stairway and hurried down. She took the dazed Stan, disarming him first so he wouldn't get a round off at the worst possible time. Holding him with his good arm over her shoulder so he couldn't grope her, she walked him up the steps and deposited him in one of the seats. Sarah was right behind her, carrying the wounded pilot in her arms.

Then it was Travis and Jack and Sam, grunting under the weight of a contraption covered with a tarp.

But they weren't ready to go yet, even with streams of tracers arcing across the darkness, reaching for them like snakes. The rounds were hitting the ground all around them and Jen flinched when some found the fuselage of the plane in a series of sickening crunches.

Next came a man bound and gagged, carried like a rolled-up rug by Travis and Sam. They dumped him on the cabin floor.

"That's it," Travis said. "Let's go."

"Where's Jack?" Jen asked.

"He'll be along. Let 'er rip."

Jenny passed the word to Hunter and the DC-3 lurched forward.

Travis jumped the steps to the ground with his last flare.

"You ready, Jack?" he called.

"Born ready, Boss."

Mikhail saw the flares, fired in rapid succession, climbing into the sky toward the low hill where the others were pouring machine-gun fire and rocket grenades into the white rocky bowl where they assumed the invisible devils were huddled behind the truck. The truck was off its wheels now, sitting flat on the ground it had been shot up so much.

Mikhail shielded his eyes against the flares to preserve his low-light vision. He was not with the others. He hunted alone and had found himself a stand all his own. He was kneeling on a small mound well to the west of the others. He had been studying the enemy position all along, but he had not fired a shot. He wasn't like the others, the rabble who followed the Prophet. He was *Spetsnatz* and that meant making your shots count, not just spraying rounds like a fireman with a hose.

The flares were a nuisance as he tried to make out the aircraft rolling toward the truck. Their brightness made it difficult for him to pick up details of the aircraft, even through his scope. He waited for the flares to die and he heard the engines rev on the old airplane he now recognized as an ancient American model from the Great Patriotic War.

They had flown them into Berlin after the war, he remembered from his school days. And now they were going to fly away with Pretsky's machine. But he didn't think so.

"Not unless you have a spare pilot," he muttered as he stood up and braced himself for the shot.

The flares were almost gone now and he could see the nose of the old plane clearly. Looking through his scope, he tracked the crosshairs smoothly up from the nose to the window of the cockpit. He could see the pilot's face, a smartass American face with a big smirk and blond hair. The crosshairs centered on the face and he began his soft, smooth caress of the trigger.

The last flare caught him off guard and its glare blinded him in the scope. Cursing, he lowered his rifle a couple of inches and reached up with his left hand to shield his eyes. The muffled report of the three-round short burst was much too far away for him to hear.

He didn't know he was dead until he felt the three taps on his chest like a man jabbing him with his finger to make a point.

"That's for Daniels and Stan, Comrade *Spetsnatz*," Jack said, his smile showing his tombstone teeth.

But there was no time to celebrate. The gooney bird was pulling out and it wasn't going to wait for him.

He turned and sprinted toward the open door of the plane already taxiing across the rock-strewn flat and picking up speed. He heard the gunshots behind him and the rounds hitting on every side. The men doing the shooting couldn't see him. He was invisible. They were shooting at the plane and he was running right into the line of fire. It was the only way to go.

Travis stood in the door with his hand outstretched. The plane was really rolling now, bouncing so hard over the rough ground that Travis had to hang on tight to keep from being thrown out.

"Come on, pardner! You can make it."

Thought I could until you said that, Jack thought. Tells me you got a doubt in your mind. He told himself to stop thinking, just run like hell and never mind the incoming.

Travis grabbed his hand as another rocket grenade exploded at his back, and Jack felt himself propelled through the air by one or the other and landed hard on the cabin floor.

"You all right?" Travis screamed at him over the roar of the engines and the explosions outside.

"Naturally," Jack said, fighting for breath. "Just getting limbered up."

"Tell me one thing," Travis demanded as he kicked Jack's long legs out of the way and pulled the cabin door closed.

"What's that?"

"How did you know where the Russian would be?"

Jack took a deep breath, but he didn't have to think about his answer.

"It's where I would have been."

Bin Laden cursed them all, the Americans and the Iranians and his own men and even poor Mustafa.

"You miserable dogs!" he screamed. "I give you the weapons of an army and you cannot kill these American devils."

But he collected himself. He wasn't through yet.

"The Grails!" he shouted. "Launch the Grails!"

There were three Russian SA-7 Grail shoulder-launched surface-to-air missiles, each manned by experienced followers.

But the first was too eager to do his duty. He fired as the DC-3 began to taxi away from the ruined truck. The seeker head picked up the infra-red radiation signature from the plane's engines and gave off a tone telling the operator that the missile was ready. He pulled the trigger. The launch motor sped the missile on its way. The missile sailed harmlessly through the air and detonated its HE frag warhead harmlessly among the rocks. The gunner had fired too soon, before the target reached the missile's 800-meter minimum range and the rocket booster never had a chance to kick in.

The second gunner had trouble getting a tone. The exhausts of the old gooney bird were not the furnaces of a modern jet or helicopter and he was unsure. Afraid to let the airplane get too far, he fired but his missile went wide. It exploded in an impressive orange ball of flame alongside the airplane as it raced across the rocky flat, sending the plane's tail wobbling for a moment. The men on the high ground began to cheer what they thought was a hit. But the accursed machine corrected itself and continued on its way, soon lifting from the ground and climbing into the sky.

The last gunner felt the hand of Allah on his shoulder. It was Osama bin Laden, but to the gunner it was almost the same. He waited until the wretched machine was climbing, its engines straining to lift it over the mountains that rimmed the basin. When it was thus emitting the maximum heat from its engines and he had a good tone, the gunner said a prayer and pulled his trigger.

The men on the high ground held their collective breath as the rocket booster kicked in to propel the 1.1 kilogram warhead skyward at supersonic speed.

They let out a loud cheer when they saw the missile fly to the plane and explode. A hit! Allah be praised, a hit with the last of the missiles!

From their perspective, it looked as if the plane must

surely be destroyed, but in fact the undersized warhead passed just beneath the belly of the plane and exploded on contact with the left wing. It did some damage, and the old bird staggered but did not fall.

The men on the high ground were stunned and appalled.

Osama bin Laden's rage was such that he could not speak.

2030 hours
Airborne over northern Iraq

"We're hit!" Jen cried out as the explosion rocked the plane.

"Just a scratch," Hunter said between clenched teeth as he fought for control of the plane. "A nick, really."

He looked out his cockpit window at the lacerated left wing, a chunk of its metal skin gone and the inner workings exposed. The engine clattered and coughed, but he adjusted the fuel mixture and she came around when he went back to the throttle. They were still climbing.

"When are you ever going to learn, girl?" He gave her his best bedroom smile.

"I guess they're right. It's better to be lucky than good," she said.

"What does a man have to do?"

Back in the cabin, Sarah was working over Captain Daniels and he was coming around. "Am I dreaming?"

"No, Captain Daniels. We're real."

"You're the same one in the dream," he said, smiling weakly. "With the cool hands."

"That's right."

"How bad am I?"

"You'll live."

"I know that. How soon can I fly again?"

Travis picked up the man who looked like Osama bin Laden and put him in one of the seats and belted him in. He checked his pulse and satisfied himself the man was just sleeping off the morphine Sarah had given him.

"You think that's really him, Osama bin Laden?" Sam asked.

"Fifty-fifty chance, I reckon," Travis said. "If he's not, he ought to be worth something."

"If he ain't him, throw his raghead ass off the plane," Stan said.

"Might be him, though," Travis said. "It's not like I can check his driver's license."

"Throw his ass off the plane anyway."

"What do you have to say about our bus driving surfer dude now?" Jack asked Stan, to get him off the subject of throwing people off the plane.

"Where is that son of a bitch?" Stan asked, trying but failing to lift himself off the pallet Sarah had laid out for him on the cabin floor. "I want to shake his hand. Boy's gonna make an operator yet."

"Too bad you won't remember saying that when you wake up tomorrow," Jack laughed.

Travis turned to find Jen at his side. She had made her way back from the copilot's seat and was studying the prisoner.

Jen was the only spook in TALON Force, an expert at makeup and disguise. She had studied photographs of bin Laden, and could probably even disguise herself as the terrorist mastermind well enough to fool some who knew the man. She knew how to look beyond the obvious, the beard and the turban, to the bone structure beneath and the telltale facets of a face that cannot be duplicated.

"It's not him," she said.

Travis cursed softly. He knew she would not be mistaken.

"But you're right," she added. "He is worth something. Sarah, how long will he be out?"

"Hours," Sarah said, looking up from Captain Daniels. "I gave him a pretty good dose."

"Ladies and gentlemen, I'd like to call your attention to the windows on the starboard side of the cabin. That would be your other right, Stan," Hunter called back from the cockpit. "Uncle Sam has arranged a little fire-works show for your entertainment this evening."

They looked down at the rugged terrain they had thought would be the last place they would ever see, still able to make out the white of the rocky basin in the darkness. They saw the exhausts of the F-16s as they swooped down on the coordinates Travis had given them.

"Jesus," Jack muttered. "Cluster bombs and napalm. Looks pretty from up here. Like ol' Robert E. Lee said, 'It is well that war is so terrible, or we should grow too fond of it.'"

"Couldn't happen to a nicer bunch of fuckers," Stan announced from his spot on the floor, unable to get to a window. "It's goddamn beautiful."

When Jen mentioned their satellite relay was on the blink, Sam perked up and went forward. He had it fixed in less than a minute, but didn't embarrass Hunter by telling anybody that the jack was unplugged.

"I've been thinking," Sam said to Travis when he came back into the cabin.

"Do tell."

"The reason I came along on this mission was in case there were commo problems if they generated an EMP with that gizmo."

He pointed at Pretsky's RF machine.

"So?"

"Well, either the gizmo's not EMP capable or else they just didn't think to use it. I'm guessing it's a single application design, only good for highly directional, fo-cused bursts. Like a laser, like you said in the briefing before we jumped in."

"Makes sense to me, Sam. You'd know more about that than I would."

"But if I'm right, there was never a threat to the commo systems."

"What's your point?"

"My point is, you didn't really need me at all. The HALO jump, the whole thing was—unnecessary. I could've gotten myself killed for nothing!"

"No, you're off in the ditch there," Travis said.

"Am I?" Sam was working up a sense of righteous indignation. He was a highly talented and valuable asset as a world class techno-geek, and he didn't appreciate being dragged out of airplanes and shot at for no reason.

"Yep." Travis looked him square in the eye. "This was a tough mission, a real rodeo. We needed *all* our operators to get it done."

"You mean that?" Sam's indignation softened. Travis was old school. He didn't toss the word "operator" around lightly.

"Damned right."

"Well—all right. I guess it's okay, then. I mean, you have to plan for every contingency, right?"

" 'Deed we do."

Sam nodded and turned away to find a seat and Travis looked at him, a broad smile creasing his face for the first time since the mission began.

Jack DuBois put his head into the cockpit where Jen had returned to the copilot's seat. He shook Hunter's hand and told him that was from Stan Powczuk. They both laughed about that, and Hunter asked how everybody came out. He said he knew Stan was too mean to kill but it looked like Sarah was dragging her leg a little.

Jack smiled and whispered the story in Hunter's ear and then turned and was gone.

"What did he say?" Jen asked. "Is Sarah hurt?"

"It's been a tough mission on the womenfolk," Hunter laughed. "You got your tit tore off and Doc got shot in the butt."

Chapter Twenty-six

The White House War Room was a madhouse. Even the men at the head table were on their feet. Backs were slapped and cigars were lit.

Within the span of a few minutes, the president's national security advisor's attitude about the call he was making now had swung 360 degrees, from doleful dread to pure joy and a fierce pride.

"Mr. President, it is my pleasure to inform you the mission is a success. We have wheels up and all aboard. Yes, sir, the machine too, a complete success. We are in contact with the aircraft by satellite relay. That's right, sir, the gooney bird. I have just spoken with the doctor treating Captain Daniels and she assures me he will pull through."

The president's man did not elaborate on Daniels's wounded leg. This was a good-news call. The details could wait.

"Yes, sir, we can arrange that. If you'll stand by a moment, please."

2100 hours
Airborne over the Iraq/Turkey border

Aboard the gooney bird, laboring along over the Taurus Mountains at even less than its normal speed because Hunter was babying the damaged wing, the call came through on the satellite relay.

"Boss!" Hunter called back to the cabin. "See you a sec?"

Travis made his way forward, expecting Hunter to say he'd lost the engine and they were going down. It was his job to worry about everything.

"Yeah?"

"It's for you." Hunter handed him the receiver. "It's the prez."

Travis eyeballed him suspiciously.

"No shit. The president of the United States."

Travis snapped to attention and cleared his throat.

Word passed through the ship and every member of the team who was able came to attention as well. Even the addled Stan sat bolt upright.

"Yes, sir," Travis mumbled, his voice gone soft.

"The nation is in your debt tonight, the whole world for that matter. I wanted to make sure you know that, that you heard it from me."

"Thank you, sir."

"Thank you. And please thank your team for me. Good night."

"Thank you, sir."

It occurred to Travis that "thank you, sir" was all he had said and he had said it twice. He handed the receiver back to Hunter.

"What did he say?" Sam asked.

"He said we done good," Travis drawled, showing his second smile since the mission began. "Real good."

"Looky here, it's the choppers," Hunter announced.

Glancing out his cockpit window he recognized the helicopter as an MH-60, the army's special ops version of the Sikorsky Black Hawk. Beyond it he could see another and in the distance a big MH-47 Chinook.

The pilot of the Black Hawk just off his wing hand-signaled Hunter the frequency and he dialed them up.

"Evening, gents," Hunter said.

"Right back at you, Ankara Studios. Sorry we were too late to make your wrap party. Just wanted to check you out on our way back to Adana and see if you were okay."

"We're fine, thanks."

"Copy that." The pilot of the Black Hawk gave their shot-up left wing a close look. "Sir, I realize I'm not cleared to know who I'm talking to and you might be somebody, but, uh—"

"Spit it out," Hunter said, laughing. "We're all friends here."

"Well, sir, you're leaking so much stuff I'm afraid the Turks may arrest you when you get back to Adana for polluting. You sure you're okay?"

"Like the man who fell off the Empire State Building said, so far, so good."

"Copy. Guess what I'm trying to say, sir, if you'd like to set that shot-up piece of shit down somewhere and fly home on a real bird, we'd be glad to pick you up."

Hunter studied the logo under the chopper pilot's cockpit window—Death riding on a winged horse with the moon at his back, stars in his wake, and a sword raised over his head.

He knew how the chopper pilot must be feeling, just how sorry he was not to have been able to get there in time to help the team. It didn't matter that it wasn't his fault.

"Tell you what," Hunter said. "I've gotten attached to this old bird and I'd like to take her home. But since you guys are going our way, I'd appreciate your tagging along just in case she gives out on me. Would you mind?"

"We can do that."

"I know you guys," Hunter said. "You're the one hundred sixtieth Special Operations Aviation Regiment, the Night Stalkers. If you can't do it, it ain't going to happen. It would be an honor to fly with you guys."

"The honor is ours, sir," the chopper pilot said softly. "We know where you've been."

And that was the first time since they had left Adana that Jen was truly impressed with Captain Hunter Evans Blake III.

1300 hours EDT
The Pentagon, Washington, D.C.

At the SCIF in the bowels of the Pentagon, Mac slapped his hand on the table and scared Dr. Fensterman out of his chair.

"That's a wrap, guys," he pronounced. "Mission accomplished and all's well that ends well."

He knew there was at best only a 50-50 chance that the man the operators were bringing out with them was actually Osama bin Laden, but he was satisfied either way. They had the RF gizmo and the pilot and all of them were in one piece, including the operators, whoever they were and God bless them all.

They had quashed bin Laden's plot and snatched his secret weapon. They had almost certainly ruined any deal he had in the works with Iran, they had thwarted his plan to snooker the United States into a war with Iraq, and they had killed a shitload of hostiles. It wouldn't be Christian to ask more than that.

"Come on, you two," Mac said, gathering Bob and the good doctor under his wings. "The ransom's been paid and we're free to go. Drinks are on me."

2350 hours
Adana AFB, Turkey

Hunter brought the crippled DC-3 in for a landing at Adana with his helicopter escort in the late-night darkness and taxied it as directed by ground crew into a big high-security hangar far from the flight line. The hangar doors closed behind the old bird and she was boarded by a crew of men and women in black jumpsuits who were friendly enough but hardly talkative. Captain Daniels was offloaded and taken to the base hospital for treatment of his wounds, where he would be joined the following day by his sweetheart, Stephanie, whose around-the-clock presence at his bedside would be authorized at the highest levels of the government.

Within an hour, the RF generator, Mustafa, and
TALON Force had all left Adana, going their separate
ways.

Washington, D.C.

Mustafa and the RF generator were flown nonstop by a
military transport with midair refueling capabilities to an
out-of-the-way military base not far from Washington, in
the company of a team of CIA counterterrorist specialists. Upon landing, the machine and Mustafa parted
company.

The RF generator was transferred to a smaller aircraft
that was boarded moments later by Dr. Fensterman for
the next leg of the trip to his laboratory in the New
England woods.

There, the little man who had first deciphered the telemetry from Captain Daniels' F-16 and correctly pre-
dicted that it had been the victim of RF weaponry would
be given the honor of leading a team of scientists assigned to learn the weapon's secrets. The late Pretsky's
machine embodied the advances of Soviet science in the
field, including most importantly the secrets of creating
a highly mobile device that could generate an RF beam
sufficiently powerful and focused to strike a sophisticated
target at long range. U.S. technology was decades behind
after a late start, and analysis of the generator would
effectively close the gap.

Dr. Fensterman could hardly wait to get started. He
already had formulated theories that accounted for the
machine's impressive ratio of mass to output and its effectiveness against digital computer chips but not hard-
wire analog systems. He suspected that years of trial-and-
error experimentation had led the Soviets to the discovery
of a combination of materials that made miniaturization
possible. He also suspected that, with sophisticated Western jet aircraft and weapons systems their primary targets, they had focused on identifying carefully calibrated
RF frequencies designed to destabilize and "devolve" the

programming of embedded microchips in complex modern systems. It should only be a matter of adjusting the wavelength of the generated output to expand the generator's effectiveness to other types of systems.

The possibility of broad-band RF impulses fascinated Dr. Fensterman as well. A cursory analysis of the captured generator was to prove Sam correct in suggesting that Pretsky's machine was limited to a single application, the highly directional laserlike beam generation specified by bin Laden. But broad-band generation to create an EMP-like effect? It was a fascinating possibility that could prove of enormous benefit to U.S. forces in any future conflict, large or small.

CIA Headquarters, Langley, Virginia

Mustafa found himself the guest of the U.S. intelligence community.

The fate of his master, Osama bin Laden, remained a mystery. It was clear from the tapes recovered from Striker Flight's on-board video cameras that the air strike on the hostile position at the rocky basin had been devastating. It was considered unlikely that anyone in the target zone had lived through it, but no one was willing to count bin Laden out. He had already shown a disquieting propensity for survival. At Langley, Mac and his team were on the lookout for any sign of his resurfacing, just in case.

It had been decided that Mustafa must stand trial for his crimes against American citizens and interests around the world. While other countries might have held him incognito, reserving him as an asset for possible propaganda or even prisoner exchange purposes, the United States did not operate that way. The CIA and military intelligence agents into whose custody he had been delivered did not argue when they received orders to turn him over to the FBI for prosecution in federal court. Mustafa's right to counsel and an open trial would be honored.

In the meantime, though, the intelligence types would take full advantage of the opportunity to "debrief" him before relinquishing him to the minions of American justice. They would use every sophisticated method known to their experts to encourage him to be forthcoming, including a humane but effective combination of drug therapy. Mustafa would appear before a U.S. Magistrate for arraignment within a matter of days. Press reports of his capture would evoke a wave of protest from Arab-American groups around the country. But by then his CIA case officer would know everything there was to know about Osama bin Laden's global operations, assets, associates, and contacts.

If bin Laden were to resurface, he would find his world curiously bereft of the resources he had so carefully cultivated over the years.

Epilogue

The five-star hotel was first class all the way, the steps from is veranda leading directly onto the sand of the beach itself.

Sarah Greene lay on her stomach on a chaise lounge on the veranda, a drink on the table beside her and a paperback novel lying unread on the cool stones beneath her. She was taken with the beauty of the scene, the white beach and the gentle swells of the sea catching the light of the setting sun. Yachts and sailboats of all sizes bobbed on the waves like props in a movie. The evening air was soft and warm and played over her gently. She sighed. The place was a dream.

"How you doin'?" a man asked in a Texas drawl.

Sarah looked down at a pair of black cowboy boots polished to a glossy shine, then up the muscled frame of Travis Barrett. He was dressed in black pants and a white shirt open at the collar. He was smiling.

"I'm doing fine," she purred lazily. "Couldn't be better."

"Hate to see you out here by yourself, missing all the fun," he said.

There was a casino on the veranda level of the hotel, and they could hear voices and music through the open doors behind them.

"Trav, this *is* fun," she assured him. "This is perfect."

"Thought maybe you'd like to join me and Stan, take a seat at the blackjack table."

"Taking a seat is not one of my favorite things at the moment," she said.

The bullet wound in her "upper dorsal thigh" was mending nicely, but it was still too painful to make sitting comfortable.

"Well, you know where to find us if you change your mind."

"Thanks, I'm fine."

She watched Travis walk away toward the doors that led to the casino, then turned back to the view of the sea. She sighed again.

Travis crossed the veranda and entered the casino. The place was opulent, lit by a series of impressive chandeliers against the oncoming night. Chamber music filled the air amid the tinkle of ice in drinks and the clatter of the roulette wheel. Here and there a croupier called out, "Get your bets down, please," in French and accented English.

The atmosphere was festive and elegant, with high-maintenance women decked out in jewelry and designer gowns and silver-haired men in dinner jackets. Waiters in short white jackets milled through the big room carrying drinks on trays.

Travis knew he was underdressed but he didn't care. This was R&R, well-earned rest and relaxation, and wearing a monkey suit was no part of that.

Stan Powczuk was not wearing a tie either. He was at the blackjack table and fully into the spirit of the R&R occasion. With his right arm strapped tight against his chest so he wouldn't aggravate his broken collarbone, he was trying to read his cards while managing a drink and a tall blonde who looked like a model in the seat next to him.

The blonde helped Stan out by picking up his drink and holding it to his lips. Stan showed his appreciation by returning his good hand to the left cheek of her teardrop-shaped ass and giving it a squeeze.

"Hit me," he said, smiling and licking his lips to keep from wasting any of his drink.

"I reckon that's what Angela's going to do when you

get home," Travis said over Stan's right shoulder. The blonde was all over his left.

"Evening, Trav," Stan said with a grin, looking up at Travis and nodding his head toward the blonde. "Italian blondes. Sexiest women in the world."

"That's what you said about Sicilian brunettes," Travis said.

Stan's wife, Angela, was a fiery brunette of Sicilian descent. Their battles were legendary, but Stan assured anyone who would listen that their making up was worth it and then some.

"What Angela don't know won't hurt me," Stan said. "And Sophia here is bringing me luck. Look at this."

Stan pointed with his chin at the stacks of chips on the table in front of him.

"Blackjack," the dealer said, pushing another stack of chips toward Stan.

"What did I tell you?" Stan gloated. "I'm gonna break this joint."

"I wouldn't put it past you."

"Pull up a seat," Stan said. "She's lucky enough for two."

"I might do that in a little bit," Travis said.

He left Stan with his blonde and went looking for the rest of his team. It was R&R, downtime when everybody was free to do whatever pleased him. But Travis was the team leader on and off duty, and he felt responsible for his people. Even if the mission was just to have a good time, he liked to check up on them to make sure they were on profile.

He found Jack and Sam when he sauntered around a column into a quiet corner away from the gaming tables. And he was glad to see they were not alone.

Jack was in deep conversation with a young woman who seemed to be hanging on his every word. They were at a table against the wall, their chairs pulled close together so they could whisper and be heard. Sam was at the table with a woman, too, but she was doing the talking. All Sam was doing was grinning.

The women were stunning, their trim and tanned fig-

ures displayed in expensive evening dresses that showed
them off to their full advantage.

Travis could see that Jack was taking the attention in
stride. Sam, on the other hand, had the look of a man
who couldn't believe his luck. As the two men looked
up at Travis, it was clear that Sam had put away a drink
or two of some stuff a little stronger than his customary
Mountain Dew. He looked like he was feeling taller by
the minute.

"*Bon Soir, mon ami,*" Jack said with a smile. "Won't
you join us?"

"Wouldn't want to be a fifth wheel," Travis said.
"Looks like y'all are doing all right."

"These young ladies are Marie and Justine," Jack said.
"Ladies, this is my friend Travis."

Jack made the introduction again in French for the
women's benefit and they both smiled at Travis. But it
was clear they were not looking for more company.

"I was just telling Marie here what a genius Sam is
with electronics, how he fixed me up with a sound system
for listening to my jazz. He put my old seventy-eights
onto CDS and they sound better than ever."

Justine said something in French.

"Said she loves jazz," Jack translated.

Marie said something too, never taking her eyes off
Jack.

"What did she say?" Travis asked.

"She said I am black and beautiful," Jack laughed.
"But that's another story. Sure you won't join us?"

This time, it sounded more like an invitation to leave
than to stay, and Travis took the hint.

"Maybe later. Stan's holding a seat for me over at the
blackjack table."

Jack said something in French and the two women
laughed.

"I told them that game was named for me," Jack explained. "Black Jack DuBois."

"Looks like they believed you, too," Travis said.
"Well, I'm gonna drift. Stan's got himself a lucky blonde,
says he's going to break the bank."

"Right on," Jack said.

"Right on," Sam said, still grinning.

That accounted for everybody except Hunter Blake and Jen Olsen, so Travis decided to make a swing around the casino to look for them on his way back to the blackjack table. He was halfway around when he saw heads turn toward the marble staircase that led down from the floor above.

He followed the stares and saw Hunter and Jen. Leave it to them to make an entrance.

It was a double staircase, separate flights of stairs winding down from above and coming together to form a landing before the double width of the stairs continued to the casino floor. The landing was like a stage above the heads of the gamblers below.

All eyes were turned to watch the glamorous couple descending the separate flights of stairs to meet at the landing.

Hunter Blake looked like a young blond James Bond in his white dinner jacket.

Jen Olsen looked like a movie star too, in a slinky and revealing blue dress that shimmered in the light of the chandeliers. Her blonde hair was done up and she was radiant—a real show stopper.

As they met at the landing, Hunter smoothed his impeccably knotted bow tie with one hand and took Jen's hand in the other. He raised it to his lips suavely and smiled his killer smile.

"Blake," he said. "Hunter Blake."

"Charmed, I'm sure," she said with mock sarcasm. "Where's my surprise?"

"Come with me."

Arm in arm, they descended the staircase and the hum of conversation and gambling resumed around them as they made their way to the baccarat table. Playing Bond to the hilt, Blake had managed to have seats at the table reserved, but Jen was surprised to see that the only seats available were on either side of a dumpy woman in a sequined dress with her hair piled high on her head.

Blake showed her to the seat on the woman's left and took the one on her right.

When they were seated, Blake smiled across the woman, who was intent on the game, and introduced her to Jen.

"Jennifer Olsen, I'd like you to meet the one and only, the incomparable Yvette."

"Oh, it is you!" Yvette said, suddenly realizing she was not alone. She eyed him lecherously and added in a thick French accent, "You look delicious in that tuxedo, Monsieur Hunter. I call you Blake, yes?"

"By all means. And this is the woman I told you about, Yvette. This is Ms. Olsen."

"Ah, Mademoiselle Olsen. Blake tells me you are a fan."

"More than you'll ever know," Jen said, smiling into the face she had studied so carefully in the copilot's seat of Hunter's gooney bird as she transformed herself into the woman beside her. "More than you'll ever know."

PENGUIN PUTNAM INC.
Online

Your Internet gateway to a virtual environment with
hundreds of entertaining and enlightening books
from Penguin Putnam Inc.

*While you're there, get the latest buzz on
the best authors and books around—*

Tom Clancy, Patricia Cornwell, W.E.B. Griffin,
Nora Roberts, William Gibson, Robin Cook,
Brian Jacques, Catherine Coulter, Stephen King,
Jacquelyn Mitchard, and many more!

**Penguin Putnam Online is located at
http://www.penguinputnam.com**

PENGUIN PUTNAM NEWS

Every month you'll get an inside look at our upcom-
ing books and new features on our site. This is an
ongoing effort to provide you with the most
up-to-date information about
our books and authors.

**Subscribe to Penguin Putnam News at
http://www.penguinputnam.com/ClubPPI**